DRUNK DRIVING

THE MISADVENTURES OF A DRUNK IN PARADISE: BOOK 3

ZANE MITCHELL

Drunk Driving
The Misadventures of a Drunk in Paradise: Book #3

by
Zane Mitchell

Copyright © 2019 by Zane Mitchell

ISBN: 9781797649818
VS: 05182019.02

To the love of my life.
Thank you for your endless support and
for getting me (and Drunk) out of many sticky situations.
You are my world.
I love you forever.

1

VALENTINA CARRIZO APPROACHED *ME* FIRST.

Now, I won't lie and say that I didn't find her attractive. The woman could set a wet sponge on fire, she was that hot. And truth be told, she *did* catch my eye. But let's not get it twisted.

She.

Approached.

Me.

But despite the fact that Valentina Carrizo was hot, she was by no means the type of woman I would've ever hit on in a bar. And *not* because I thought I couldn't score with someone that hot. So let's just drop that notion right now, shall we? There were numerous reasons *why* I wouldn't have approached her, *none* of which being that I thought I'd be unable to score.

No. I knew from the moment I laid eyes on her that sex was kind of a given. Her clothes kinda told the story. Red skimpy dress, clinging to every nook and cranny of her body. The slit in the front of the dress riding clear up to her lady bits. Big bulging breasts on display and as inviting as the last two peanuts in a bowl on top of a bar. They dared every man around to grab 'em for a taste, but in the back of that man's mind, he had a nagging curiosity as to how many hands had been there before him and just where, exactly, *those* hands had been.

No. Scoring was most definitely *not* the reason I wouldn't have approached Valentina Carrizo. The real reason, I actually attributed to my mother. And she wasn't even in the bar that night. She was twenty-two hundred miles and an ocean away.

Go figure.

But it was her words that rang truth and wisdom into my head that evening. "Only hookers wear that much makeup."

Thanks, Mom.

I was pretty sure her advice saved me several hundred dollars that evening and quite possibly an antibiotics prescription.

So when Valentina Carrizo approached me at the bar— and in lieu of a handshake as a greeting, her hand immediately grabbed my junk—my head tilted approximately fifteen degrees to the right. I squinted and frowned at the same time, having the instant urge to cough. I imagined the conversation she'd just been having with her girlfriend on the other side of the bar. I figured it had to go a little something like this.

"Hey, Valentina, you see that hot guy over there?"

"You mean the one with the big nose?"

"Yeah. You know what they say, 'big nose, big hose.'"

"You know, I've always wondered if that was true."

"I guess we'll find out…"

Challenge accepted.

"Well, hello to you too," I said.

She let out a giggle and then a sultry, thickly Spanish accented, "Just checking." She ran a hand through her long, wavy black hair, pulling a lock over her bronzed shoulders.

I leaned both elbows back against the bar and chuckled. "Checking to make sure I am what the beard says I am?"

She held out her hand then, her long red fingernails looking like daggers covered in blood. "I am Valentina."

Taking her hand, I gave it a small pump and then leaned into her slightly. "I'm Drunk."

She put her ear against my mouth then. "What do you say?"

"I'm Drunk," I repeated over the pounding bass.

She giggled. "Yeah, me too."

"Can I buy you a drink?"

"Sure. Rum and Coke."

I turned and flagged down the bartender whom I'd been chatting with before Valentina had arrived. "Rum and Coke." I held up my tumbler and gave it a little shake, making the ice that was left clink against the sides. "And I'll have another."

The bartender grinned at me. I was sure he thought I was some poor shmuck that didn't know a hooker from a ho when I saw one. He probably assumed I thought I was getting lucky tonight by buying the woman a drink. But that's not what I was doing. I was actually buying the woman a drink so she wouldn't be offended when it was time to excuse myself.

Is that wrong?

Well, then, let's just put it to a vote, shall we?

Ladies, would you be offended if a man bought you a drink just so you wouldn't be offended that he *didn't* buy you a drink?

I didn't think so. A free drink's a free drink.

I was playing it safe, folks. I'm not stupid. The bar scene used to be my jam. And I knew how to work a room.

Rule #1. Keep the women happy.

Rule #2. Don't take home hookers. Just don't. I don't care how hot they are. Just don't do it.

Rule #3. Tip your bartenders well.

And rule #4. Never eat the peanuts.

I slid the bartender some cash and handed Valentina her drink.

She took a sip, then smiled up at me, batting her long dark eyelashes. "Thanks. So what do you do, handsome?"

"I'm in security."

She cuddled up to my side. "I feel safer already."

I smiled at her. She was cute. That much was for sure. "I like your accent. Where's it from?"

"Colombia," she said, sounding a little like a cross between Sofia Vergara and Charo.

"You're sure a long ways from home."

She took another sip of her drink and shrugged. "You are American?"

"Yeah. Why?"

"You're a long way from home too. Maybe we were destined to meet."

I could play along. "Were we?"

She nodded. "We could go back to your place and get to know each other a *leettle* better."

"Mmm, I don't think my better half would like that very much," I said, giving her a tight grin.

"Aww, you're married?" Though her bottom lip plumped out when she said it, her body language said the opposite. She cuddled up closer to me as if the idea of me being married had made her *more* interested.

"Something like that."

She stood on her tiptoes, nuzzled my ear, and whispered, "I don't care." Her hand cupped my junk again.

I glanced over at the bartender. He was smiling. This was his silent *I told you so* moment, even though he hadn't said a word. Only his shit-eating grin had spoken for him. Without moving, I looked down at Valentina. "Do I get a discount for all these free feels?"

She giggled. "Oh, honey, if that's not a rolled-up sock in there I'll do it for halfsies."

"Halfsies, huh?" I sighed and glanced around, wondering

just where exactly my other half was when I needed him. That was when I spotted him.

Eighty-seven-year-old Al Becker was a small man with hunched-over shoulders that made him *barely* five feet tall. Aside from the two small patches of white hair behind his ears, he was bald. He wore his usual uniform. Khaki shorts. A white ribbed tank top under a Hawaiian button-down. White New Balance sneakers and long white socks pulled up to his knobby knees. He hobbled over to me at the bar.

"Al. What took you so long?"

When he looked up at me, his whole torso moved, like he had a stiff neck or something. "We gotta go, kid." He said it low, like he'd been chased to the bar by a mafioso.

"Go? Why?"

"The line for the john's too long."

"You been in line this whole time?"

"I mean it, Drunk. Let's go."

"Why we gotta go?"

"Which one of us has the bad ears here? You or me? I told you. The line to the john's taking too long."

"Your point?"

"Do I really gotta spell it out?"

"Fuck, Al. I can't take you anywhere. We just got here."

"Don't 'fuck, Al' me, kid. We've been here for over an hour."

I glanced backwards at the bevy of beautiful women on the dance floor. I hadn't even gotten started yet. I was still waiting for my first three drinks to kick in and give me rhythm. "An hour? That's nothing."

"An hour in a bar is like dog years to a hooker. Trust me, it's plenty."

My eyes widened and I glanced down at Valentina. "Did you seriously just say that, Al?"

"I did. Now can we go?"

I cleared my throat. "Hey, Al. I'd like you to meet my friend, Valentina."

Valentina's right brow rose, but she extended her hand to Al.

Oblivious to the fact that her hand had just been cradling my boys, he took it and gave it a polite shake. "It's nice to meet you, Valentina."

"Valentina's a hooker, Al."

He cupped his ear. "A what?"

I leaned closer and hollered, "A hooker."

Al's brows lifted up towards his bald head, lifting the bags beneath his eyes and making his watery blue-green eyes more pronounced as he looked her up and down. "I'll be honest. That doesn't surprise me."

Valentina didn't even pretend to look offended. She leaned in a little closer to me. "I'm sorry. Who is this man?"

I tipped my head towards Al. "My better half."

She quirked a smile. "You are kidding."

I grinned cheekily.

Al's head gestured towards the door. "Come on, Drunk. We're leaving. I need to make. Those taquitos you forced me to eat aren't sitting right with me."

Al started towards the exit, but my hand shot out to grab his arm. "You're not even gonna say goodbye to our new friend?"

He nodded amicably to the bombshell clinging to my side. "It's been a remarkable pleasure, Valentina." Then he turned his narrowed eyes on me. "Now let's go, kid. I gotta take the kids to the pool."

When he'd disappeared into the crowd, Valentina looked up at me curiously. "He is your grandfather or something?"

"Nah. My wingman."

"He's fun," she said dryly.

I tried to pry myself out of her viselike grip. "He's a cool cat. He's just not used to leaving the resort. Especially after the sun goes down."

"Resort?"

"The Seacoast Majestic. That's where I do security."

"Oh, so you *live* on the island?"

"I do now." I didn't think she needed to hear the whole story of how I'd come to move here from the States. I was over all of that. I was an official Paradise Isle resident now. For better or worse.

She curled into me again and purred, "Niiiice."

I chuckled while trying to escape again, but shaking Valentina was like trying to flick a booger off your finger. "Sorry, Valentina. I gotta go before Al deuces in the resort rental and we get our driving privileges revoked."

"How about a raincheck?"

I glanced back at the bartender again. He'd moved on to a group of college-aged girls down the bar and wasn't watching me and Valentina anymore. I shrugged. Just like I'd bought Valentina a drink so as not to offend her, I decided to agree on a raincheck for the same reason. Hell, she didn't need to know I had no intention on cashing it. "Sure, a raincheck would be great."

Magically, she plucked a business card out of her cleavage and handed it to me.

"Valentina Carrizo, Professional Escort." I looked up at her in surprise. Though I knew prostitution was legal on the island, this was my first experience with it being so blatant. I smiled at her. "You have *fucking* business cards?"

"In case you ever need a date to the ball, but the fucking part is extra," she said, giggling.

"Next ball I go to, I'll look you up."

"Promise?"

I grinned. "You have my word." Valentina grabbed my face and kissed me on the lips then. It was pretty PG and not anything I would've been embarrassed for my mother to have seen, but somehow it made me uncomfortable. I pulled my head back and cleared my throat. "It was nice to meet you Valentina."

As I started to walk away, she called out to me. "Hey. What's your real name?"

"Drunk."

"It's really Drunk?"

"Sure is."

She smiled at me. "Well, it was nice to meet you, Drunk."

Outside, Al waited for me in the resort car that Artie Balladares, the owner of the Seacoast Majestic, had let us borrow. It wasn't the first time we'd been loaned the car, and it always came with the stipulation that Al had to be present when it was used, and I had to be the one driving. I wasn't sure if that was Artie's way of making sure Al was always entertained or if it was his way of making sure I always had a chaperone.

I crawled into the driver's seat. "Jeez, Al. I barely got a chance to look around."

But Al wasn't one to be sidetracked. "What took you so long? Those taquitos bought my stomach a one-way ticket to Shitsville."

"Hey, man, I'm sorry. You didn't have to eat 'em. I mean, you know what they say. 'Greasy in, easy out.'"

"You said you ordered them for the table, Drunk. I was being polite."

"In that case, you get two gold stars. You were extra polite."

"Let's just go. I gotta find the nearest john."

I pointed to the nudie bar next to the Blue Iguana, where we'd just been. "I bet Club Cobalt next door has a bathroom you could use."

Al's eyes widened. "Are you nuts? You don't sit on a toilet seat in a place like that unless you wanna get pregnant, and I'm too weak to squat."

"You're also too old to get pregnant."

Al pursed his lips. "Are you gonna start this car, or do I have to get out and push?"

"In your current condition, I advise against pushing. You'll shit your shorts."

Al shook his head. "I think it's time you bought your own vehicle, kid. I can't keep hauling you around like this."

I tried to restrain my smile as I started the engine. "You can't keep—" Steering the vehicle out of the parking lot and onto the main road, I shook my head. "Who's hauling who around here?"

"Look, you've got the cash. How about I take you shopping for a new ride one day this week?"

I shrugged. The thought had crossed my mind a time or fifty. Only every time I wanted to run into town for something and had to ask Artie's permission to use a resort car and then persuade Al to ride along. I'd tried to convince Artie to give me my own private business car, but he said he'd seen the bullet holes we'd gotten put into Gary Wheelan's ride my first week on the island and he didn't trust me to keep his small fleet of cars safe. They were for guests to be shuttled around in, not for my personal escapades.

"I'm not sure I wanna part with that kind of cash, Al."

"You're not exactly a pauper, kid. You can afford to spend a little of that money."

"But it's my nest egg." Al was referring to the money I'd made solving a big theft my first week on the island. Even though I'd made off with nearly seven million bucks, I'd lost the majority of it in the fucking Atlantic—a ransom drop gone bad. And the small amount that we'd been able to fish out of the ocean had gone to pay for the damages to the Cruz brothers' fleet of boats. In the end, I'd wound up with only the interest I'd earned on the money for the couple months that I'd had it. It wasn't enough to live the rest of my life on, but with

Al's help, I'd invested it properly and it was already growing steadily. I really didn't feel like touching it.

"You need your own car, kid." Al held up his hand and pointed at his little finger. "Besides. You owe me."

"Oh, come on. You're gonna bring *that* up?"

"The fact that you got my finger cut off? Yeah, I think I earned the right to bring that up a time or two a week for the rest of my life."

"It's not like I was the one that cut it off, Al."

"Really? That's how you're gonna spin it?"

"Spin it? I'm not—look. I put it on ice for you, didn't I? They sewed it back on. It hardly looks used. Well, except for all those wrinkles on it. But those are your fault, not mine."

"Hardly looks used? I can't bend it anymore, kid!"

I fought back a laugh. Watching Al drink a cup of coffee now was like having a tea party with the queen. I had to look away to convince my lips to cover my teeth again. When I had myself under control, I turned to Al.

"Fine. I'll look at cars."

Al's head bobbed as if it was settled. "We'll go see Steve Dillon this week. I think Artie knows the guy. He'll give us a good deal."

I glanced over at Al as I hit the main road that would take us back to the resort. "You're kinda bossy, you know that?"

"Yeah, well, you're pain in my ass." He was quiet for a minute. "And you drive like an old woman."

I pulled the car over at the first convenience store I could find. "Yeah, well, I took lessons from you."

2

EARLY THE NEXT MORNING, MY SNEAKERS PRESSED RHYTHMICALLY into the wet sand, leaving the scant imprint of my size thirteens along the shoreline. The air, riding in on a balmy ocean breeze, smelled fresh, maybe even a little sweet. With the rising sun at my back and the Caribbean Sea on my left, my legs carried me along at a steady clip. Tom Petty's "Running Down a Dream" pounded in my ears, blocking out the sound of the surf breaking next to me and the gulls screeching overhead.

My arms pumped by my side as I ran, my lungs demanding more oxygen the harder my calves worked. Getting back into shape felt good, like I was finally getting my life together. And after a few months on Paradise Isle, I was finally at the point where I felt like *this* was where I belonged. My life had gone from this chaotic messy pile of crap to something Zen and, dare I say, *enjoyable.*

I mean, let's be real. I got to wake up on a fucking tropical island every day. I was the head of security at a resort where very little ever happened. I had money in the bank, and an endless supply of women at my doorstep, though most of them were pushing eighty and smart enough to turn me down flat every time. But truth be told, I wasn't sure how life could *be* any better.

I kept my head up scanning the horizon. From my peripheral vision, I caught Evie Becker's broad wave from the porch of her beach front cottage. As she was every morning at this time, Al's little missus was seated against a pillow on her Adirondack, likely reading the latest Dean Koontz or Nora Roberts, always in hardback. I swore the books weighed more than she did.

I waved back but kept running until I hit the rocky coastline. Hooking a right and breathing heavily, I headed up the loose, sandy beach towards the Pepto-Bismol-pink duplex-style cottages and cut between cottages ten and eleven. I paused next to cottage eleven long enough to catch my breath, grab my tank top off the railing, and tug it on over my head, covering my sweaty torso.

At one point, cottage eleven had been my place, but when Vic and Shirley Hoffman had returned to the island and wanted their cottage back, Artie had gotten me a permanent place next to his in the back of the resort. Now the Hoffmans were back in the US once again, this time to attend their first great-grandchild's christening, so their place sat empty until Artie was able to rent it out.

I added the black fedora and shades I'd left on their steps and plugged my earbuds back in, grabbed a dog biscuit from the coffee can next to their back door and picked up a jog once again. Running into the sun now along the cobblestone driveway, I slowed next to cottage five and unplugged my buds. Sure enough, I could hear the barking growing progressively louder. I eased myself around the corner and Scully, Gary Wheelan's pint-sized Pomeranian, came tearing out, yipping at my ankles. To prevent him from following me back up to the resort, I threw the dog biscuit up onto Gary's deck, and Scully took off on a mad dash to retrieve his present.

Leaving my buds dangling around my neck, I jogged past

the resort cottages until I got to the bottom of the steep hill snaking between the main resort hotel on the left and the three-storied motel buildings on the right. I slowed to little more than a walk to catch my breath and then began the arduous climb. The steep, shaded corridor was landscaped with palm trees and low shrubbery on both sides. Lizards and island birds played in the road, not intimidated in the least by the resort guests and golf carts that zipped past regularly.

"Oh, Daniel!" shouted an old woman from just outside one of the motel room doors. The hunched-over woman had a cane in one hand and struggled to push a small red canvas laundry cart with her other hand.

"Need some help, Mrs. Agostino?"

, I wasn't even sure why I asked. Of course she needed help. She *always* needed help.

"I'm sorry to bother you," she said without looking the least bit apologetic. "I did a load of wash in the laundry room and need to get it up to my room. It wouldn't be an issue if you had a laundry room on the top floor."

Mrs. Agostino was an eighty-five-year-old widow from New Mexico with hip problems. Two years ago, she'd subleased her apartment in Albuquerque to her niece and was now spending the rest of her days traveling the world. The fact that she still managed to travel alone shocked the hell out of me, but she was so feisty that I imagined her family had a hard time corralling her.

I jogged over to her and her squeaky cart. "It's no bother." I looked down into the basket. There was a small load of wash inside and a miniature bottle of detergent.

With two shaky fingers, Mrs. Agostino beckoned me to follow her before turning around to slowly face the wooden flight of stairs. Her cane tapped the first step, then she hefted her left leg up, then her right trailed behind next. She had to stop there to take a big breath before attempting the next step.

It was painful watching her walk up the stairs, one step at a time. I half-debated just picking her up and tossing her over my shoulder in a fireman's carry to speed up the process. Instead, I tucked her clothes and soap under one arm and jogged up the stairs ahead of her. "Can I just put them on your bed Mrs. Agostino?"

She waved her arm after me. "Yes, room …"

"Room 337, I know. You want me to grab you some ice while I'm up there?"

"Ice?" Her crackly old-lady voice dragged the word out, putting emphasis on the question mark at the end as if I'd never gotten her ice before and the idea intrigued her. But I knew the drill. I'd be at the bottom of the stairs, halfway back into my jog, and she'd shout back down at me. "Daniel, while you're over here, would you mind getting me some ice?"

I held up a palm and tipped my head sideways. "Only if you need some."

"Oh, well, yes," she agreed, nodding. "Extra ice would be lovely."

I nodded, unloaded the clothes in her room, grabbed her ice bucket and strode down the length of the exterior deck to the ice machine. I refilled her ice bucket and placed it back in her room. By the time I'd finished all of that, Mrs. Agostino and her cane had just gotten to the top step. She stood a little more erect to look at me and to smile sweetly.

"Such a sweet young man. I bet you make your mother proud."

I lifted a shoulder. "She tolerates me."

Mrs. Agostino's cackle followed me back down the stairs. I gave her a backwards wave and took off running again.

That was when Caesar Bishop, the new maintenance guy Artie and I had hired, spotted me. Caesar was a short man with a protruding belly and a severe case of plumber's crack. He'd just gotten out of a golf cart and slung his tool bag over his shoulder when I ran past.

"Mornin', Caesar," I hollered.

He looked up. When he saw it was me, he lifted a hand. "Oh, Mr. Drunk, there you are! I needed to speak with you."

I glanced down at the Fitbit on my wrist. "My run's not over, Caesar," I huffed, not bothering to stop.

He chased after me, running several more paces before realizing he couldn't keep his pants from falling down *and* his tool bag from bouncing on his hip all while trying to run. When I didn't stop, he turned around and ran back to his golf cart, catching up to me in it.

"Mr. Drunk, I'm working on installing those new security cameras you ordered for the employee parking lot," he hollered at me from behind the wheel.

My head bobbed as I jogged next to him. "Good."

"You said you wanted no gaps in the coverage, but there's one spot that no matter what I do, I can't get covered."

"Then order another camera."

"How do I do that?"

"Get a purchase order from Mariposa. Fill it out. Put it on my desk, and I'll sign it."

"Mariposa?"

"At the front desk."

Caesar smiled at me and brought the golf cart to a stop on the road, waving. "Thank you, Mr. Drunk."

"Hey, Caesar," I hollered, turning around to run backwards up the hill.

"Yeah?"

"Just call me Drunk."

"Yes, sir. Thank you."

The top of the hill was hopping as it usually was around this time. Checkout time. Airport shuttles, cabs, and resort cars zipped around the circle driveway in front of the resort's lobby, which was tucked back into a swathe of palm trees and low growing shrubbery on my left side. To my right, on the far side of the driveway which overlooked the pool and beach down below the hill, I noticed a pair of gardeners tending to the landscaping. Sticking out from between two hibiscus bushes, a perfectly heart-shaped bottom swayed from side to side, making my head tip slightly to the side. None of the gardeners I was aware of had asses quite like that. I veered to the right to investigate.

"Hey, Carlos, what's happening?" I said, stopping to check out the brightly colored hibiscus flowers. I looked down at the person buried beneath the bushes.

"*Hola*, Drunk. *Nada*. Just training the new girl."

"New girl? I didn't know we were hiring new gardeners."

"Well, she's just going to be helping out for the summer."

Oooh. I liked the sound of that. Temporary summer help. I was down for a summer fling. "Oh, well, I don't want to be rude to a new employee. You should introduce me."

Carlos quirked a brow. "I don't think Mariposa would like—"

"Tut-tut-tut," I argued, wagging my finger in the air. "Gardeners aren't *on* Mariposa's staff. She doesn't have a say." As part of my commitment to turn over a new leaf and get my act together, I'd agreed to leave Mariposa's staff alone. No more fraternizing with the cleaning girls *or* the front office staff. But she had absolutely no say over any gardeners hired. Especially not gardeners with asses like that.

"But, Drunk…"

"Carlos, please. We don't want to be rude," I interrupted.

He shrugged and then cleared his throat. "Giselle," he began, "I'd like you to meet the head of resort security."

The heart-shaped ass in the bushes began to wiggle, backing out of her position just as the resort's sliding glass doors slid open and Mariposa Marrero came flying out, scuttling across the circle driveway towards us. "Drunk! Oh no you don't! Don't you dare! You just stay away from her."

I frowned as I saw all the bellhops and Desi, the concierge, turning around to stare. "Mari, you're making a scene. I was just getting introduced to the new *gardener*. Relax."

"I know *exactly* who you're about to get introduced to."

I glanced over at the new girl, who was now on her feet. She was tall and thin, with high cheekbones and dark eyes, very modelesque. Her onyx hair was pulled back in a tight bun, showing off just how young her face really was.

"Giselle, this is the man I warned you about," said Mariposa to the girl.

"Mari! So now you're warning the staff about me?" I felt insulted. I looked at the girl. "Please, don't listen to Mariposa. I'm a really nice guy."

The girl giggled. "This is Drunk, Mom?"

3

"MOM?!" MY EYES WIDENED AND I GLANCED OVER AT MARIPOSA in shock. *This* was her daughter? One of the *little* children she always spoke about?

"Yes, *Mom.* This is my daughter Giselle. Giselle, this is Drunk, the man I told you to stay far, far away from."

"I'm offended, Mari. Really offended," I said, touching my fingers to my chest. "You really think I'd hit on your daughter?"

"Yes," she said, her eyes hard.

I caught Carlos nodding his head too. I stared at him in disbelief. "Carlos!"

His eyes floated up and away and his lips puckered, in whistling fashion. He pulled a pair of pruning shears from his belt and pretended to clip the hedges.

I looked at Giselle and extended a hand to her. "I'm so sorry for whatever your mother told you about me, Giselle." I paused for a second as she giggled. Then I narrowed my eyes. "What exactly *did* your mother tell you about me?"

Letting my hand go, she shot a furtive glance in her mother's direction. She smiled at me, blushing. "I'm sorry, Drunk. It wouldn't be polite to repeat what she said about you."

I sighed. "I'm not like that anymore. I swear. That's the *old* Drunk. You know that, Mari. I've cleaned up my act."

Mariposa gave me a tight smile and a little head nod. "You're doing better, yes. But my daughter is off-limits. She's only seventeen years old."

"Well, *obviously* she's off-limits," I said, rolling my eyes. "I don't date seventeen-year-olds. I'm not a pedophile. Plus she's *your daughter*. I like you, Mari, but I wouldn't want you for a mother-in-law."

That made Giselle giggle.

"So, Giselle. Your mom got you a summer job here?" I asked, trying to steer the conversation away from me being such a manwhore that Mari thought she had to warn her seventeen-year-old daughter to stay away from me.

"Yeah, I'm trying to save up money for college," she explained. "Mom said I could work as many hours as I wanted this summer here."

"Nice. Good for you."

"Yeah. So, I hear you're from the US? How do you like it here?"

I smiled. "I love it. It's really grown on me."

"I'm kind of surprised to hear that. Mom said you've had your hands full."

I tipped my head to the side. "You mean…"

She laughed. "I mean with all the problems you've had. You know, between your ex getting kidnapped and that dead guy they found in your room."

"Oh, that stuff." I grinned. "Yeah, it was kind of crazy for a while. Things are settling down now, though. I'm starting to enjoy myself." I glanced over at Mari. She had one brow lifted while she watched us interact. "So, when's college?"

"In the fall. I got into PIU, but we're short some cash."

"Well, I'm sure Carlos will keep you busy." Catching Mari's continuous skeptical stare, I threw up my hands. "What?! I'm just making conversation. I can't even *talk* to Giselle?"

"I'd prefer you didn't."

"Look, Mari. She's seventeen. I swear, I'm not looking at her like that. She's like a niece or something."

"A niece?" asked Mari, putting a hand on her hip.

"Yes." I looked at Giselle. "Just consider me your good old Uncle Drunk. Okay?"

Mari shook her head. "No, no. I don't think so, Drunk. There are some bad uncles out there."

I shook my head. Mari really didn't trust me. I felt hurt. "Those are cruncles. I'm not a cruncle."

"What is this 'cruncles'?"

"Creepy uncles?" I thumbed my chest. "I'm more of a funcle, myself."

Giselle giggled. "A fun uncle?"

"Yeah. See, you're already laughing. That's me. The fun uncle. I'm the guy you come to when you want to do something your mom won't let you do. Or when you need a favor or help with something."

Mariposa wagged her finger in my face. "No, Drunk. She doesn't come to you to do something I wouldn't approve of. My Giselle is a good girl. You just leave her be. Understand?"

"Sure thing, Mari." I shot a wink in Giselle's direction, making her laugh again. "Well, I better get inside. I've got work to do. It was a pleasure meeting you, Giselle."

"It was nice meeting you too, Funcle Drunk."

I chuckled. "See, Mari? Doesn't that have a nice ring to it?"

Mariposa glared at me, a frown resting on her face. "No. Not really."

I pointed at her as I backed away. "Lighten up, Mari. You're too tense." I gave her and Giselle a little wave. "See ya, ladies."

I took off towards the resort lobby before Mari could make any other disparaging comments. I waved at the concierge, a tall, broad-shouldered man with short dreadlocks and space to fit a straw between his two front teeth.

"Hey, Desi."

"Good morning, Mr. Drunk."

"Hey, J.R.," I said, pointing at a bellhop who was helping to load suitcases onto an airport shuttle that had just pulled up beneath the porte cochere.

"Hello, Drunk," said the young man, giving me a winning smile.

The lobby's glass sliding doors opened, and a blast of frigid temperature-controlled air enveloped me as I walked inside the navy-and-white nautical-themed check-in area. The place was abuzz with both new guests checking in and current ones heading to breakfast in the main dining room. I gave a wave to Alicia and Roxie, the front desk girls, just as a man in a security uniform chased me inside.

"Drunk!"

I paused, my hand resting on the employees-only door. "Hey, Davis. Just heading home?"

"Yes. Do you have a second? I was wondering if I could have next Thursday off. It's my wife's birthday and I'd like to do something special for her."

"You got anyone in mind to cover your shift?"

"Wilson said he'd trade shifts with me if it was alright with you."

I threw up a hand. "That works. Fill out a shift exchange form and put it on my desk."

"Thanks, Drunk."

I pulled down on the door handle and had nearly gotten away when I heard her call out.

"Drunk, wait up!"

My head fell and my shoulders slumped. *Mariposa.* "What's up, Mari?" I tried not to let the heavy sigh be too apparent in my voice.

"I'm serious about you messing with my Giselle," she began again.

I held up a hand to stop her. "Look, Mari. I was serious too. Seventeen is too young for me, alright? I might date a lot of women, but I'm not a creep. Okay? Even I have my limits. You have a beautiful daughter, but I would never go there. You can hold me to my word."

She squinted one eye at me but then finally nodded, like she wanted to believe me. "Fine. Thank you. I appreciate that, and I'll do my best to trust you."

For the first several months that I'd been on the island, I'd done everything I could to get Mariposa to like me. I'd given her rides to her car when she'd gotten off work. I brought her expensive imported chocolates after I'd discovered our mutual affinity for the sweet treat, and I always came running when she needed something work-related.

And yeah, sure, I admit it, I slept with almost every woman on her staff, sometimes in pairs, but I'd completely stopped, and in addition, I wasn't drinking as much as I had been to start with. I was working hard at the resort. I'd begun to work out again. But even though I'd drawn a hard line in the sand about getting involved with the wrong women, Mari *still* got on my case.

"You know, I just don't know what else I can do to get you to believe that I'm really trying hard to clean up my act."

She shrugged. "I guess only time will tell. Maybe it's a little too soon for me to really believe it. But I do believe that you wouldn't go there with my Giselle."

I sighed. That was the best I was probably going to get out of the woman for a while. "Thank you. Now while you're here, Mrs. Agostino in 337 stopped me again. We really should get her into the main building. The woman can barely make it up the stairs to her room."

Mariposa lifted her dark brows and ran a hand over the top of her hair, smoothing her bun. "Oh, we've tried. She won't budge. She said she likes her view and she likes the exercise."

I sighed. "Well, then, I guess I'll just have to keep being her errand boy. Artie in?"

"Yes, in his office. Mr. Becker's in there too. You want me to let him know you want to speak with him?"

"Nah. I need to stop in my office first. I'll handle it. Thanks, Mari."

4

I SWUNG INTO MY SHOEBOX OF AN OFFICE AND DROPPED MY shades, my earbuds and my iPod onto my desk. I grabbed a Dr Pepper from the little mini fridge under my desk and a candy bar from my top desk drawer before heading over to Artie's office. I gave it a little rhythmic knock and then burst in without waiting for a response.

"Drunk," said Artie.

"Hey, Artie, Al," I said, giving them both a wassup nod.

I took the chair next to Al.

He held a hand up to his nose and leaned away from me. "Hell, kid. You smell like skunk balls."

"Fuck you very much, Al. You smell like Bengay. You're not supposed to bathe in it. You know that, right?"

Ignoring our usual playful banter, Artie leaned forward. "Well, speak of the devil. Al was just telling me about the hooker you were trying to buy last night at the bar."

With pursed lips, I glanced over my shoulder at Al. "I wasn't trying to *buy* a hooker last night, Al."

Al's brows lifted and he looked away. "Coulda fooled me."

Artie shook his head and wagged a finger in my direction.

"You see, Drunk, this is why I don't trust you with the company car."

"Oh, come on, Artie. Who're you gonna believe, the guy who never knows what day of the week it is, or me?"

"Well, that's easy. I believe Al."

Al chuckled. "That's the breaks, kid."

"Thanks a lot." I leaned back in my seat. "And quit calling me kid, Al. I'm thirty-five years old."

"Puh," breathed Al. "I have underwear older than that."

"Yeah? I think it's time to throw those out."

"But they're sacred underwear."

"Why? Because they're holey?"

"No. Because when I wear them, my wife says, 'Boy, Al, you sure are blessed!'" Al chuckled proudly at his lame attempt at a joke.

I rolled my eyes. "You been sitting on that one for a while, Al?"

"Hehehe," Al and Artie chuckled together.

"Can we be serious here for a second, fellas?"

Al chuffed, waggling his head. "Ohhh, Mr. Big-Shot Thirty-Five-Year-Old wants to be serious, Artie."

Artie shook his head. "I never thought I'd see the day."

I lifted my fedora off my head and ran a hand through my sweaty hair. "Don't quit your day job, boys. Between the two of you, you have half a sense of humor."

Artie leaned back in his seat, making his chair squeal in protest. Artie was a large fellow. So large he couldn't shop for his linen suits in big and tall stores and instead had to special-order them. He wore a big white Panama Jack hat with a black band around the crown, and his beet-red face sweated profusely all day long. He wheezed when he walked, but it was okay because he rarely walked, and when he did, he never went far. He had his own personal golf cart and used that to drive around the property whenever there was an issue that required his attention.

"So, Drunk, what's up with you picking up a prostitute? Mari drained the water outta your dating pool, so you're shooting fish in a new barrel now?"

I shot Al an annoyed glance. "I'm most definitely *not* shooting fish in a barrel. The woman was hitting on *me*. I was just standing there waiting for this guy to come back from the john."

Al leaned forward. "Look, Artie. I can't keep hauling the kid around. It's not good for my image."

"For *your*...!"

Al held a hand up in the air to silence me. "If Evie would've seen me cavorting with a prostitute? I'da been sleeping in the doghouse last night."

I shook my head. "Hell, Al. I thought we were buddies."

"We are, but that doesn't mean our balls are tied together. I need my space."

"You need *your* space?" I couldn't believe it. My eighty-seven-year-old best friend was trying to ditch me. "Shoot me straight, Al. Are you breaking up with me?"

"Jeez, kid. Does everything have to be so dramatic with you? I'm not breaking up with you. I told you last night. It's time you got your own ride. I'm too old to be staying up late and eating taquitos and taking you to hoochie bars."

"That's what this is about, isn't it? The taquitos? I told you I ordered them for the table. You didn't have to eat them."

"It's not about the taquitos." He was quiet for a second. "Well, it's a little about the taquitos. The acid reflux is still giving me hell." He looked up at me and Artie and then was silent again like he'd forgotten where he was going with that. "What was I saying?"

"That you're too old to eat taquitos and go to hoochie bars," said Artie, prodding him along.

"And apparently to remember what you were saying," I said under my breath.

Al cupped an ear. "What?"

I waved my hand dismissively. "Nothing, continue."

"Artie, the kid needs his own vehicle. I wanna take him to see Steve Dillon."

Artie shrugged. "Well, go ahead. You don't need my permission."

"I know I don't, but you mentioned something to me a few weeks back about Steve offering you a good deal on a new vehicle. I wondered if maybe you wouldn't be able to pull some strings and help the kid out. He's not as loaded as he once was."

"Thanks, Al," I grumbled. Losing that almost seven mil still smarted, I never enjoyed being reminded.

"Eh, rub a little dirt on it, you'll be okay," said Al. "So, you think you can help us out here, Artie?"

"I don't know. I actually don't even know the guy. He sent me an email out of the blue last month. He called the deal a business owners' special. I'm not sure he'd extend the offer to my employees. But I can certainly call him."

Al nodded. "We'd appreciate it, Artie."

5

"FUCK THE STICKER PRICES ON THESE THINGS," I BALKED, strolling through the lot at Steve Dillon's Automart almost a week later. I just about couldn't believe what I was seeing. Why in the hell would islanders pay these outrageous prices for vehicles?

Al cupped his hands and peered into the window of a new Toyota Yaris. "They certainly don't give these things away, that's for sure. I've never seen prices this high back in the States. I wonder if it wouldn't be cheaper just to buy something over there and then have them ship it in."

"We're about to find out," I said as a young black guy in khaki slacks and a white polo joined us out on the lot.

"Hello, gentlemen, my name is Samuel. How can I be of service today?"

I shook his hand. "Hey, Sam. I'm Drunk. This is my buddy Al. I'm new to the island, and I was thinking it was time I bought myself a vehicle, but I gotta be honest. I'm feeling a little sticker shock right now. I'm used to US prices. These prices are astronomical in comparison."

Samuel nodded, giving a little knowing smile. "Yes, the tariffs on our vehicles are quite high. I hear it all the time.

Makes a man wonder if he shouldn't just buy something somewhere else and import it in, doesn't it?"

I shot a glance at Al, wondering if there was a hidden camera somewhere on the lot. I cupped a hand against the back of my neck. "Well, yeah, yeah, it actually does make a guy wonder that."

"Unfortunately, you'll find that the import tariff is so high that you're going to wind up paying more that way. You'll not only pay the cost of the car and the tariff, but you'll also be paying a shipping company to deliver it to you."

I groaned. Going through all that sounded like a headache anyway. "So you're saying it's actually cheaper to get it on your lot."

"You got it." He put his hands behind his back and rocked on his feet. "So, what kind of a vehicle were you interested in?"

I shrugged. "I don't know. I kind of like the look of the sportier SUV styles." Francesca Cruz's little Suzuki Samurai flickered in my brain. I wanted an off-road vehicle like that, but rugged and with more meat on its frame.

He nodded. "Like a Wrangler?"

My bottom lip popped out and I nodded. "Yeah. A Jeep would be alright."

"Yes, those are very popular here on the island. I've got our Jeeps parked around on the other side. Follow me." Samuel led us to the other side of his dealership where they had a fleet of Jeep Wranglers in every color lined up.

"Oooh, these are nice." My head bounced appreciatively. I could almost see myself cruising around the island in one of those. Driving with the shell off, I could feel the island breeze blowing through my hair.

Al shot me a look. He'd told me on the car ride over I was to show no emotion. And since Artie hadn't been able to score us a deal with Steve Dillon himself, Al was in charge of the business end of the deal.

Al, who had been a Case IH implement dealer his whole life, claimed to know a thing or two about negotiations. Of course *he'd* haggled with farmers over tractors and combines, but it was basically the same thing. And as he'd told me in the car, the first rule of business was not to get excited. The second they could smell your excitement, they tightened the noose.

Trying to play it cool, Al shrugged. "Meh. They're not that great. I bet they're hell on gas."

"You'll get about twenty-five miles per gallon highway and about seventeen city," said Samuel. "It's not horrible."

"You got any preowned? We're not about to lose ten to twenty percent of the value just by driving a new one off the lot."

"Sure do."

Samuel led us over to a strip of Jeeps. "How do you feel about green, Drunk? We just got this Sahara in on a trade the other day. It's only got ten thousand miles on it. It was barely driven. The owner decided it was too big for his needs."

I lifted a shoulder. "I don't mind green. That's kind of islandy."

Al grunted. "You're not gonna be driving *me* around in that John Deere–green bucket of bolts."

I looked down at Al. "So you're encouraging me to buy it?"

"I'm serious, kid. You aren't getting a John Deere–green vehicle if I have anything to say about it," he said staunchly.

"Okay, Dad." I sucked in my breath and my gaze skipped across the lot. I pointed down the line. "What about that one over there on the end?"

"The yellow one?" asked Samuel.

"Yeah."

"That one is a Rubicon. It's two years old and I believe it has about seventeen thousand miles on it. It has been very well taken care of. It looks like a new vehicle."

I looked down at Al. "What do you think?"

Al was quiet for a moment. He crossed his arms over his

chest and widened his stance slightly. "You know, Drunk, sometimes buying a car is like voting for a president. You have to pick the lesser of two evils. It's flashy and I wouldn't drive it personally, but the banana boat is a helluva lot better than that John Deere–green one."

"Ha. Banana boat, I like that." I smiled, nodding my head. "It'll go with my banana hammock."

"Banana hammock?" said Al, lifting a brow.

I grinned and shot Al a wink. "Let's just say you're not the only one with sacred underwear." I looked over at Samuel, grinning. "I'll take it."

6

It was two days later, and my new yellow Jeep Rubicon was parked outside my cottage in the back of the Seacoast Majestic. I'd just gotten home after closing up the bars down at the pool. A warm island breeze blew in through my open front window, making my sheer white curtains dance like ghosts tethered to the wall. I dropped my keys and hat on the side table and then flipped on the television. Characters rattled on dramatically in Spanish. I didn't understand a word, but I didn't care. Their voices canceled out the silence.

Flipping on my kitchen light, I noticed a blue-and-yellow zebra-faced macaw perched on the edge of my kitchen counter. "Hey, Earnestine."

The bird danced on my counter, her little feet clicking on the Formica. "*Welcome home, asshole, welcome home, asshole, rawck!*"

I stopped moving and stared at her. A dumb grin covered my face. "Aww, you missed me." Pride swelled my chest. I felt like a father who'd just heard his sweet little girl say Da-Da for the first time. We'd been practicing that fowl phrase, pun intended, for several weeks, but it was the first time she'd said it without my coaching. I stopped and gave her a little under-the-beak scratch as a reward. "You're such a good girl."

She closed her eyes and reclined her head, making a little clicking sound in the back of her throat before crooning, "*Pretty bird. Pretty bird.*"

Earnestine and I had first met when I'd moved into my cottage. She'd adopted my place as her own, and after a bit of a rocky start, specifically her early wakeup calls and ill-timed insults, I was finally used to her. In fact, I partially credited Earnestine for my lifestyle changes. She woke me up at sunrise whether I liked it or not, prompting me to get my jog on the beach in before starting work.

One would think that because I spent my day surrounded by people, I'd appreciate my nights alone, but I didn't. I was a fairly social guy, and coming home to an empty cottage was the one drawback to being newly single. So I purposely left my cottage windows open all day in the hopes that Earnestine would be there to hang out with me when I got off work. Of course leaving the windows open all day made for a warm, humid cottage in the evenings, but I didn't mind. I liked it better than the alternative, a lonesome air-conditioned icebox.

After showering a little bird love on my feathered friend, I went into the kitchen and popped open the fridge, plucking out a beer. Though I did still enjoy the occasional drink, I wasn't getting hammered every night like I had when I'd first gotten to the island. One hard-and-fast rule that I'd made for myself was that I wasn't allowed to drink while I was doing security at night. I found I had far fewer hangovers that way, plus I wanted to be prepared in case there ever *was* a security issue that I had to deal with.

I set my beer on the counter as I pulled out a package of ham, some mayo, and a slice of cheese. By the time I'd turned around again, Earnestine had opened my bottle for me.

"Thanks, sweetie," I said, giving her another beak scratch.

"*My pleasure,*" she squawked back.

I'd no sooner made myself a sandwich and taken that first deliciously cool swig of beer than there was a pounding on my door. I glanced down at my Fitbit. It was after two a.m. Who in the hell would be pounding on my door at two in the morning?

I took a quick bite of my sandwich. I half-expected it be Al, Artie, or maybe, if I was lucky, one of the many women I'd slept with since being on the island. Of course I hoped it was the latter. As long as it wasn't one of Mariposa's girls, I was down for a late-night booty delivery service. Before I even got to the door, the pounding started up again.

"Yeah, yeah," I hollered through a mouthful of food. "Coming."

I opened the door and just about choked on my food.

Giselle Marrero stared back at me.

She was the *last* person on the island I expected to see standing on my doorstep at two in the morning, and for damn sure the last person I *wanted* to see.

"Giselle," I gasped, letting out a chortled cough.

She looked concerned. "Are you okay?"

My eyes watered as I nodded. I held up a finger and went back into the kitchen to slug down half of my beer and wash away the bread that was caked against the back of my throat. When I had myself under control, I cleared my throat and motioned her inside.

"Come in."

"You sure you're okay?" She stood in my living room, wringing her hands and wearing what I assumed was a fashionable skirt and top, but to me looked like little more than a matching pair of black leather Band-Aids.

I nodded. "I'm fine. I'm just surprised to see you here. It's after two. Why are you out so late? What's going on? Is everything okay?" And then a thought hit me. "Is it your mom? Is Mariposa okay?"

Still fidgeting with her hands, Giselle glanced around the

room nervously. "Oh, yeah. Mom's fine. But I—I've got a problem, and I didn't know who else to go to."

"Go to? What's going on?" I shut my front door and then turned to face Giselle again. Her dark hair was down around her shoulders. Her lips were bright red, and a thick layer of dark eyeshadow was glommed to her eyelids. She looked nothing like the fresh-faced girl I'd gotten to know over the last week or so. Her makeup paired with her outfit made her look so much older and not nearly as innocent. "And why are you wearing so much makeup?"

"When we first met last week and you said that I should think of you as my *fun* Uncle Drunk, did you mean it?"

My mouth gaped. I certainly hadn't meant *fun* in a "come over to my place at two a.m. looking like *that*" kind of way. I held up my hands and kind of shook my head.

"Giselle, I didn't mean *fun* like—" My hands bounced back and forth between us. "You know, like you and me—"

Her eyes popped open wider when she understood what I thought she meant. "Oh, gawd, I didn't mean it like that, Drunk." She rolled her eyes and sighed. "You said I could come to you for help and talk to you about stuff that my mom might not approve of. Did you really mean that?"

Now that she was actually taking me up on my offer, I teetered on the edge of regret. Especially now that she was at my place dressed so suggestively, I felt like I'd already crossed a line, even though I hadn't done anything even remotely inappropriate. "Well, I mean, I'm happy to help you with anything, of course, but Mariposa would kill me if she kn—"

Fear flickered across Giselle's dark eyes. "No, no. You can't tell my mom I was here."

"I can't tell your mom? I don't know that I can do that. I mean, I promised Mariposa—"

Without another word, Giselle made a break for the door. I took two steps backwards to get there before she could open it and put a hand on it. "Now, hey, just wait a second," I said calmly. "Where are you going?"

"If you're just going to tell my mom, then I came to the wrong person. I thought you were serious that I could come to you if I had a problem. I thought you were the right guy for this. But I was wrong."

"Right guy for what? What's going on, Giselle?"

Biting her bottom lip between her teeth, she shook her head. Unshed tears welled up in her eyes. "I can't tell you if you're going to tell my mom."

I took my hand off the door then. My cop training kicked in, and against my better judgment, I decided it was better that someone knew what was going on with the girl, rather than letting her handle whatever the problem was on her own.

I sighed. "Fine, I won't tell your mom."

She looked up at me then, her eyes big and watery, but mostly hopeful. "Really?"

I nodded.

"You promise?"

I held three fingers up in the air. "Swear."

"*Go to hell, you motherfucking asshole,*" squawked Earnestine.

Giselle's eyes widened as she looked past me into the kitchen. "What was that?"

I smiled at her. "My parrot. Sorry. I taught her to curse on command. I'm alone here most nights. I don't have a lot of other things to do when I get off work." I rushed for Earnestine. "Let me just put her in my room so we can talk. Why don't you have a seat?"

I grabbed Earnestine and took her to my room. When I came back into the living room, Giselle was seated on the far edge of my cushioned rattan sofa. She had her knees pressed together and was leaning forward with her chin in her palms and her elbows on her knees. The skimpy black Band-Aid top she wore smashed her chest together, making me feel incredibly uncomfortable.

I pointed at her uneasily. "What's up with the outfit and all the makeup?"

She looked down at herself, noticed her rampant cleavage, and sat up right. "Oh, I was at a concert."

"You want a t-shirt or something?"

She lifted a shoulder. "No, I'm okay."

I made a face and glanced at the door. A nagging fear that Mariposa was about to come bursting in through my door ate at me. "You look cold to me. You should borrow one of my shirts." I left the room and in seconds was back with the first shirt I saw. I handed it to her, and she shrugged it on over her head.

"Thanks."

That's when I noticed I'd given her my favorite tank top. It had a Red Cross insignia on the front and read Orgasm Donor. I probably should've looked at it before I'd handed it to her, but seeing her covered up put me a little more at ease. I let out a heavy breath.

"You bet. I was just making myself some dinner." I went into the kitchen and grabbed my sandwich and beer. "You want anything?"

"No, thanks. I'm fine."

I carried my dinner into the living room and put it on the coffee table, then sat down on the chair next to the sofa. "Mind if I eat while we talk? I haven't had anything since lunch and I'm starving."

"Oh, no. Go ahead."

I nodded and took a big bite of my sandwich and then leaned back in my chair. "Okay. Now you can tell me what's going on."

As if someone had flipped a switch, tears began to run down Giselle's cheeks. "It's my friend Jordan. She's missing."

7

"MISSING? WHAT DO YOU MEAN SHE'S MISSING?"

"Well, she was supposed to go with me to the Island Wanderers concert tonight. It's her favorite band. But she never showed up."

I frowned and took a drink of my beer to wash down my sandwich. "I don't know if I'd call that missing. That's not that big of a deal. Maybe her plans changed."

Giselle shook her head. The tears were flowing now, making her mascara paint long lines of black down her cheeks. "I don't think she would have willingly missed that concert."

"Okay, then maybe she was there, but you just didn't see her. It wouldn't be hard to miss someone at a concert."

"Our seats were together, though. But that's not all."

I stood up and went into the kitchen to tear a couple paper towels off the roll and walked them over to her.

"Thanks," she whispered before blotting her face.

"Okay. What else?"

"She hasn't returned any of my calls or texted me back since Friday," whispered Giselle.

"When was the last time you saw her?"

"Friday. We hung out. We kind of got into a disagreement. That was when she stopped returning my texts and calls."

I threw up my hands. "Well, then it makes sense that she didn't go to the concert. You two weren't getting along. Maybe she just didn't want to see you."

Giselle blotted her eyes and wiped her nose. "Jordie's not like that. It wouldn't matter if she was *that* mad at me. She'd still go to the concert and sit right next to me. She might ignore me the whole time, but she'd still go."

"You don't know for sure."

"I do know for sure, Drunk. Something happened to her. I know it."

I took a drink of my beer and then sighed. This was not how I wanted to spend my Monday night. "Look. Maybe she just doesn't want to be found right now. Maybe she's taking a little break. You know, putting some space between the two of you."

"That's not it, Drunk. Even if she wanted some space, she wouldn't make me worry. She'd at least text me back and tell me she was okay."

I sighed. "Giselle, just out of curiosity, does your mom know that you're out right now?" I lifted my brows and tipped my head in her direction. "And that you're, you know, dressed like that?"

Giselle's eyes widened. "Of course not! I told you you can't tell her any of this. You promised!" She stood up, like she might bolt again.

I held a hand out to her calmly. "Relax. I was just curious. What does she think you're doing right now?"

Giselle sat back down and gave me a little shrug. "She knows about the concert."

"Surely she doesn't know you're dressed like that."

"No," she admitted, her dark eyes sling-shotting down to her hands in her lap.

"And I have to assume she's smart enough to know concerts don't get over this late?"

Giselle sighed. "She thinks I'm staying over at Jordie's."

"Ah." I nodded. "Well, did it ever occur to you that Jordan is exactly where *she's* supposed to be? Maybe she's just at her house, ignoring your messages."

Giselle shook her head. "When she didn't show up for the concert, that was the first place I went. She's not there."

"Well, surely if she was missing, her parents—"

"She lives with her aunt. Her mom died when she was little. She doesn't know who her dad is."

"Well, have you asked her aunt if she's seen her?"

"Her aunt is in the US. Her grandma has been sick. She went there a couple weeks ago to help take care of her. Jordie's been staying in their apartment by herself."

"You're sure she didn't go with her aunt to the US?"

"Positive."

"And you checked her apartment tonight?"

"Yeah."

"If Jordan's not there and her aunt's not there, how'd you get in?"

"The lock on their balcony door is broken. It's how Jordan and I used to sneak in and out of her apartment when her aunt was home. There's a picnic table under her window. If you stand on it, you can basically climb up to their balcony and over the railing. So I snuck in. Jordie's not there, and I don't think she's been there for a while."

"How can you tell?"

"She's got a cat. Gabby. Gabby's like Jordan's baby. She has pictures of her all over her IG account. She even dresses her cat up for holidays and stuff. Gabby's food bowl was completely empty when I got there, and her water dish was bone dry. She practically attacked me when I came in. She hasn't had food and water for a while. It was pretty obvious."

"Huh," I said, taking another bite of my sandwich while I

rolled all this information around in my mind. When I was done chewing, I tipped my head to the side. "How old is Jordan?"

"Sixteen."

"Has she ever gone missing before?"

"Not that I know of."

"Does she have a boyfriend?"

"Nope."

"A boy that she's been hanging around with?"

Giselle shook her head. "No one like that."

"How about other family on the island? Cousins. Siblings. Other aunts or uncles?"

Giselle shook her head. "No. She doesn't have any brothers or sisters, and as far as I know there were no cousins or other aunts and uncles. It was just her and her aunt."

"What about your other friends? Maybe with her aunt being gone, she didn't want to stay in the apartment alone. Maybe she went to stay with someone else?"

Giselle lifted a shoulder. "That's really doubtful. I'm her best friend. I don't think she has any other girlfriends that she'd feel close enough to stay over at their house. And even if she did, she'd come back to feed Gabby. Drunk, something's wrong. I'm telling you."

"Well, if you're that *sure* that something's wrong, then why did you come to me? Why not go to the island cops?"

Giselle's eyes bulged. She scooted over on the sofa so she was closer to me. "Drunk, I can't go to the cops. And you *absolutely* have to promise me that you won't either."

"Giselle, I can't promise anything. I mean, if there's a missing girl—"

"I mean it, Drunk. You have to promise me!"

I sighed heavily. "I'm not promising anything until I understand what's going on here. And why can't your mom know about this? Doesn't she like Jordan?"

"No, Mom likes Jordan, even though she does think

Jordan's a little wild. But we've been friends since we were little. If she knew that I wasn't really staying over at Jordan's house tonight, she'd freak out. Plus, she might not trust me and Jordan to hang out anymore. I just don't want to cause any problems unnecessarily."

"And why can't we go to the cops?"

"Well, obviously, my mom might find out about all of this then."

"But if your best friend's missing, I'd think you'd want to do everything you could to find her."

"I am doing everything I can to find her. I came to you. You're a cop. You saved that woman. And you figured out who killed that guy and took Mr. Balladares. I just don't want to go to the cops and get Jordan in trouble if I don't need to."

"You know, you said yourself that Jordan's kind of a wild child. Maybe she ran off."

"Jordie wouldn't do that."

"You can't be sure. I mean, her aunt and her grandmother are in the US. Maybe she decided to hop a plane and go be with them."

Giselle pursed her lips as she mulled that over in her head. "But then why isn't she texting me back?"

"Seriously? Why does anyone not text someone else back? They're busy. Their battery died. They're mad. They don't have a signal. They didn't pay their cell bill. You want me to continue?"

A small, sheepish smile played around Giselle's lips then. "No. I got it."

I nodded. "I'm sure Jordan is just fine. Okay?"

"But that still doesn't explain Gabby. Look, will you do some checking for me? Just to make sure?"

I sighed. I really didn't want to waste my time looking for a kid who'd probably run off to be with her aunt in the US. "Will it make you feel better?"

"*Much* better," she assured me. Her hands went to the

center of her chest, and she clasped them together and gave me her best sad puppy dog eyes. I was pretty sure there wasn't a girl in the world I could say no to with those sad puppy dog eyes.

I slumped forward. As much as I *didn't* want to go look for some runaway sixteen-year-old wild child, I also wanted to be the person that people could rely on for help. After all, hadn't I been the one to tell Giselle that she could think of me as her Funcle Drunk? The guy who she could come to when she needed something? This was my own fault.

Put up or shut up, Drunk.

"Fine. I'll do a little poking around. See what I can find out. But no promises."

Giselle squealed and launched her thin frame into my arms. "Omigosh, thank you! You have no idea how relieved I am."

With her arms wrapped around me, I shot a glance at the door once again. Being alone in the same room with Mariposa's underage daughter made me uncomfortable. Having her arms around my neck made me downright uneasy. I patted her back stiffly and then unpeeled her arms from my neck.

"Yeah, I'll help. But for now this stays between the two of us. I don't need your mom giving me a hard time."

Giselle's eyes brightened. "Duh. I told you I don't want her to know. Of course I wouldn't tell her."

"So, do you have a picture of Jordan and some details about her? Full name. Address. Links to her social media accounts, stuff like that?"

Giselle nodded and unlocked her phone. Swiping through her pictures, she settled on a close-up of a short brunette with big brown eyes and smooth shoulder-length brown hair. She held an orange tabby cat in her arms.

"This is Jordan. Her last name is Lambert. And that's her cat, Gabby."

"I assumed," I said, nodding. She looked innocent enough.

I was confident I'd find her safely in the US. with her family. I walked into my kitchen and jotted down my cell number on a slip of paper and handed it to her. "Send the picture to me and text me whatever you can think of that will help. I'll see what I can dig up tomorrow."

"Thanks, Drunk. I owe you big."

8

AFTER MY RUN AND A SHOWER THE NEXT MORNING, I WENT IN search of Al. I found him down by the pool paying miniature golf with Gary "The Gunslinger" Wheelan, Big Eddie, and Ralph the Weasel, three of Al's card-playing buddies. It was a strange sight to see them all out of their natural habitat, the breezy shade of the clubhouse's covered back porch. Now leaning on their golf putters beneath the bright Caribbean sun, they all had beads of sweat on their brows and were deep in a heated conversation over whether Al's last shot had been talent or just dumb luck.

But when I approached, all conversation immediately ceased and everyone turned to smile at me like I was the prettiest girl at the dance. Somehow, by no means of my own, it seemed, I had become a bit of a BMOC around the Seacoast Majestic. At thirty-five years old, I wasn't exactly a spring chicken, but Al's buddies, who had been all around when dirt was invented, were a little jealous. They wanted to be young and carefree again, but their hip replacements, osteoporosis, and sagging moobs wouldn't let them. Which was why they enjoyed living vicariously through tales of the many women I'd dated and stories about things I'd seen as a rookie cop when I'd worked for the Kansas City PD back in the States. But it was the stories about how I'd saved Artie, my ex, and Al's finger that made for the majority of repeated bedtime stories.

"Heya, Drunk," said Gary, a full-time resident who lived in the cottages down by Al. Gary was a tall, thick man with a receding hairline and a potbelly. He accentuated his rotundness by tucking his polo shirts tightly into his denim shorts. Today his polo of choice was salmon-colored. There were only three things in life Gary liked to talk about: his 1978 FJ40, his annoying little ankle biter, Skully, and his former life in the military and then as a security guard at the Mall of America. He bent over, clubbed a ball through a hole beneath a windmill, and then looked up at me again. "How's security?"

"Tight as always, Gary," I said, giving him a little salute. Maybe it was a corny ritual, but it always made Gary smile and salute me back.

"It's a hot one, eh, Drunk?" said Big Eddie, his moniker being a misnomer of course. In reality, he was a shriveled-up old man with thin bird legs, a former computer geek who struck it rich working for Dell in their glory days. Big Eddie had skin the color of new-fallen Missouri snow, which was hard to believe considering he'd lived full-time at the Caribbean resort for the last two years. He wore a button-down white linen shirt with a pocket protector. He was the guy that always carried two mechanical pencils in that pocket, a palm-size steno pad, and his black browline reading glasses. Today he wore a sun visor pulled down low over his face, and I could tell that he wore sunscreen on his arms and the back of his neck because the white cream was still visible on his skin and he smelled of coconut and zinc oxide.

"It's always a hot one, Eddie. We live on a Caribbean island," I said, looking up at the sun through my knock-off Ray-Bans.

"Seems hotter than usual is all," he said, shuffling over to take his turn hitting the little ball.

"That's because you're actually standing in the sun today. What happened to cards?"

"The rest of the guys had other stuff to do this morning. No point in playing if I can only take *their* money," said Al, nodding his head towards his buddies.

Ralph the Weasel, a tall black man with fuzzy white hair, a flat nose, and an uncanny resemblance to Morgan Freeman, smiled at Al. "Speaking of money, I'll be taking your money after this shot." He gave the ball a whack, sending it through a hole beneath a plywood monkey's ass. His hands went up into the air. Victory. "That'll be fifty cents each, fellas. Pay up."

I shook my head. Oldies amazed me. "You know, I can't decide if I'm looking forward to the day when I have nothing better to do than to bet fifty cents on the outcome of a miniature golf game or if I'd rather kill myself if that day ever comes to fruition."

Al pointed at me. "Don't knock it, kid. There's something to be said about a relaxing game of golf."

"Alright, well, when you're done playing put the ball in the clown's mouth, I got a case I thought you might wanna help me with."

Al's head snapped up then, his eyes bright and hopeful. "Some kind of mystery to solve?"

I shrugged. I wouldn't go so far as to call it a mystery, but if it made Al look cool in front of his friends, I could play along. "Something like that."

His once-bright eyes narrowed to pinpricks. "This isn't just your way of getting me to ride along in the banana boat, is it? I'm not in the mood to pick up more hookers."

Gary, Big Ed, and the Weaz all looked up at Al with interest.

"Al! What's Evie got to say about you picking up hookers?" asked Gary.

"Hey, don't look at me." Al pointed a gnarled finger in my direction. "It was all Drunk. I was just there for moral support." He shook his head. "Supporting the kid's morals is a full-time job, you know."

I stared at Al. "Shit, Al. Listen to what you're saying. This is how rumors get started. I'm trying to clean up my image around here." I lifted my hat to run a hand through my damp hair. I put the hat back on and let out a heavy sigh. "Look, guys. We didn't pick up any hookers, alright? Al's full of shit."

"What's the matter, Drunk? Hooker shoot you down?" asked the Weaz with a bright-eyed chuckle.

I frowned. "Anyone ever tell you guys you're assholes?"

"Only every day," said the Weaz.

"Hey, Drunk, next time you and Al pick up hookers, you should bring us along," said Gary with a straight face.

I started to walk away, swatting a hand backwards over my head. "Alright. Alright. You fellas have fun playin' with your balls. I'm outta here." I took long strides towards the golf cart that I'd borrowed to give me a ride down to the pool.

Seconds later, I heard my name behind me.

"Jeez, kid, I don't have legs that long. Slow up."

I stopped and looked over my shoulder to see Al hobbling as fast as he could towards me. "Look, Al, never mind. I'll handle this on my own."

"What's the matter? You can't take a little shit anymore?"

"I can take plenty. I'm just tired. I was up late. There's a sixteen-year-old kid missing. A girl. I was asked to help find her."

Al's face sobered up then. "Oh. You really do have a case to solve? Well, why didn't you just say so? I wanna help."

"Alright, but you need to give this hooker shit a rest."

Al nodded his head. "Alright. Alright. I'll let it go. So what's the story?"

I pointed at the golf cart. "Get in. I'll tell you everything on the way."

9

"So, lemme get this straight. You *haven't* told Mariposa that her daughter's best friend since childhood is missing?" asked Al as we drove my new-to-me Wrangler off the resort property and towards town. Finally having my own wheels on the island felt good, and it was especially nice not having to ask Artie to borrow a vehicle.

With one elbow resting out the window, I glanced over at Al. He seemed smaller than usual, seated in the passenger's seat of my new ride. The seat dwarfed him, reminding me a little of Edith Ann, a show I remembered my mom watching when I was a kid.

"No. Giselle asked me not to tell. So, that means you can't tell either."

Al shook his head. "I don't know, Drunk. I'm not very good at holding in secrets."

"You're not very good at holding gas in either, but should that keep you from trying?"

Al frowned. "I'm serious, kid. I can't *not* tell this to Evie. I tell her everything."

"Did you tell her that you met a hooker last weekend?"

Al's mouth snapped shut. With his weathered old lips pressed together, he gave me a stinky side-eye.

I gave him an exclamatory nod. "I didn't think so."

"That was different, kid."

"No, it wasn't," I said with a chuckle. "But whatever. You can tell Evie, but she can't tell Mariposa. Once we find Jordan safe and sound, then maybe Mari can know. Until then, mum's the word. Okay?"

Al nodded. "Alright." He looked out the window. "So where are we going to start looking for this girl?"

"Giselle gave me the address to her aunt's apartment. I think we'll start there. I also put a call into Lola over at the airport. She's checking the manifests for me to see if Jordan flew off the island. Hopefully I'll hear back from her soon."

"So do you think she just ran off?"

I shrugged. "I have a feeling Lola's going to call me back, and we'll see she went to find her aunt in the US."

"So you think she's alright?"

"We really have no reason to think otherwise. But we'll check out her apartment and see if we can't pick up her scent."

JORDAN LAMBERT LIVED in an apartment building just two blocks away from where Camila Vergado lived. Camila had been the witness to a murder months prior. Her place had been in a not-so-great part of town, and Jordan's neighborhood wasn't much better. Her apartment building was a pale yellow two-story rectangular box. Green shutters flanked every window, and each second-floor apartment had sliding glass doors that opened to a small balcony with a white railing. Outside, an iron fence ran around the perimeter of the property, and two newly planted palm trees stood out front like sentinels.

"Giselle said Jordan's apartment is in the back. She said she always got in through the balcony door. I'll run around back and see if I can't get in that way. Meet me in the hallway upstairs and I'll let you in."

Al nodded. "Be careful, kid."

I slipped around the back of the building and found the picnic table Giselle had spoken of beneath one of the balcony windows. My eyes scanned the backyard, hoping no one was looking out their windows as I climbed on top of the table and scaled the balcony. The sliding glass balcony door didn't even pretend to offer resistance, instead sliding open easily.

As if she'd been expecting my arrival, Gabby greeted me immediately. "Meow." The orange tabby cat rubbed her fur up against my legs as if she were starved for attention. I reached down and scooped her up. "Well, hello, beautiful. Are you lonesome?" Scratching her behind her ears immediately kick-started her internal purring mechanism. With her cradled in my arms, I walked to the door and poked my head out into the hallway.

Al stood at the opposite end of the staircase with his arms pinned behind his back.

"Al! Over here." I waved at him with my free arm.

When we were both inside Jordan's apartment with the door closed, I handed Gabby to Al. "This is Gabby. She needs some attention."

He frowned. "Well, what do you expect me to do about it?"

"I don't know. Take her out for a drink. Buy her some flowers. Tell her she smells nice."

Al looked at down at the cat uncomfortably.

"For fuck's sake, Al. It's a cat. She just wants to you to pet her."

"Oh." Al patted the top of the cat's head like it was a basketball and he was just learning to dribble.

"Not like that," I said, heavily exasperated. "Like this." I scooped Gabby back up and snuggled her closely, scratching her under her chin. "Haven't you ever had a cat before?"

"The girls had cats. When they were little. I was never much of a cat person, though."

I could tell. I sighed. "Fine. I'll hold the cat. You snoop around."

"Where should I start?"

I nodded towards some papers on the kitchen counter. "Why don't you go through those? I'm gonna go look through her bedroom."

"What are we looking for?"

"I don't know. Anything that might explain where she went or why." Gabby and I went down the hallway. I poked my head in the first doorway on my left. It was a small bathroom. It was obvious that women lived here. Makeup and hair products covered the small white vanity. Dirty clothes littered the floor. A towel was slung over the shower rod. I put up a hand to feel it. Dry as a bone.

I went back into the hallway. Across the hall was a bedroom. The bed was made up with a blue floral quilt. There was a lamp on the nightstand and an alarm clock. I pulled open the top drawer to see a Bible and a flashlight. The closet had lots of empty hangers. I was fairly confident I'd discovered the aunt's room.

Back in the hallway again, I went to the end of the hallway and took a left. It was the smaller of the two rooms and most definitely Jordan's. Clothes were strewn everywhere. There were posters and photographs on the wall. A partially eaten bowl of cat food was near the bed with a little bowl of water next to it. I put Gabby on the floor and refilled the cat food bowl from the container next to it. Then I began to poke through Jordan's stuff.

If taken out of context, one might have thought the messy scene before me was due to a burglar ransacking the place, but based on the messy bathroom and the aunt's clean bedroom, I had a feeling this was just Jordan's normal way of doing things. I picked up a long red plastic backscratcher lying next to her bed and began to poke at her clothing, turning things over, unsure of what I was looking for but hoping I'd find it. But everywhere I looked, I only discovered a floor at the bottom of the pile.

When digging through her clothes didn't pan out, I went to her nightstand and opened the top drawer, thinking maybe I'd luck out and find a diary or a note of some sort. But to no avail. I only found a stack of *Cosmopolitan* and *Vogue* magazines. I flipped through each one quickly, but no notes materialized. The second drawer wasn't any better. It was stuffed full of underwear. And the bottom drawer was stuffed full of bras.

Her dresser was completely covered with makeup, a blow dryer, and other girl hair necessities. I looked up and stared at my reflection in the mirror. My sunglasses clung to the brim of my hat. I combed the hair around my chin with my fingers. My beard had gotten so thick that it was starting to get hot, but it was almost at the end of its growing cycle. Soon I'd cut it and start all over again.

My attention traveled to the perimeter of Jordan's mirror. Pictures covered every inch of it, like a frame. There were pictures of Jordan with Gabby. Jordan with Giselle. Jordan with an older woman that I had to assume was her aunt. Jordan with other girlfriends. In every picture, Jordan smiled like she didn't have a care in the world. I couldn't help but wonder why a girl who seemed so carefree would run off without so much as a word to her best friend.

On the right side of the dresser was a small blue jewelry box. I opened the lid to find it jam-packed with rings and earrings. I moved it slightly and noticed a slip of folded paper tucked beneath it. I pulled it out and unfolded it. It was an invitation. *You are invited to a private party at Club Cobalt. Saturday. After 10 p.m.* I stuck it in my pocket and kept looking.

Al stuck his head in the room then. "Hey, Drunk, come here. You should see this."

"Yeah, okay." Gabby purred at my ankles again. I bent

down, picked her up, and headed for the kitchen. "What'd you find?"

Al had opened bills spread across the counter. "They're behind on everything. Their utilities. Their cellular phone bill. There's even an eviction notice here for their apartment."

"Huh." I stared down at the large overdue balances.

"Maybe Jordan decided to leave before she could be evicted."

"Maybe. That might explain why she didn't say anything to Giselle. Maybe she was embarrassed," I said, nodding. "But you'd think she'd take her cat. Or at least find her a good home."

"Did you find anything?" asked Al, shuffling sideways to look at me.

"Not really. I found an invitation to a party at a club in the District. I don't know if that's anything, but we can check it out."

"So what should we do about the cat?" asked Al.

"We'll leave her here. I'm sure now that Giselle knows Jordan's not feeding her, she'll come over and take care of her."

My phone rang. "Drunk here."

"Hi, Drunk, it's Lola at Paradise International."

I set Gabby on the counter and leaned a hip up against it. "Of course it is. I'd recognize that beautiful voice anywhere."

Al rolled his eyes and scooted towards the door. "I'll be in the banana boat."

I waved Al on as I heard Lola giggle. She was definitely someone I wanted to take out one of these days. "So do you have anything for me?"

"I looked up that name you asked me to, Jordan Lambert. I couldn't find anyone by that name flying in or out. At least not in the last two weeks. Do you want me to check further back than that?"

I frowned and let out a little sigh. "No, that's fine."

"Sorry, Drunk. Is everything okay?"

"Yeah, just a customer trying to skip out on their tab. I'll figure it out. Thanks a lot for checking. I owe you one. How about I take you out for a drink sometime?"

"Sure. I'd like that. When?"

"I'll give you a call when I get this whole thing I'm working on resolved. How about that?"

"Yeah, sounds good. Take care, Drunk."

"You too, Lola."

Now that I had a date with the lovely Lola planned for when I found Jordan Lambert, I was more determined than ever to find the girl.

I gave Gabby another quick scratch, locked the front door, and pulled it shut behind me. So Jordan hadn't left the island. Now I was really curious as to where she was hiding.

Back in the vehicle, Al looked over at me. "So? Did Jordan leave the island?"

I put the Jeep in drive. "If she did, it wasn't on an airplane."

"So now what?"

"Now? Now I think it's time to pay Frankie a little visit. What do you think?"

Al turned and looked at me suspiciously. "Fine, but just remember, kid, this is for business, not pleasure."

I grinned at him. "Are you kidding? Where Frankie's concerned, you can't *have* one without the other."

10

FRANCESCA CRUZ WAS A POLICE OFFICER FOR THE PARADISE ISLE Royal Police Force. She'd helped me on a couple of other cases in the past, and I felt confident that she'd be able to help me out once again. I parked my Jeep in the parking lot across the street from the PIRPF, next to a tricked-out black Escalade.

Inside, Officer Jefferson, a young, pudgy-faced fellow with one wandering eye, was seated at the front desk as usual.

"Hey, Officer Jefferson, what's going on?" I said, coming in hot with my hand extended.

The man smiled at us. He was a likable enough fellow, and though not many of the other police officers seemed to appreciate my specific brand of cereal, Officer Jefferson was always friendly towards me.

"Not much, Drunk. It's been a pretty quiet day."

I nodded. "That's always good to hear. Hey, I'm looking for Officer Cruz. Is she in by any chance?"

"Oh, yeah, she's at her desk. I'll get her."

"I'd appreciate that."

We waited while Jefferson called her to the front. Minutes later, she appeared in front of us. As always, the sight of her took my breath away. Even in her police-issued uniform,

Frankie's athletic curves stood out. She had dark, exotic eyes and a sleek black ponytail. Truth be told, I was immensely attracted to Ms. Francesca Cruz. And not just in an I-wanna-bone kind of way. No, I had too much respect for the woman to look at her like that. Not that I'd never thought about what it would be like to take her to bed. I mean, come on, I wasn't a choirboy, after all. I had to have a lot of self-discipline when she was around. Otherwise, it was too difficult working together if I allowed my mind to wander freely.

"Danny, Mr. Becker—hey, what are you two doing here?"

Al was the first to give her a hug. "Please, Francesca, call me Al."

She chuckled. "Good to see you, Al."

When it was my turn, I opened up wide for a hug. "Damn, Frankie, looking good as always."

She laughed as I enveloped her.

Squeezing her tightly, I whispered in her ear, "I missed you, woman."

"Yeah, I noticed how much you missed me. All those missed calls and texts on my phone and all—"

"I'm sorry," I said, pulling back to give her a sheepish smile. "I've been doing some soul searching. I figured I had a lot to prove to myself before we could hang out again."

"Oh yeah? Have you finished yet?" She smiled, her hands on her hips.

"I'm getting closer."

"Well, good. I wouldn't mind catching up."

"For sure. We'll catch up. But first, Al and I are working on something. We were wondering if maybe we could ask you a couple questions. Kind of off the record."

"Off the record?" Her shoulders crumpled. "Come on, Danny. I can't keep doing these projects with you off the record. Every single thing we've worked on together has put me lower and lower on the totem pole around here. If I get any lower, I'll be scraping gum off the bottom of Sergeant Gibson's shoes."

I balked. "You're kidding. That last arrest didn't do *anything* to help you move up rank towards inspector?"

"I don't know about it helping me to move up rank," she said with a chuckle, "but it certainly didn't earn me any brownie points with Gibson."

"Ugh. What's his issue?"

She shook her head. "He just doesn't like me. Never has."

"Because you're a woman?" I asked.

"Because he's a chucklehead," blurted Al, glancing around like he was listening but not invested in the conversation.

Frankie grinned and her head kind of bobbed. "All of the above and maybe because I lived in the States for a while. Maybe he looks at me like I'm an American? I don't know what else it could be."

"Okay, well, you don't have to get involved. I just need to ask you a couple questions. That's it. Then you can wash your hands of me."

She chuckled. "Who said I want to wash my hands of you? We just can't partner up anymore."

I smiled. "That's fine. I've got Al here. We can figure this out together."

She looked at me and then at Al thoughtfully. Finally, she sighed. "Just a few questions?"

"Yeah, it'll only take five minutes, I swear."

"Fine. Come on." She beckoned for us to follow her.

We walked past several closed office doors including Sergeant Gibson's before we got to her office, which was little more than a partially enclosed cubicle amongst other partially enclosed cubicles—some with officers and/or criminals in them and some without. The whole room buzzed with activity, and the familiar pungent smell of coffee and stale cigarette smoke filled my nose, reminding me to be thankful that I wasn't a cop anymore. Now I got to smell salt, sand, and seaweed, and I was all the better for it.

Al and I both took a seat in front of her desk. I pointed to her boss's office. Sergeant Gibson, a stocky man with skin the color of obsidian and a voice just as deep, sat behind his desk, chatting with a very tall, broad-shouldered man in a slick black suit. The man had dark wavy hair and shiny black shoes, and he looked like if Javier Bardem and Negan from *The Walking Dead* had a triplet brother. "Who's the VIP?"

"Rupert Villanueva. He's the commissioner of customs."

I tipped my head sideways as I looked over at Al. "No shit? That's the guy I need to thank for raising the tariffs so high that I could barely afford to buy a new vehicle."

Al patted my knee. "Let it go, kid. What's done is done."

"Danny. You bought a new car?" asked Frankie.

I tore my eyes off the commissioner and looked at Frankie. "Yeah. A Jeep. I was tired of bumming rides off people and borrowing the resort's car."

She nodded. "It's a small island, but everything is so spread out you need a vehicle to get anywhere. It's probably long overdue."

Al pointed his finger at her. "That's exactly what I said. He just didn't want to spend the cash."

"Hey, frugal is sexy." I shrugged and gave Frankie a playful smile. "Especially after *someone* decided to give all my money to their *brothers*. I'm not naming any names, though."

She chuckled. "Hey, you owed them. You blew up my brother's boat!"

"And I would have taken care of that obligation."

"Really." She looked at me like she doubted me.

"Of course I would have. I'm a nice guy, Frankie."

She leaned back in her seat and nodded. "I know you are, Danny. And I believe you would've taken care of your obligation to my brothers. Maybe I was wrong for coercing you into give them *all* of the money."

I shrugged. "Coercing?" I balked. "You told me I could either give it to them or to the cops!"

I was sure I saw her blush. "And that was wrong of me. I was just trying to make it right with my brothers. I didn't want them to get screwed over in the end because then I'd never hear the end of it."

I leaned back in my seat. "I didn't come here to argue with you about that, Frankie. Like you said, it really wasn't mine to start with anyway, so it wasn't mine to lose. Plus, I'm not completely broke. Not yet anyway."

She nodded. "I'm proud of you for taking it so well, Danny."

"I am too, kid," agreed Al, patting me on the shoulder. "Good for you. I like your attitude."

"Thank you." I leaned forward then. "Now. About the reason we're here…"

Frankie lowered her brows and nodded, her face taking on a more somber look. "Yeah, what's going on? Is everything okay?"

"I don't know. First of all, I promised I would handle this on my own, so I need you to promise that this is off the record. At least for now."

"Has a crime been committed?"

"We don't know," said Al.

"Not yet anyway. That's what we're trying to figure out. There's a girl. No one has heard from her for a while. I'm just trying to track her down."

"A girl? How old is she?"

"Sixteen."

Frankie nodded. "It happens. Seems like there are more and more every year."

"You're kidding," said Al. "Why is that?"

She shook her head. "You know, I couldn't really tell you. Most of them are runaways. Gibson doesn't like wasting a lot of department resources on kids that run away and end up coming back on their own."

"But you couldn't—" I began.

She shook her head and cut me off before I could finish my sentence. "I can't do anything Sergeant Gibson doesn't want me to do. It's just the way it is. He's the boss, and if I ever want to get ahead, I've got to play by his rules."

"So you just let young girls like that stay missing?"

"No, we start files on them. We do what we can do, but you don't understand, Danny. Most of them return home, but occasionally there's that one that doesn't."

"That's just terrible."

She nodded. "I completely agree."

"Well, I'm not going to let this girl stay missing. I promised I'd do my best to find her, and that's what I'm going to do."

"That's very noble of you, Danny. Who's the girl?"

"A woman that I work with has a seventeen-year-old daughter that just started a summer internship at the resort. It's her best friend. My coworker doesn't know that her daughter came to me. Teenage girl stuff, I guess. But I promised I'd keep it close to the vest until we got further in the investigation."

Frankie threw up her hands. "You want me to run a background check on her?"

"I was hoping you could do that," I said, nodding. "And maybe see if she's in any local lockups?"

"Sure. What's her name?" Frankie leaned forward in her seat and awakened her computer.

"Jordan Lambert."

She typed the name into her computer system while we sat waiting. Finally, she gave me a tight grin. "Sorry, Danny. I don't see anyone in the system with that name. As far as I can tell, she's never been arrested."

I sighed. "Damn it. I was hoping maybe she was sitting safely in a jail cell somewhere. That would've made it easy to find her."

Frankie gave me a sympathetic smile. "Have you tried her extended family?"

"She doesn't have any other family on the island, and I've checked the airport. If she left the island, it wasn't by plane."

"I wish I could help you more."

I shook my head. "No, you've done enough. Al and I are going to have to get creative," I said determinedly. "Right, Al?"

His head bobbed. "We're going to do our best."

I stood up then. "Okay, we'll get out of your hair, Frankie. Thanks. If you hear anything about this girl or get any tips, would you keep us in the loop?"

"Oh, for sure. You didn't even have to ask, Danny. I'll keep my ear to the ground for you."

"Thanks, Frankie."

I held my arms out to give her another hug, but she glanced around the room full of other police officers and criminals and held out her hand instead. "It was good to see you again, Danny. Al."

I chuckled as I squeezed her hand. "You too, Officer Cruz."

11

LEAVING THE COP SHOP WITH LITTLE TO GO ON, AL AND I DECIDED
to follow up on the only other lead we had—the invitation to a
private party I'd found in Jordan's bedroom. Club Cobalt,
located in what the locals referred to as "the District," was a
twenty-one-and-over establishment, and the fact that Jordan
had an invitation to a party there made me wonder how she'd
gotten it and if maybe she'd met someone there that she didn't
want Giselle to know about. I held out hope that we might find
someone there that would say they'd seen her recently and
might be able to give us a clue as to her whereabouts.

It was barely eleven o'clock when we pulled up in front of
Club Cobalt. The sun shone brightly, the palm trees that lined
the empty streets casting long, lonely shadows. The District
looked like a ghost town without any cars or pedestrians
in sight.

I shut off the engine and leaned forward against my
steering wheel so I could look at the club's darkly tinted glass
front door. "It doesn't look like they're open yet."

"You should check anyway," said Al.

Opening my door, I hopped down out of the vehicle and
walked over to the door. It was locked. The sign said they

didn't open until noon. I got back inside the Jeep and restarted the engine.

"They open?"

"Nah. Not until noon."

"I could go for some lunch," said Al, glancing down at his watch.

"It's not even eleven yet."

"Restaurants open earlier than bars, kid."

Marveling, I stared over at him. "I don't get it. You literally eat all day long, and yet you never grow."

He shrugged. "I have a high metabolism."

"You have an *old* metabolism. There's a difference. You're growing backwards. Pretty soon you'll be so small, you'll just be like a black hole."

"I had a black hole once." Al looked over at me and cracked a smile. "It was in my black sock." He chuckled.

I rolled my eyes. "Those are the kinds of jokes that'll get you sent to dad joke jail, Al."

He grinned. "You know when a regular joke graduates to being a dad joke?"

I lifted a brow curiously, but before I could respond, Al answered for me.

"When it becomes apparent." He chuckled.

"Oh, jeez. You make me wanna drink."

"Let's go get lunch, then. You can have a margarita. I'm in the mood for Mexican, but no more of those taquitos."

"Yeah, you don't have to tell me twice." I'd only driven a few blocks when my phone rang. "Drunk here."

"Hey, Drunk. It's D. How's it going?"

"Diego, hey man. It's going alright. What's up?" Diego Cruz was one of Frankie's older brothers.

"Miguel asked me to call and see if you had a minute. We got something we wanna chat with you about."

"Is that right? Well, Al and I are in town. We just saw Frankie, actually."

"Oh, yeah? Where at?"

"At the station. We're heading to lunch now."

"Lunch?" Diego sounded surprised. "It's not even eleven o'clock yet, bro."

I shot a sideways glance over at Al. "I'm aware. But we can probably hold off a minute. Where are you? Over at the marina?"

"Yeah, man. We'll all be here for the next hour or so if you have time to stop by."

"Alright. We'll be over shortly."

"See you then."

I hung up the phone and looked over at Al. "That was Diego. The Cruz brothers wanna have a word with me. Can we swing by the marina before we do lunch?"

Al threw up his hands. "If we must."

"Alright. Let's go."

THE KING'S BAY MARINA wasn't far from the District. I parked in their parking lot next to a white van with a big fish-shaped magnet on the side that read Cruz Bros. Commercial Fishing and Charter Fleet.

Waiting for Al on the side of the vehicle, I looked around. The Cruz brothers had made some serious improvements since the last time I'd been there. I was pretty sure the van was a new addition as I hadn't seen it before. The narrow wooden walkway that connected the parking lot to the little marina building had doubled in width and the marina building itself looked to have new siding, new windows and a new front door, and if I wasn't mistaken, the entire building looked bigger than it had the last time I'd been there. I wondered if they hadn't added onto it.

"Wow," said Al as we walked towards the office building. "They've made some serious upgrades around here."

"No shit," I grumbled. "I bet my money had a little something to do with that." Though I wouldn't come right out and say it, I was still a little salty about the way things had gone down.

"I'd say it did," agreed Al, bobbing his head.

"I imagine that's why I'm here. They probably wanted to rub my nose in their good fortune."

Al patted me on the back. "Stay cool, kid."

"Yeah, I know." I gritted my teeth and forced a smile on my face as I pushed open the front door to the marina office, where Solo and Beto Cruz worked. "I got this," I mumbled under my breath.

"Hey, Drunk! Al!" said Rico, the shortest of the Cruz brothers. He rushed over to give us each a bro hug, but Al was old-school and Rico had to settle for a handshake.

"How's it going, Rico? Hey, fellas," I said, nodding at the rest of the burly Cruz brothers, who were all standing around in the middle of the marina office, talking loudly and laughing. We all took a minute to exchange bro hugs or handshakes and hellos. Except Solo, the oldest and most somber of the Cruz brothers. He sat at his desk with his feet up, calmly watching the commotion. When I approached him, he made no effort to get up. He did, however, offer me a hand.

"Drunk. Good to see you."

"You too, Solo. How's the family?"

"They're good. Thank you for asking."

"I just came from seeing Frankie. She's looking good as always."

The almost imperceptible smile he'd had vanished, leaving behind traces of a frown. I was sure he didn't like hearing that I was still in contact with his sister. But ultimately, he'd promised to let her lead her own life and keep his opinion to himself.

With his lips smashed together, he gave me a bit of a nod. "Mmm. Yes." He looked over my shoulder at Al. "Mr. Becker, how are you?" Solo went out of his way to get to his feet to shake Al's hand. Whether it was a diss to me or a tribute to being raised by his mother to stand when greeting an elder, I wasn't sure. I decided to take it as the latter.

"Good to see you, Solo. I like what you've done with the place," said Al, his eyes scanning the place.

Solo's head bobbed as he sat back down at the desk and folded his hands across his chest. "Yes, I think it all turned out nice."

I took a step back so I could see all the brothers clearly. I put a hand on either hip and nodded. "You can definitely tell that you've infused some money into things."

Miguel, the second-oldest of the brothers, a wide man with a round face and huge muscular arms, nodded. "That's why we asked you to come over, Drunk."

I did my best to fight back any feelings about that. I'd been right. They'd called me over to rub my nose in my loss and their gain. But out of respect for Frankie as well as for them and what they'd done to help me save Al and my ex, I simply nodded. "Well, it all looks great. Really. You guys did a great job. I'm glad you were able to put the money to good use."

Diego smiled at me. "Nah, Drunk. We didn't call you over to just to show you the improvements."

My brows knitted together as I frowned. "Okay? Then why am I here?"

Miguel glanced backwards at Solo, who gave him a little head nod as if to say, *Go ahead, you tell him.* "For starters, we replaced the boat that got blown to pieces."

"And we bought two more," added Diego. "Rico's running his own charter now."

I shot Rico a genuine smile. I knew that was something he'd been wanting. "Hey, good for you, Rico. That's great."

"We'll be hiring another captain to handle the fourth one."

"Wow. Four boats. You really do have a Cruz brothers fleet now."

Miguel nodded. "Sure do."

Beto gestured around. "Plus, as you noticed, there was enough left over to fix the marina up."

I swallowed hard, nodding. "You really stretched the money, that's for sure."

"We couldn't have done it without you, Drunk," said Miguel.

"Yeah, we owe you a lot," agreed Rico, nodding. "I wouldn't be captaining my own boat if it wasn't for you. Thanks, man."

I glanced over at Al. "Well, my buddy Al might not be here if it wasn't for you guys helping me out. And Pam, she'd probably be at the bottom of the Atlantic, you know? So, it's all good."

Al looked up at me and gave me a tight smile. I knew what he was thinking without him even saying it. He was saying, *Good job, kid. Way to take one in the nuts.*

Miguel nodded. "We know it was a team effort, but we don't think it's fair that we all came out so good and you didn't. You did a noble thing saving your ex. Especially after she did you wrong. So, we've decided we want to cut you in on the business."

My head tipped to the side. "Cut me in on the—"

"Yeah, man, we want you to be a silent partner in the Cruz Brothers Commercial Fishing and Charter Fleet business," added Diego excitedly.

My jaw dropped. I wasn't sure if I was hearing them correctly. I glanced over at Al. A smile had already spread across his face. Apparently I'd heard them correctly. They wanted to cut me in. "Are you serious, guys?"

"Dead serious," said Diego, sporting a hundred-megawatt smile. "The Cruz brothers don't joke around about money."

Except for the low hum of the air conditioner, the whole room had gone silent. From where I stood, I could see boats docked out in the harbor and the sun reflecting off the smooth, glassy water. My mouth hung open. I was speechless.

Al smiled. "Wow, fellas. This is amazing. You did something even I can't do. You got this guy to stop talking."

Several of the Cruz brothers chuckled.

After an extended silence, I finally shook my head. "I'm in shock. I didn't expect this at all. I'm just—fucking shocked," I repeated with an ear-to-ear smile. "Thank you. I mean, I've got some great ideas. You know what we could do? We could—"

But Miguel held a hand up to stop me cold. "Drunk. We said a *silent* partner. That means we make all the decisions, but we cut you in on the profits. *Comprende?*"

I clamped my mouth shut. As the words *silent partner* sank in, I couldn't help but nod. I clicked my cheek and shot Miguel a wink. "Yeah, I got it."

"We figured we wouldn't be where we were without you, so it was only fair that you get a part of the proceeds. We'll send you a check quarterly. This is your first cut," said Miguel, handing me a check. "It's not much. We've mostly been working on getting our equipment up to speed. Next will be growing our clientele and focusing on advertising, so hopefully next check you'll see a bump. Beto's working on the paperwork for the deal. We'll get it to you to sign next week sometime."

I looked down at the check. It was for six hundred bucks. Hardly a return on such a handsome investment, but I didn't care. It was a start, and I was ecstatic. "Guys, you know what this means, don't you?"

"That you're not broke after all?" asked Rico, his face covered in a smile.

I chuckled. "Well, yeah, that too." I shook my head, smiling. "It also means that we're tied together now. It's like I'm a Cruz brother."

From his desk, Solo rolled his eyes and let his head loll

back on his shoulders. I knew he didn't like the sound of that, but I didn't care.

Diego and Rico laughed.

And then suddenly, Solo's head lifted. "Well, I guess you being a Cruz brother isn't all bad."

I was shocked that he'd come around to my idea so quickly. "Yeah? You like that, huh?"

He shrugged. "Well, if you're one of my brothers, that means you can't date my sister, now doesn't it?"

"Ohhhhh!" cried Diego, holding a fist in front of his mouth and laughing. "He gotcha there, Drunk."

Shaking my head, I smiled and wagged my finger at him. "This is true. You got me there, Solo. Maybe I need to rethink if I really wanna be a Cruz brother after all."

Al held up a finger then. "Drunk, if you really wanna be a Cruz brother, the right way to do it would be to marry their sister. Then you'd be their brother-in-law."

Solo sat up and cleared his throat. He didn't like the sound of that. "How about we just stick with silent partner for now, eh, Drunk?"

I chuckled, shooting Al a wink. "We'll leave it at that for now, Solo. *For now.*"

12

I COULDN'T STOP SMILING AS AL AND I DROVE AWAY FROM THE marina minutes later. I was a silent partner of a charter and commercial fishing business. And almost as good, Frankie's brothers had *voluntarily* cut me in. That had to mean they liked me, even if it was just a little bit.

"You ever gonna lose that stupid smile on your face?" asked Al, grinning just as widely.

"Not today," I said, rubbing my hand across my bearded jaw. "I went in there thinking they were rubbing my nose in everything I lost, and I walked out as a partial owner of the company. I'm still in shock, I think."

Al's head bobbed. "Good for you, kid. I'm happy for you."

"Thanks, Al."

"But now we've got real business to take care of," he said, focusing on the road in front of us. "We need to get back over to that club and see if we can't find anyone that's seen Jordan Lambert."

I glanced down at the clock on my dash. That meeting hadn't even taken a half hour. "They're still not open. How about we grab lunch first?"

Al's head bobbed. "Deal."

I BLAME Al for taking us back to the same Mexican food place that had, not that long ago, served us the questionable taquitos. What is it they say about doing the same thing repeatedly and expecting different results? But, ultimately, it was Al who had to pay the price for our insanity. By the time we'd finished eating and pulled up to Club Cobalt, Al was already whining about his stomach.

"Well, now we know it wasn't the taquitos," I said. "Maybe it's their food in general. Or maybe they imported some Mexican *agua* just to make the experience more authentic."

"Could be," said Al, nodding and rubbing his stomach.

I looked over at him. His brow had a glossy sheen and he looked miserable. "Hey, Al. I'm sorry you feel like shit—uh, no pun intended. I told you we should've gone somewhere else."

"I know. I know. It was my fault. I had a hankering for fish tacos." He shook his head. "I love the food at the Seacoast Majestic, but their fish tacos leave a lot to be desired."

"Alright, well, you can stay out here if you want," I suggested, pulling my Jeep to a stop along the curb. "I'll just go in and show Jordan's picture around a little. I won't be that long."

But Al had already sprung into action and thrown his door open wide. "Nope, I gotta find the nearest john."

I looked down the street in both directions. "I think this is the only place open down here."

"It'll have to do."

"I thought you were worried about their john knocking you up?"

He slid out of the vehicle. "I'll chance it."

"Suit yourself," I said with a shrug.

The inside of Club Cobalt was much like any seedy bar in the District. It was dark, even in the middle of the afternoon, so when you were inside, you couldn't tell what time it was.

The music played a little too loud, and even though they'd only unlocked their doors thirty minutes ago, there was already a half-naked girl dancing around on a pole onstage.

Al patted my arm and pointed towards a bathroom next to the stage and then shuffled off in its direction.

I removed my Ray-Bans and slid them around the band of my hat. When he'd gone, my eyes swept the room, looking for anyone that looked like they might be a regular. I walked up to the bar.

"What can I getcha?" asked the bartender, a white guy wearing a black V-neck t-shirt with rolled-up sleeves that revealed a tribal tattoo wrapped around his bicep.

"Mmm. I'll take a whiskey sour," I said, pulling out my wallet. As I waited for the bartender to make my drink, Al came shuffling over to me. "Well, that was fast."

Al's face was sweatier than it was when we'd come in. "John's broken."

"Way to go."

"I didn't break it. It was like that when we got here."

"Sure it was."

"Jeez, kid. I'm serious. We're gonna have to leave if they don't have another one."

When the bartender returned, I leaned forward. "Your shitter's busted. You got another one around here somewhere?"

"Nope."

"C'mon, man. This guy's in bad shape. He got ahold of some bad Mexican food."

The bartender glanced over at Al. His eyes were as big as quarters and he was sweating and fidgeting back and forth. "'Round the corner." He nodded towards a set of double doors. A guard stood in front of them. "Tell that guy. He'll take you to the employee john in the back."

Al didn't even pause for niceties but instead took off on a mad shuffle towards the double doors.

I looked up and gave the bartender a friendly smile as I

handed him the cash for the drink. "Keep the change." Leaning backwards against the bar, I took my time sipping on my drink. The place was almost empty with the exception of the dancer, two guys sitting at darkly lit tables on opposite ends of the stage, a muscle-bound guy at the end of the bar, and a waitress. When I'd finished my drink, I put it on the bar.

The bartender, now drying a tumbler with a bar towel, walked back down to me. "Need another one?"

"Yeah, I'd take another one." I pulled out the cash for the drink, making sure to tip him handsomely. Then I pulled out one of the photographs I'd snagged off Jordan's mirror and showed it to the bartender. "Hey, you haven't happened to see this girl around here lately, have you?"

The bartender's hand stopped twisting inside the glass long enough to give me a once-over. Then for the briefest of seconds, his eyes dropped to look at the picture. "Nope. Haven't seen her." His eyes were on me again.

I frowned. "You sure? Maybe have another look?"

The bartender's eyes dropped once more before pinging back up to stare at me. "She looks too young for this place."

I nodded. "Well, that's what I thought too, but I found this in her stuff." I pulled the invitation out of my pocket and showed it to him. "Know anything about a private party that was here on Saturday?"

The bartender considered me for a second. "Just a sec." He walked down to the end of the bar and said something to the muscle-bound guy.

That was when the waitress who had been across the room appeared next to me. She was young and blond with a tight little black dress on, carrying a drink tray. I noticed almost immediately the faded remnants of a black eye and a scar across her cheekbone.

I turned towards her and gave her my most charming smile. "Hey, gorgeous. Come here often?"

She grinned. "Only six days a week."

I lifted the picture of Jordan up off the counter and showed it to the woman. "Well, then, hey—maybe you can help me. I'm trying to find my kid sister. Someone she knew thought she might've been in here not that long ago." I showed her the picture of Jordan. "You seen her?"

The waitress froze as she stared at the picture. Then slowly, a hand rose to touch her hair. She cleared her throat. "No, huh-uh, haven't seen her."

"You sure?" I pressed.

"I said I haven't seen her," she muttered before glancing up at the bar.

I turned to follow her line of sight to see the bartender staring back at the two of us.

"Sir, I'm going to have to ask you to leave."

I frowned. "Leave? I haven't even gotten my second drink yet."

The bartender pushed my money back across the bar towards me. "You'll have to get it somewhere else."

"Bu—"

But before I could even complain, the guy at the end of the bar stood up and motioned with his head towards the guy guarding the double swinging doors that Al had gone through. They both got behind me, intentionally invading my personal space bubble. "Sir. We don't allow customers to harass our waitresses," grunted one of them.

"I wasn't harassing her. I just wanted another drink," I protested. I glanced over at the waitress. Her eyes were cast downwards. She couldn't even look at me. And then the two guards had their hands under my elbows, and I felt the weight lessen on my legs and feet.

Within seconds, I was facedown on the pavement outside Club Cobalt. My palms and knees burned from the force of the fall, and my hat and sunglasses had fallen off my head and onto the concrete. I stood up, dusted myself off and put my hat back on, then leaned against my Jeep, waiting for Al. I could only hope he wouldn't be met with the same forceful exit that I had.

It was another ten minutes before Al came hobbling out the door. He looked both ways down the street before he noticed me leaning against the vehicle. He shuffled towards me. "There you are. You couldn't even wait for me?"

"They kicked me out. What took you so long?"

"You have to ask? I'm an old man. Things take a lot longer when you're an old man."

I opened his door for him. "Get in."

As soon as we'd taken off, Al looked over at me. "Why'd they kick you out?"

"They said I was harassing the waitress, but I wasn't. I just showed her Jordan's picture and asked if she'd seen her." I sighed and slumped back against my seat back. Something about that entire interaction didn't sit right with me. "Who kicks someone out of their establishment just for showing around a picture?"

"Someone with something to hide," said Al knowingly.

I nodded. "Exactly. I'm willing to bet Jordan went to that party and they knew she was underage. I bet that's what's going on. They could get in trouble for having underage girls at their club, and they didn't like me asking questions about it."

"You might be right. I'm pretty sure Jordan isn't the first underage girl that they've ever had in their club," said Al.

I looked over at him. "Oh yeah? What makes you say that?"

"The walls down the hallways in the back were lined with framed pictures of really young girls in skimpy lingerie."

"You're kidding. How young?"

"Too young," said Al knowingly. "Teenagers—fifteen-, sixteen-year-old girls."

"You're kidding?"

Al shook his head. "I wish I was. They weren't all recent pictures."

"Yeah? And how in the world would you know that?"

"I recognized one of the girls in the pictures. She's older now."

I looked over at him in surprise. "Al! Is that what took you so long?"

"I wasn't trying to look at them. It was right across from the john when I came out."

"So who is she?"

"She's a realtor on the island."

"You know her name?"

"Monica Arndt. She works for Vista Realty. She showed Evie and me a couple condos last year when we were debating whether we should get our own place or live at the resort."

I lifted a brow. "You sure that's all? You seem to know a lot about this half-naked girl. Anything else you feel you need to share, Al?"

Al shot me the stink-eye. "Yeah, the woman's face is plastered all over half the billboards on the island. Tell me you haven't seen the name Monica Arndt before."

I was silent as I drove. I didn't pay a lot of attention to billboards, but I did seem to have a recollection of a dark-haired young woman with a nice smile photographed in front of a house for sale. I wasn't sure what man on the island hadn't noticed her face before. She was an attractive woman, but young. Maybe barely twenty-five. "Yeah, alright. I think I know the one."

Al pointed at the road. "If you wanna go up to the corner and take a right, I think there's a billboard at an intersection down there. We'll take a look."

I followed Al's directions, and within a few minutes, we were parked on the side of the road, staring up at a pair of ten-by-twenty-two-foot billboards. One of them had bright blue and pink lettering splashed across a colorfully painted helicopter and read "Hidden Beaches Aerial Tours, Paradise Isle's *only* Doors-Off Adventure Tour." The second billboard featured a woman with her arms crossed, standing in front of a house for sale, just as I'd remembered.

Al poked his finger in the air as if to punctuate his rightness. "Yup. That's her alright. I wonder if she has any idea that she's on full display in the hallway of that club."

"You've gotta believe she knows the picture exists if she posed for it."

"But she might not know it's hanging up in the employee hallway of a strip club."

"I'd wager she does. In fact, I'd even bet that she knows a little something about the operation they've got going on there."

"Think we should ask her what she knows?" asked Al.

My head bobbed. "I don't think it would hurt. What other leads do we have to follow at this point?" I pulled out my phone and dialed the number the billboard advertised in two-foot-tall print.

Within minutes, Al and I had a four o'clock showing scheduled with Ms. Monica Arndt for an oceanfront three-bed, two-bath vacation condo.

13

THE THREE-BEDROOM VACATION CONDO WAS ON THE GROUND floor of an eight-story nearly-all-glass building fronting the beach. Palm trees and other island vegetation provided privacy for a pool and a tennis court just off the main parking lot. Little cabanas dotted the long run of sand between the condo and the beach, and whitecapped waves rolled right up to the shoreline, filling the air with the calming sound of breaking waves.

Al and I sat on a cedar bench in front of the building while we waited for Monica Arndt to show up. At exactly one minute to four, a pearl-white Jag tore into the parking lot and came to a screeching halt in a spot marked for the building manager. A twenty-something willowy brunette emerged from the car, wearing neck-breaking high-heels, a slim-fitting turquoise pencil skirt, and a white sleeveless blouse. She strode towards us assuredly.

"Hello! Are you here to look at the condo?"

"Yes, ma'am," I said, jumping to my feet. I reached back to tug Al to his feet too and then I reached out to shake the woman's hand. "Are you Monica?"

She gave us a wide smile. "I am. And you are?"

Pumping her hand, I said, "I'm Calvin. And this is my partner Hobbs."

"Oh, your partner. How sweet," she said, giving both of us a handshake. "You know, we have a lot of LGBTQ couples here in the condo. I think you'll find it to be a very welcoming community." She smiled then. "A bit of a May-December romance, too, I see. My boyfriend is twenty-five years older than me, so I completely get it."

I looked down at Al and smiled before putting my arm around his shoulder. "Hobbs and I sure appreciate your openness, Monica."

"Of course! Now, why don't you follow me, and I'll show you the place." Monica's smile looked like it might burst her face, but the second she turned her back to us, Al kicked me in the shin.

Grimacing, I doubled over to rub the sting from my leg. "Owww!"

Monica kept walking but turned her head to look at me curiously.

I stood up and laughed it off, swatting the air. "Hobbs, sweetie. Really! Save a little of that enthusiasm for later." I shot him a wink.

Monica put her key into the door at the end of the hallway. "You two are just so adorable." She opened the door and gave a sweeping gesture. "Go on in, please."

The furnished condo was pretty basic and smelled a bit stale. Like whoever had lived there before had either had a pet or had smoked, and they'd used some kind of chemical air freshener to hide either one or both of those facts. We spent about ten minutes moving from room to room behind Monica, pretending to be interested. When we got to the end of the tour, and I still hadn't come up with a way to infuse any questions about Club Cobalt into the conversation, I finally just had to come right out with it.

"You know, Monica, I feel like I've seen you somewhere before."

Monica smiled. "I get that a lot, actually. I think it's all the billboards around the island."

I frowned and cupped my chin with my thumb and middle finger, tapping my index finger against my nose. Shaking my head, I disagreed, "No, no, no. I don't think it's that." And then I sucked in my breath and pointed to her. "I've got it. Have you ever been to Club Cobalt?"

Almost instantly, the smile dissolved off Monica's face. "Club Cobalt?" She cleared her throat. "You mean in the District?"

"Yeah. You know the place?"

"Well, it's a small island and I'm a realtor. I know most places."

I smiled at her. "Oh, of course. How long have you been a realtor?"

Monica's green eyes shifted over to Al, who was just casually strolling through the kitchen once again with his arms pinned behind his back and kind of pretending not to be paying attention. "Umm, just the last two, two and a half years or so."

"Wow, that's all? You've really done well for yourself in such a short amount of time."

"I've done alright," she agreed, unsure of where the conversation was going.

I wagged a finger then. "You know, I think I just remembered why I'm putting your face and Club Cobalt together. They have kind of a wall of fame there. In their back hallway. You've got your picture hanging up. Framed," I added.

She swallowed hard and turned to look out the sliding doors to the beach. She winced, like the light hurt her eyes, but in reality, the light wasn't that bright. "Umm, no, I think you've got the wrong person." She let out a nervous giggle.

"Really? You never did any modeling for them?"

"Modeling? No, I—" She ran her fingers through the underside of her hair and then tossed it back over her shoulder.

"But you've been there before," I said.

"I mean, maybe when I was younger, but that was forever ago."

Al stopped walking and looked at her. "Little lady, you don't know what forever ago *means* until you get to be *my* age. Then when you say something was forever ago, you mean it."

She kind of giggled. "Oh, yeah, I'm sure. Well, it was quite a while ago. When I was into the whole *bar* scene thing. But that's not me anymore."

I frowned. "Well, you can't possibly be *that* old. What are you? Twenty-three or twenty-four?"

She cleared her throat. "Twenty-four."

I pointed at her with a flourish. "See! There you go. You've only been of legal island drinking age for the last three years. That's not been that long ago, now has it? Shoot, I'm surprised you've even outgrown it already. I mean, I didn't outgrow the bar scene until I was—well, how old am I again?"

"Thirty-five," said Al.

"Right. I guess until I was thirty-five years old, then." I chuckled.

She giggled nervously and then tried to turn the conversation back to business. "Well, Calvin, would you and Hobbs like to see another place, or are you interested in this one?"

I ignored her question and kept talking. "Although, you know I guess I could see how you might be over the bar scene by now if you'd started going out *earlier* than twenty-one. Some people do. You know, I have heard that Club Cobalt allows underage girls in."

A hand went to her throat. "Well, I wouldn't know—"

"You wouldn't? You never went there when you were underage?"

"I mean, I might have—that was forev—" Her eyes darted

over to Al, and she seemed to change her mind about her choice of words. "That was years ago. I really don't recall." She glanced back at me again. "Now, if you're ready to go—"

But I felt like I'd already crossed a line that I couldn't uncross. At this point, I felt like I should just cut to the chase. "Can I just be real with you Monica?"

"Real?"

"Yes. You know, cut through this whole song and dance." I sighed. What did I have to lose at this point? She was already getting annoyed with me. I could see it in her face. "Look. My little sister is missing. She had this in her room." I showed her the invitation to Club Cobalt. "I need to know what happened to her. And if they're letting in minors, then she could've gone in there and gotten herself into some trouble. All I want is to find her. I'm not trying to get anyone in trouble." I held up her picture. "This is her. Her name is Jordan."

With her breath hitched in her throat, Monica stared at me, wide-eyed for a long second. Then she glanced over at Al, who had stopped pacing and was now looking at her pleadingly.

"Please, Ms. Arndt. Anything you know and would be willing to share can only help us find her. Jordan's only sixteen years old. Her friends and family want her back."

But Monica's face, once bright and shiny, was now dark. She'd gone to a difference place in her mind, and I wasn't quite sure how to get her back. "I have no idea what you're talking about. Now, if you'll excuse me, I have another showing on the other side of the island. I have to be going." With a stiffened spine, she strode over to the front door and opened it, giving the air a sweep with her free hand.

Al tightened his lips and left the condo first. I followed behind him slowly. "Please, Monica. We need your help. If you know anything—"

"I don't," she snapped, unable to even look at me now.

As Al and I walked down the hallway, I could hear her

keys jingling in the lock behind us. We walked out of the building first, followed by Monica.

I turned and opened my mouth, preparing to offer her my name and number if she thought of anything that might help us, but before I could even get a word out, she breezed past us in a mad dash back to her Jag. Al and I both stared after her as she climbed in and tore out of the parking lot.

"Well, that didn't go as I'd hoped," I said with a frown.

"Was it just me, or did she seem like she was hiding something?"

I nodded. "Oh, she definitely seemed like she was hiding something. Kind of like the people at Club Cobalt acted when I started asking questions about Jordan."

"She seemed scared to me. Something is going on in that club. I think we gotta get back in there and have a look around. Whaddaya say?"

"But how? They just kicked me out. There's no way they're going to let me back in there to snoop around."

Al grinned as he started walking towards the Jeep. "You know anything about plumbing, kid?"

14

THE NEXT MORNING, AFTER MY USUAL JOG, I SOUGHT OUT GISELLE Marrero. I wanted to make sure that she hadn't heard anything from Jordan before Al and I followed through on our plan for the day. I found her planting flowers in planter boxes down at the clubhouse by the beach.

"Giselle! Hey, you got a second?" I hollered at her.

She turned around and gave me a gloved wave. "Hey, Drunk. Have you found Jordan yet?"

My shoulders slumped. Those five words told me everything I needed to know. Jordan was still missing. "No, I haven't. I was hoping you'd heard from her."

"No. I haven't, and trust me, I've still been trying."

"Damn it."

"Have you found anything yet?"

"Some," I said, nodding. "I'm fairly confident she didn't leave the island."

Giselle nodded. "I told you."

"Yeah. And she's not in jail."

"You called the cops!" Giselle eyes sprang open. "Oh my God, Drunk. I told you you couldn't call the cops!"

I held up a hand. "Whoa, whoa, whoa. Slow your roll. I

have a contact at the PIRPF, she's a friend of mine. She just did me a favor. I didn't like *report* Jordan missing or anything."

"But what if she passes that on?"

"Relax. She's not going to pass it on. I told you, she's a friend of mine. I can trust her to keep things tight."

With her gloved palm to her forehead, Giselle spun around so that her back was to me and she was facing the front of the resort clubhouse.

"What?"

"Nothing," she grumbled in a low voice.

I'd come to learn a thing or two about women during the course of my life. I wouldn't say I knew *everything* about them —I mean, hell, women don't even know everything about women—but I definitely knew a thing or two about them. When they say *nothing* in that tone of voice, it most definitely does not mean what the word implies. In reality, it means *something* and you have to play detective.

I sighed. I wasn't a fan of this game. With my hands on my hips, I looked around. Manny at the swim-up bar gave me a little heads-up nod. I nodded back. Trinity, one of the snack bar girls, was sitting on one of Manny's barstools, chatting with him. I gave her a little wave. She smiled and waved back. I had to get on with this. There were far too many people watching me chat with Giselle. I didn't want any rumors getting started.

I walked around her so that I faced her. "Okay, let's have it. You're upset because I went to my friend at the police department?"

She lifted a noncommittal shoulder. "Sorta."

"Sorta?"

She nodded.

I didn't have much experience dealing with teenagers, but I was quickly discovering that I didn't like it. "What does sorta mean? You either *are* or *aren't* mad at me. Which is it?"

She sighed. "I'm not mad at you. I'm just—scared, I guess."

"Scared of what?"

She shrugged and made that little sound in the back of her throat that implied *I don't know.*

"Okay, fine. Are you scared that we might not find Jordan?"

"Yeah," she said softly.

"Is that all you're scared of?"

She was quiet for a really long, drawn-out second before she finally shook her head.

"Okay. Help me out here, Giselle. I have to find your friend, and guessing games aren't helping. If there's more to the story that you're not telling me, I need to know."

She looked up at me. Her dark eyes were full of something. If it was fear or anxiety or sadness, I couldn't tell.

"Please, Giselle. Whatever it is, you don't have to worry. I won't tell your mom. I won't tell the cops. I won't judge. Okay?"

With her breath dammed up behind firmly pressed lips, her head bobbed.

"Good. Okay, so what's the big deal about me going to my friend who's a cop? Why does that matter so much to you?"

"Because they made us promise," she whispered, her eyes throwing cautious glances around the pool area.

"Who made you promise?"

Wide-eyed, Giselle shook her head. It was obvious she was afraid of something. Or someone. I had a sudden sneaking suspicion that there was more to the story of Jordan's disappearance. And for the first time since she'd shown up on my doorstep, I wondered what Giselle and Jordan had gotten themselves involved in.

"It's a really long story."

"Fine. Tell me. I have the time."

She looked around. "This isn't the best place to talk. My mom has spies everywhere. Can we go back to your cottage?"

As much as I didn't like that idea, I knew Giselle was right. Her mother actually *did* have spies everywhere. We couldn't talk like this out in the open. "Fine. Can you take a quick break?"

She pulled out her phone and looked at the time. "I get a fifteen-minute break in a half hour."

"Okay. Then I'll meet you at my place in a half an hour." I pointed a finger at her. "And don't let anyone see you heading over there."

I REALLY WANTED to invite Al over to my place for the meeting with Giselle—for two reasons. One, so I wouldn't have to repeat everything she told me, and two, so I had a witness to Giselle's visit lest anyone think any funny business was going on between us. But because Giselle was so skittish the way it was, I thought inviting him in on the conversation might just scare her away or prevent her from being completely honest. I'd just have to remember everything she said so I could fill him in later.

When she knocked on my cottage door a half an hour later, I poked my head outside and scanned the road in both directions. "Did anyone see you coming over here?"

Looking over her shoulder, she shook her head. "No, I don't think so."

"Okay, well, have a seat. You want something to drink?"

I went to the fridge and pulled out a bottle of Dr Pepper and a Milky Way bar from one of my kitchen cupboards. Breakfast of champions. Walking back in the living room, I held up the soda.

She shook her head. "No, thanks."

Shrugging, I unscrewed the cap and took a big guzzle and then sat down across from her. "Alright. You said it's a long story, so we better get started. I've got plans in an hour, and you only have a fifteen-minute break."

She cleared her throat and nodded. "Well, something

happened a couple of weeks ago that might kind of explain where Jordan is."

"Wait a minute," I said, leaning forward and frowning. "Lemme get this straight. You *might kinda* know where Jordan is and you didn't think to tell me this before?"

She shrugged. Her cheeks were pink. "I don't *exactly* know where she is, but maybe. I don't know."

"Giselle! Why wouldn't you have told me this when you first came over here? You could've saved me a bunch of time."

"I'm sorry, Drunk. It doesn't exactly sound very good. I was embarrassed."

I fought the urge to palm my forehead. "Fine. Go ahead. I'm listening."

"Okay, well, a couple weeks ago when school was just getting out for the summer, Jordan and I were hanging out at one of our friends' beach houses. They were having this really big end-of-the-year party," she began. "Jordan and I were sitting outside when this really, really nice red sports car drove up and this girl got out. She was blond and beautiful and she was wearing this killer dress, and she just looked—I don't know—really, really cool. Jordan and I both made it a point to sort of *accidentally* bump into her before the end of the night so we could find out who she was."

"And did you?"

"Yeah."

"What was her name?"

"Crystal. At least, that's what she told us her name was. I don't know if that's her real name or not."

I nodded for her to continue with her story.

"So, we told her we liked her car and asked if it was hers. She said it was a gift from her boss. We were both like, 'Wow. That's some boss.' We got to talking and one of us asked her where she'd gotten her dress, and she told us she'd bought it at this little boutique downtown. Of course there was no way either me or Jordan would ever be able to afford to shop there.

That's a tourist boutique. Too expensive for us. And we said something like that to her, and she said she made really good money where she worked. I asked her what she did, and she said that it varied. But sometimes she did modeling and she made three to five hundred per gig. We were like shocked. I mean, who makes three to five hundred dollars *a day*? She asked us if we were interested in getting a job there because they were always hiring pretty girls."

I sighed. This already sounded like a bad idea. But as I looked at Giselle, telling the story, I could tell that she already knew what I was going to say.

Giselle held her hand out to keep me from saying it. "I know, Drunk. I know. Hearing it now, it sounds shady, but we just saw dollar signs. And it wasn't to go on some dumb shopping spree. I'm saving for college. Jordan's paying her own bills right now with her aunt gone. She *really* needed the money."

I nodded. I knew I couldn't be judgmental; I'd seen the delinquent notices in Jordan's apartment. "Okay, I understand. Keep going."

"So, Crystal handed us each a slip of paper. It was an invitation to a private party at this club down in the District. It's called Club Cobalt. She said when we got there to ask for her."

So far I wasn't shocked. I'd already pieced most of that together, except the part about the invitation being for a job. "Don't you have to be old enough to get into a place like that?"

Giselle shrugged. "Crystal said the invitations would get us in the door. And she was right. The bouncer didn't even flinch when we showed it to him, and we just walked in. We found her there, hanging out. She seemed excited to see us. And when we asked about the job, she told us to take the invitations down this hallway and give them to the guards there and they'd take us where we needed to go. We asked her what we'd be doing, and she just kind of waved us off and said the boss would explain everything."

"You sure you don't want a bottle of water?" I asked, interrupting as I took another drink of my soda.

She shook her head. "No, really, I'm fine."

"Okay, sorry. Keep going."

Giselle nodded. "So, we did what Crystal told us to do and we took our invitations to this hallway, and there were these two big guys guarding the doors. They took us down to the end of the hallway, where we met this other guy. They called him Vito. He was kind of intimidating, I mean, he had this, like, flat nose," she explained, pressing her palm against her own nose. "And he looked really serious. He looked us up and down and said, 'So I hear you want to make some good money.' We told him that Crystal had said something about modeling. He said that the girls who have been there for a while move up to the modeling gigs, but the newer girls kind of have to work their way up. He said he needed a couple of girls to work a private party a friend of his was hosting and that we'd get all the details when we got there. He said his driver would give us a ride to the party and bring us back to the club when it was over."

I couldn't hold it back anymore. I let my head fall into my hands. "Tell me you didn't just get in a car with these creeps?"

Giselle's hands flared out in front of herself. "I didn't want to! But Jordan really needed the money. I did too. We figured, what's the big deal? He said he'd bring us back! So we went. But the whole thing was weird. They had us ride in this long stretch limo with darkened windows and we couldn't see out, so we had no idea where we were going. Then when we got there, the limo pulled into a garage and there was this kind of creepy butler guy who took us down this hallway and said we'd need to get our pictures taken if we wanted to be considered for future modeling jobs. Which, of course, was what we both wanted. So, he put us in this room and pointed to a closet and said we could put on anything in the closet, but we couldn't wear our own clothes for the pictures." That was when Giselle started to tear up and her chin began to shake. "But they weren't *clothes* in the closet, it was just all really skimpy lingerie." Tears trickled down her cheeks then.

I groaned. Some asshole had taken advantage of a couple of teenage girls so he could put their pictures up on his club's wall of fame. I wanted to put a fist in his face. But I had to remain calm. Giselle needed me to remain calm. I slid around to the sofa and put an arm over her shoulder. She leaned her head on my shoulder and cried. I squeezed her shoulder, all the while wishing I could storm out of there and find the guy who had made her cry. "It's okay. We'll figure all this out."

She sat up and blotted her eyes with the hem of her shirt. "I didn't want to wear that stuff," she cried. "But Jordan convinced me that it was just like wearing a string bikini to the beach. It was no big deal and models wore that kind of stuff all the time. She was like, look at the Victoria's Secret models, they strut around in their underwear on stage. What's the big deal? They just wanted to know that we had nice bodies and pretty faces." Giselle sniffled and blotted her eyes again. "And you know, when I thought about it, she was right. But there was still a creepy factor that wearing a string bikini to the beach didn't have."

"But you let them take your pictures like that anyway?"

Giselle's head bobbed. I could tell she was fighting tears again, but she wanted to get the rest of the story out. "They took us to this other room. There was this like padded table on one side and some photography equipment on the other side," she explained. "They had this photographer come in and take our pictures. Jordan was excited about it, she kind of played it up, like pretending she'd been modeling her whole life. I was way stiffer about it. I was so embarrassed. I kept thinking if my mother ever saw those pictures, she'd kill me. But I told myself that if I really wanted to be a model, Jordie was right. I needed to relax because real models did this kind of stuff all the time. At least we weren't naked or something."

I gritted my teeth and mumbled under my breath. "Yeah, thank God for small favors."

"Huh?"

I shook my head. "Nothing. Keep going."

"So, after they took the pictures, they told us to stay in there and their client was going to be in shortly and our assignment for the evening was to give him a massage."

"In the lingerie?" I balked.

She only nodded.

"Oh my God. You're kidding me."

She shook her head, biting her lip. "When it was over, we each got three hundred cash and they took us back to Club Cobalt and told us we could come back anytime we wanted to make more cash."

I wasn't sure how to ask her the next question. The obvious, glaring one. So I swallowed hard and just asked. "Did they want you to do anything, you know, *sexual*?"

Giselle looked down at her hands. She shook her head. "No. It was just a massage."

"You're sure?"

Her head bobbed up and down, but she refused to look me in the eyes then. I couldn't tell if she was lying or just embarrassed at what she'd been through.

I slid sideways on the sofa and put a hand on either of her shoulders and gave her a little shake. I wanted her to look me in the eye. I had to be able to tell if she was being honest with me. "Giselle. Tell me the truth."

She looked up then, her eyes still brimming with tears. "I swear. We just gave him a massage. It was just... it was just really uncomfortable and super awkward. And it felt wrong. And I hated every second of it."

"I don't blame you one bit. I'm glad you came to that realization."

"Yeah, totally. When we got back to our car, I told Jordie how glad I was to be out of there and that we were never doing that again. She agreed with me and I thought we were both on the same page about it. I, personally, never wanted to speak of it again. It was just a weird and uncomfortable thing. But then last Friday, we were hanging out at her apartment, and I found this stack of cash. It was like more cash than I'd ever seen before. I asked her about it and she got really defensive."

Dread filled the pit of my stomach. "Had she been going back to Club Cobalt?"

"I mean, I automatically assumed that's what was going on. And I asked her, but she wouldn't say. But where else would she get that kind of money that quickly? Before that, she was completely broke."

"Is that what your disagreement was about?"

Giselle nodded sadly before hanging her head. "Yeah," she whispered. "She didn't like the fact that I was bugging her about it. She said I was judging her and friends don't judge."

"So do you think that Jordan's disappearance has to do with whatever she got herself mixed up in?"

"I mean, kind of. Don't you?"

"It definitely sounds like it could be connected." I sighed. "Look, Giselle, I know you don't want to, but we have to go to the cops."

Giselle's eyes widened and her head shook. "You can't go to the cops, Drunk. I told you."

"Yeah, well, you never really explained why."

"They said they'd release the pictures they took if we ever told anyone that we'd gone over there."

"I mean, I get that, but Jordan could be in some serious trouble over all this. Don't you want to make sure she's safe?"

"It's not just the pictures," she whispered. "They said we couldn't go to the cops."

"Who? Who said you couldn't?"

"The people at Club Cobalt. And Crystal, she..." Giselle's voice trailed off.

"Crystal told you not to go to the cops?"

"When they brought us back to the club and we were walking to our car, we saw her again. She asked us if we were going to come back. We both said no, probably not. She said that's fine. But whatever we do, don't talk to anyone about the private party. That's part of our fee. We're paid for our silence."

"Giselle, that's ridiculous. They can't possibly think that—"

"She was all beat up, Drunk. Her face. It was bruised and she had a black eye. She'd covered it up with makeup, but after we came back, she took us into the bathroom so we could see her face better. She said that's what they do if you do something they don't like. Something like talking to the cops. They told us that at the private party too. That we weren't allowed to talk to the cops."

And then the pretty blond waitress with the scar across her cheekbone and the faded black-and-blue eye I'd seen at Club Cobalt sprang into the forefront of my mind. I'd bet anything that was Crystal.

"I can't believe you got mixed up in all this, Giselle. You seem like a smart girl."

"I *am* a smart girl, okay? I had a lapse in judgment. Mom's going to kill me if she finds out about all this. Look. I just want to know that Jordan's okay. We don't need to go to the cops if she's okay and doing all this by choice. But if she's not doing it by choice, and something happened to her—"

I was quiet for a long moment as I thought about all the things that Giselle had told me. I needed to get back over to that Club Cobalt and find Jordan before something *did* happen to her. Finally, I stood up. "Is there anything else you need to tell me, Giselle? Anything at all. Now's the time."

She shook her head. "No. Not that I can think of."

"Because if you're not telling me everything, then I reserve the right to go to the cops."

"Drunk, I swear—"

"And you have no idea where they took you that night?"

"None."

"No names that might help me out?"

"Just Vito, that was the only name we got that night."

I nodded. "Okay, I'll handle this."

"You're going to keep looking for her?"

"Of course I am."

"And you won't go to the cops? I can't have them hurt her."

"I'll be careful. I only wish you would have told me all this when we spoke before."

"I'm sorry. I—I was scared. And embarrassed."

"I know. I know. I also hope that you learned a lesson."

Her eyes widened and she nodded her head. "I did. I really did. There's no way to make a quick buck. You just have to work hard. My mom's told me that all these years, but I guess I never really understood. I understand now. I just wish Jordan had learned with me." Giselle stood up.

I gave her a hug. "I'll do everything I can to find Jordan and bring her back. Okay?"

She nodded. "Thank you. For everything."

"Okay, now I need to go. I have a plumbing call I need to make."

Giselle looked confused. "A plumbing call?"

I nodded, my brows lowered. "Yeah. I've got some pieces of shit I need to flush out."

15

FIRED UP AFTER MY TALK WITH GISELLE, I GAVE DIEGO A CALL and asked him to meet Al and me at the marina at ten. Then I headed down to Al's place to pick him up. On the ride over, I recounted Giselle's whole story to Al. By the time we got to the marina, I was fuming mad once again about the jackasses that had taken advantage of a pair of young girls' naivety, and I was ready to find out what in the hell was going on over at Club Cobalt. Al, though just as upset, seemed to be able to hold his temper better than I could.

"What's up with you, Al? You don't even look fazed," I said as we pulled into the marina parking lot. "Don't you care what Club Cobalt did to Giselle and Jordan?"

"Of course I care. I have granddaughters! I hate that there are monsters out in the world like that, but it doesn't help anyone to go off half-cocked."

I frowned and gripped the steering wheel tighter. My anger still seethed just below the surface. "Yeah, but it sure feels good."

Al closed his eyes, lifted his brows, and shrugged. "Maybe. In that moment it might feel good, but nothing good comes out of anger. Except maybe determination, but you can be determined without anger." He pointed at himself then. "Look at me. I'm determined and I'm keeping my emotions under control. We have to be clear-headed for this, kid. We can't let our emotions run the show. We have a sixteen-year-old girl to find."

My head drooped forward onto the steering wheel for a brief moment. The logical side of my brain knew that Al was right. I had to calm down so I could think clearly. Unfortunately, the emotional side of my brain sent the logical side of my brain a message that said, *Easier said than done.*

There was a knock on my window.

I opened my left eye and turned my head slightly. It was Diego. I sighed. I needed to shake it off.

I gave him a tight smile, and Al and I got out of the vehicle. "Hey, D."

"Hey, fellas," said Diego.

"Thanks for meeting us on such short notice." I gave him a bro hug as Al came around the corner of the vehicle to shake Diego's hand.

Diego couldn't take his eyes off my new ride. "Nice set of wheels, Drunk," he said, his eyes bright. "You just get it?"

I grinned. "Yeah, Al insisted."

"You picked a good one. It's flashy. I happen to appreciate flashy myself." Diego straightened the collar of his colorfully printed short-sleeved Hawaiian shirt. He walked around the vehicle, looking it over carefully. "It looks brand-new."

"Fairly new. I couldn't exactly afford new with the prices of vehicles on the island."

Diego nodded and gave a nod towards the white van in their parking lot. "Oh yeah, man. Aren't those tariffs the worst? We paid an arm and a leg for the van when we got it."

With my hands on my hips I nodded. "Yeah. Hey, speaking of the van, I was wondering—do silent partners get to borrow the van from time to time?"

"You need to borrow the van?" asked Diego.

"Yeah, sorta. Just for a couple of hours."

"Oh, not a problem, man. It doesn't smell the best, but you're welcome to use it."

"Hey, thanks, we appreciate it."

"Yeah, no problem. I'll just go grab the keys from the marina."

He turned to walk away, but I held a hand out to him as another thought popped into my head. "Say, you don't happen to have any coveralls we could borrow too, do you?"

Diego's grin covered his face. "Listen, Drunk, if you can handle the smell of dead fish, I gotcha covered."

I glanced over at Al. "Hey, if I can handle the smell of this guy after a week of eating Kashi cereal for breakfast, I think I can handle the smell of a few measly dead fish."

Al frowned. "Hey, your protein powder bombs don't smell like roses either."

Diego chuckled. "Alright, fellas. I'll be right back. Don't say I didn't warn you."

WITH OUR WINDOWS down and our heads stuck out the van's windows, we pulled to a stop in front of Club Cobalt at exactly eleven o'clock that day. After leaving the marina, we'd made two pit stops—a sign shop and a plumbing store. From the sign shop, we'd grabbed an order I'd placed over the phone the day before, and from the plumbing store, we'd picked up a tool bag and a few plumbing necessities.

So now, instead of being parked in front of Club Cobalt in my flashy yellow Jeep, we drove a white van with a magnetic logo on the side that read *P.U. Plumbing—We're #1 in the #2 business.* Of course, Diego had been right. The van reeked like the rotting carcasses of a school of dead fish, as did the coveralls we'd borrowed. The stench had almost done me in on the ride over. It was only because we'd driven with our heads out the windows that we hadn't succumbed to choking on our own vomit.

Al leaned forward and looked around. "They're not even open this early, kid. You weren't planning for us to break in, were you?"

"This is why I get paid the big bucks and you don't." I gave my newly shaven chin a little scratch and smiled. "I'm way ahead of you. I called yesterday and made an appointment. I told the guy who answered the phone that someone had called us to fix the john, and that we preferred to fix it when they weren't open. He said he'd have someone meet us here at eleven."

Al's head bobbed. "Now that's using your head. Good thinkin', kid."

I got out of the van and went around and opened up the back. I pulled out the bag of supplies we'd purchased at the plumbing supply store and then stepped back onto the sidewalk, adjusting the tool bag on my hip.

A tall, muscular guy with a narrow waist was walking up the sidewalk towards us. He had his cell phone pressed against his ear. I recognized him immediately, mostly because he reminded me of a dark-haired version of Johnny Bravo. I'd seen the guy the day before, when he'd decided I should be lying facedown on the pavement as opposed to sitting on a barstool inside.

"Shit," I barked, swiveling sideways to give him my profile.

Al's eyes flicked up to look out the windshield. "What?"

I nodded my head towards the man. "That's the same guy that bounced me off the pavement yesterday. Do I look different enough without my hat and beard?"

Al looked me up and down. "You're wearing coveralls and a tool bag, kid. You look like a plumber."

"Fine," I said, rolling my eyes. "Did I look like a plumber yesterday?"

"Were you wearing coveralls and a pipe wrench on your hip yesterday?"

"So you're saying I look different?"

Al threw out his hands. "Of course I'm saying you look different. Jeez. Do I have to spell it out?"

I stared at Al then. He didn't look much different, except that he was wearing coveralls and I'd put a baseball cap on him to cover up his baldness. I could only hope that the guy wouldn't recognize either of us. "Hey, Al, do me a favor. Let me do the talking. Stay behind me, alright?"

"Yeah, sure, kid. Whatever flushes your tank."

"Whatever flushes my tank?" I lifted a brow. "Is that another one of your granddad jokes?"

Al waved a hand at me as the bouncer stopped in front of Club Cobalt's front door to unlock it. "It's plumbing lingo, kid. We gotta sound like the real deal."

I rolled my eyes and walked over to the guy opening the club up. "Hey, uh, we're here to fix the toilet," I said, unintentionally deepening my voice.

The guy spoke into his phone. "Hang on, babe." Then he turned to look at me. "You're shittin' me." He said it flatly, with dull eyes before cocking his head backwards towards the street. "Pretty sure the van was a dead giveaway."

I glanced back at Al, who was climbing out of the passenger's seat but had his head lowered slightly. "Oh, uh, yeah. Right. We'll be out of your hair as soon as we can."

The bouncer nodded and put the phone back up to his ear but held the door open with the toe of his boot. Even though I could only hear his side of the conversation, it was apparent that he was getting chewed out by his woman. "Look, babe, I've got a plumbing emergency to deal with down at the club. … I told you I'd be there…. Your mother isn't always right, you know…."

Standing there awkwardly, I finally pointed towards the club. "I'll just be in here."

He nodded and waved me on. As he strolled away from the door, I looked back at Al, who had just slammed the van door shut. Catching his eye, I shot him a *hurry up* look.

He shot me back his *this is as fast as I go* look.

Seconds later, the two of us stood in the middle of Club Cobalt, smelling like dead mackerel and wondering how we were going to weasel our way into the boss's office without Johnny Bravo noticing. I could only hope that his woman was the windy sort. "Come on, Al, we don't have much time. That bouncer could be back any second."

We'd just started for the set of double swinging doors to the back hallway when Mr. Bravo joined us in the club. He shook his head at us and waved us over to the other side of the bar. "Nah, guys. The head's over here." He led us towards the bathroom by the stage.

I nodded. "Oh, right."

On the way to the bathroom, the guy waved his hand in the air, fanning his face. He stopped and looked back at me. "You two smell like the devil. Do you always smell like that?"

"Oh, we were, uh, responding to a sewage emergency before this. Had to crawl through some pretty nasty stuff."

His nose wrinkled and he frowned while he held a hand up to his nose and mouth. "That stinks, literally."

I shrugged. "All part of the job. You know, if you'd rather wait for us outside—"

Johnny Bravo seemed not to hear my offer. "So, you guys gonna be long?" He glanced down at his watch.

"Depends on the problem," said Al. "If we gotta bust up the floor and lay new pipe, it could be awhile."

The guy's shoulders slumped as he grimaced.

"You got somewhere else you need to be?" I adjusted my tool bag.

He groaned. "Eh, my lady's pissed because I'm supposed to meet her and her mother for lunch," he admitted with an uncomfortable nod. "I was hoping maybe we'd be in and out of here in a few minutes."

Al shook his head. "Oh, there's no way we'll be out in a few minutes."

I nodded in agreement. "This is gonna take at least an hour for sure. Maybe longer."

The guy groaned. "Shit."

"Look, we know what we're doing. We're professionals," I assured him. I pointed at Al. "I mean, look at this guy. He's been plumbing since the invention of the outhouse."

Al's torso leaned back so he could look up at me with a somber face.

"What I'm trying to say is we don't need a babysitter. Just go have lunch. By the time you come back, we'll be done."

The security guard lowered his head. "I appreciate the offer, but nah, the boss'll be pissed if he finds out I didn't stick around."

I made a face. "Who's gonna tell the boss? I know I'd never mention it to anyone. I tell you what. What time do you guys open?"

"Noon."

"We're charging you for an hour of labor one way or the other. It's our minimum service call fee. So we'll stick around until noon. You make it back by then and you'll be square with the boss. He'll never even know you stepped out."

The guy thought about it for a long moment and then finally smiled. "You know what? You two seem like a couple of trustworthy fellows. I think I'll take you up on that deal." He got serious again and pointed a finger at us. "You touch the alcohol or anything else besides the plumbing and I'll break every bone in your body. Got it?"

"Considering that I can't afford the hospital bill for something like that, I think I'll keep my hands to myself," I promised, holding both hands up and giving him my best winning smile.

"Great. I really just need to make an appearance, you know, punch my card. I'll do my best to get back here a little early. Hey, thanks, man. I appreciate it."

"Hey, no problem." I extended a hand to Mr. Bravo.

He looked down at it with a wrinkled nose, as if my hand was covered in the Ebola virus. Instead of shaking it, he gave me a little bump with his elbow. "Alrighty, fellas. See you soon."

When we heard the lock click behind us, I was finally able to relax a little. "Well, that worked out. Thank God." Letting out a sigh, I looked over at Al.

"And what was your brilliant plan if he hadn't gotten a call and had to leave?"

I shrugged. "Getting into the building was as far as I'd gotten."

"Seriously, kid? You gotta be two steps ahead at all times." Al shook his head as if he were disappointed in me and started walking around the bar again.

I followed after him. "Are you kidding me? I was the one that got us the van and the overalls. I was the one that called yesterday and ordered the logo for the van. I made the appointment to have someone let us in. What have you done?"

Al stopped and shuffled around in a circle to look at me. "I told you the john was broken. If I hadn't told you that, we wouldn't even *be* here."

"You want credit for discovering the fucking john was plugged?" I looked at him incredulously. I shook my head. "You want credit for breathing too?"

"At my age? I think I deserve credit for that, yes. Now come on. We have work to do."

I TURNED ON THE FLASHLIGHT ON MY PHONE TO FIND THE LIGHT switch to the back hallway. Once the lights were on, Al led me to the row of photos he'd seen on his way to the bathroom the day before. There were at least a dozen framed pictures, all of young girls wearing little or nothing.

Al pointed at the one he'd seen of Monica Arndt. "Here she is."

I looked at her closely. Her hair was dyed blond in the photograph, but it was most definitely Monica. I'd recognize those legs anywhere. "It's her alright. But she looks younger." All of the pictures were taken against a simple white backdrop, like they'd all been taken in the same studio. I wondered if that wasn't the same place that Giselle and Jordan had been taken. Maybe if we could find the photographer, we'd be able to find the location. I pointed at a watermark in the lower right-hand corner of the picture. "Joseph Ayala Photography," I said.

"Oh, good eye," said Al, nodding and holding his glasses so he could read the nearly imperceptible typeface. "I didn't notice that before."

"If we can track down this photographer, maybe he'll be able to tell us more about what's going on at Club Cobalt."

Al patted my shoulder. "Hey, uh, you got the investigation under control, don'tcha, kid? I think it's time to check out the john."

I stared at him. "We're not really here to fix the plumbing, Al. That was just our cover story to get in."

Al patted his stomach. "I wasn't planning to fix it. I was planning to destroy it, if you catch my drift."

I wanted to groan, but instead I just let out a sigh. "Just don't take forever. Our bouncer friend could come back at any moment."

Al nodded and shuffled down the hall to the bathroom.

While I stood comparing watermarks on the pictures, I suddenly became cognizant of the fact that there was absolutely no air movement in the hallway. Not only was I starting to get really hot, but the combined smell of my sweat mixed with the smell of my fishy coveralls and the stagnant air really started to get to me. I felt nauseous and suddenly claustrophobic.

"Ugh," I groaned to myself. "I don't know how the Cruz brothers do it. I can't take this smell anymore." I unzipped the onesie and let it fall to the floor. Stepping out of it, I kicked it over to a corner, making a mental note not to leave it behind when we left.

Putting my shirt up over my nose, I wandered down to a doorway at the end of the hallway. I remembered Giselle describing her trip to Club Cobalt and how they'd had to pay the manager, Vito, a visit. I wondered if it wasn't Vito's office on the other side of the door. I turned the knob slowly, surprised to find it unlocked, and pushed it open. I stuck my head inside and found the room dark.

"Hello?" When I got no response, I pushed the door open further.

With no exterior windows to provide any light, the room was almost completely dark. I flicked on the light to find a pretty bare office. There was a basic grey metal desk in the middle of the office with a computer on it. A worn brown sofa and a coffee table sat on one side of the room and a big wooden armoire on the other side. Behind me, on the wall over my head, was a row of television screens. I assumed that was the club's security monitors. I was happy to see that they were switched off. I could only hope it wasn't still recording.

Vito's desk was fairly cleared off, except for the sticky notes posted all over the place. *Pick up Gio's shoes* was scrawled across one blue sticky note and stuck to the monitor. *Milk, butter, flour, eggs, chorizo*, read another note and was stuck to his desk planner. *Dinner Miriam 8pm* read a third. On and on they went. The guy had an obsession with sticky notes. I was surprised there weren't notes that said *don't forget to blink* and *remember to breathe*. I flicked on his computer monitor and a password-protected screen popped up.

Damn.

I opened the drawers in the desk, hoping maybe the password would be written on a sticky note inside, but found no such treasure. Really, there wasn't much to see. One drawer had files of club business in it. Receipts. Liquor invoices. Employee files. The top drawer just had pens and pencils, an engraved Zippo lighter that read *Vito, you light my fire! Love, Miriam*, a tube of cherry Chapstick, a key to something, and a pair of gold cufflinks engraved with the initials PGC and encrusted with chipped red rubies and diamonds.

Shutting the drawer, I walked over and opened the armoire to find it full of lingerie and other sexy little numbers. I shook my head, whispering to myself, "Vito, Vito, Vito. Does Miriam know?"

Then I noticed a garbage can just beside the armoire. I got down on one knee and picked through the crumpled waste. More sticky notes ranging from grocery lists to a reminder to pick his car up from the shop were crumpled up inside. I frowned. Nothing helpful. And then at the bottom of the can, I noticed a crumpled-up slip of white paper. I pulled it out and unfolded it to see an invitation to the private party at Club Cobalt. It was the exact same invitation I'd found in Jordan's room.

Even though it didn't tell me much, I shoved the little slip of paper in my pocket. Maybe I'd be able to use it to at least prove to the cops that something was up if I needed to.

And then, out of nowhere, I felt a pair of arms thrust under my armpits. It happened so fast that they had time to snake back around to the back of my head, putting me in a full-nelson headlock. I was immediately yanked into a standing position. Unable to move my head, I stood slightly stooped, like a ragdoll, held up only by the will of the person behind me. I was forced to spin around, and though I couldn't see my puppet master, a stocky guy with dark greasy hair and a flat nose stood in front of me.

"Who the fuck are you? And what are you doing in here?"

A momentary blitz of panic sent my pulse pounding through my veins. "Oh, hey, fellas. How's it going? I'm the plumber," I said, wishing like hell I hadn't taken my overalls off. I held my hands up as the stocky guy took an offensive step towards me, fists balled. "I'm here to fix the toilet! I swear!" I hollered.

"Didn't look like you were fixing a toilet to me." The stocky guy shoved his fist into my gut then, knocking all the air out of my lungs and instantaneously rendering me unable to breathe.

"I'm the plumber," I reiterated in an outward gasp as my eyes rolled back in my head and my knees went weak.

"There ain't no reason for a plumber to be snoopin' around in here," said the stocky guy.

The bouncer tightened his grip around the back of my head, widening my shoulders and making my arms flail out more all while I struggled to suck in oxygen.

"I was throwing something away—" I gasped, now forced to stand up straighter.

My eyes widened as the stocky guy balled his hand into a

fist and pulled back. I closed my eyes, preparing to take a hit to the face, when I heard a toilet flush. My eyes popped open to see stocky guy's head now turned. We both saw the bathroom door open, and Al appeared in the hallway with the pipe wrench slung over his shoulder.

"Where ya at, kid? There ain't nothing wrong with that toilet. It's working just fine." He looked both ways down the hallway until he caught sight of me in Vito's office.

We made eye contact and through a single blink, I thanked him for coming to my rescue when he did. "See?" I managed to whisper, looking at Vito again. "I told you. We're here to fix your toilet. We got a call. Go look. My van's out front."

Stocky guy frowned and then gave a nod to his accomplice, who promptly unlocked his grip behind my head. I felt the weight of my body return to my feet. I rubbed the ache out of my shoulders as they were let back down into their normal position.

"Thanks a lot," I grunted, turning to see that my puppet master was none other than one of the two guards that had kicked me out the day before and Johnny Bravo's partner. I kept my head tilted downwards slightly, hoping he wouldn't recognize me.

"Just because you're the plumber don't change the fact that you're not supposed to be in here," grunted the stocky guy. "My office is off-limits."

So it was official—I'd met Vito. I nodded. "I was looking for another bathroom."

He pursed his lips and pointed down the hallway. "The broken john's over by the stage." He gave his bouncer a head nod. "Andre, show these two jokers to the other bathroom."

Andre nodded and gave me a shove from behind as I started towards the hallway.

I turned to look at him, giving him a bit of a pout. "Watch it." I bent over and grabbed my coveralls from the floor.

"Oh, hey," called Vito, seated at the desk in his office now. "How'd you get into the building?"

I glanced down at Al.

Al hooked a thumb over his shoulder. "A different big guy let us in."

"Cal? Where'd he go?"

"We were out of plumbing tape," said Al. "He offered to go grab some for us so we could get started."

"Good employee you got there," I added.

Even though Vito looked puzzled, it seemed to satisfy him. "Huh. Okay."

Andre walked us out of the back hallway and across the club to the stage. He pointed to the bathroom that Johnny Bravo had shown us earlier. "We open in a half hour. This needs to be wrapped up by then."

"A half hour?" I bellowed. "You're kidding me? Why in the heck didn't someone call us to come in sooner? There's no way we'll be outta here by then." I looked down at Al. "I guess we'll have to come back tomorrow."

Andre shrugged. He didn't care. He wasn't using the broken toilet; he had an employee bathroom to use that worked fine. "Suit yourself. You can call the bar and set up a time."

I grinned. "Sounds like a plan." I tipped a nonexistent hat at the man. "You take care now, Andy."

17

BACK IN THE VAN, I LOOKED OVER AT AL. "OH, MAN, I OWE YOU one, buddy. That guy was just about to break my jaw."

"We're partners kid. It's what we do."

"Yeah, well, your timing couldn't have been more perfect. So, thanks. Now what we need to do is figure out what was going on in there. Vito didn't like me snooping around in his office, that's for sure. I definitely think we need to pay that photographer a visit—see what he knows."

Al's head bobbed. "I agree, but I don't think he's gonna want to talk. Anyone who's taking those kinds of pictures of underage girls isn't going to be too forthcoming about what they're involved in."

"Yeah, I think you're right. Well, then, maybe we need to make him believe that we wanna get in on the action. I think it's the only way he'll talk."

"We can sure give it a shot," said Al.

A QUICK INTERNET search revealed that the Joseph Ayala Photography studio was located on the street level of a three-story brick building in the heart of Paradise Isle's historic downtown area. The area was lined with cobblestone, and though many of the arched brick doorways had been painted over, many also remained untouched, exposing the original brick that had been used when the buildings were first built. The second-story balconies were an updated feature, along with the addition of eye-catching brightly painted shutters and hanging baskets of flowers. The posh shopping area was mostly frequented by tourists due to the nearby harbor where incoming cruise ships docked and the duty-free shopping the island provided.

The front door of Joseph Ayala's shop was propped wide open with a carved stone statue. And as Al and I entered the studio, I found that I was unprepared for what we discovered. The walls were covered in ornately framed portraits of beautiful beach weddings and breathtaking landscapes, as well as outdoor portraits of couples of all ages, women in hats walking along the beach, and children playing in the sand and surf. My mouth gaped slightly as I stared at the walls. I wasn't sure exactly what I'd thought I'd walk into, but it certainly wasn't what I was looking at now—a very wholesome photographer that didn't seem the least bit seedy or raunchy.

"Wow," I mouthed, staring up at the walls in awe.

Al stood next to me with his hands behind his back, staring up at the artwork. "Yeah, he's good."

A brunette woman wearing a white camisole tucked into a floaty red skirt and sandals whose straps wrapped around her ankles and calves came breezing into the studio from a back room. "Hello, may I help you?"

"Yes, we're looking for the artist. Joseph Ayala? Is he in?"

The woman gave us a tight smile. "I'm sorry. He is not. Mr. Ayala is currently on location shooting a wedding."

"Oh," I said, nodding. "I see."

"May I leave him a note or schedule an appointment for

you?" The woman opened a three-ring binder and flipped open the well-worn pages of an appointment book.

I stared down at it for a second. "Is that Mr. Ayala's schedule?"

"Yes, sir. Is this for a wedding or are we looking for a portrait session?" she asked.

My lips pressed together as I put an arm over Al's shoulders. "Yes, a wedding." I gave squeezed his shoulder. "When you know, you know."

Al stared up at me, his mouth set in a straight line.

"Oh," she said, a big smile on her face. "When's the big day?"

"It's coming up quickly. But before we talk dates, my partner here was just saying how he needed to use the little boys' room. Do you have a restroom here he could borrow, by any chance?"

"Of course," she said, giving Al a smile.

Al's torso turned and he looked up at me curiously.

"Honey, weren't you just telling me that you needed to go?" My eyes widened as I spoke the words, trying to tell him quietly to just play along.

"Oh. Yeah. I forgot." He smiled at the woman. "Hazards of getting old."

"Right this way," she said, leading Al down a hallway towards the back of the building.

When they'd both disappeared, I wasted no time in spinning Joseph Ayala's appointment schedule around. I flipped back a page to the current month and then ran my finger down the page until I landed on the current date.

Grainger/Smith wedding. Coco Bay Beach Resort.

Bingo.

I swiveled the planner back around again just as the woman returned to the front counter. "Okay. So, shall we start talking dates?" she asked, shooting me a wide smile.

"Yes, the wedding is next Saturday," I said with a nod.

Her eyes widened. *"Next* Saturday?"

"Yes, ma'am," I said, brightly. I leaned over her counter. Resting my chin in the palm of my hand, I smiled at her. "Why wait when you're having fun?"

"I'm sorry, sir, but as you're probably aware, Mr. Ayala is one of the most sought-after beach photographers on the island. During wedding season, he's booked months out, sometimes a year in advance. I might have something for you in the fall—"

"Oh, darn it, the fall. I don't think I can wait that long," I said, shooting Al a look as he rejoined us at the desk. "What do you think, dear? Can we wait until fall to make it official?"

"I might not be alive that long," said Al. He looked up at the woman with nothing short of a dead serious face. "Every day is a gift at this point."

She gave him a sad look, plumping out her bottom lip, while I fought off a laugh at Al's ability to keep a straight face. "Oh, I completely understand. I'm really sorry I can't help you out, fellas. I might be able to give you an idea of some other photographers that could help you."

I shook my head. "It's alright. Maybe we'll just hire a videographer instead. Thank you so much for your time."

She waved at us as we high-tailed it back to our vehicle. When we were out of earshot, Al leaned over. "What in the heck was that about?"

"I got a look at Ayala's calendar. I know where he's at. Coco Bay Beach Resort."

Al's mouth gaped. "You can't be serious, kid. You wanna interrupt a wedding to find this photographer?"

I nodded. "Damn straight."

COCO BAY BEACH RESORT wasn't difficult to find considering it was one of the more popular resorts on the island. Signs for it abounded, and when we got there, they'd made it even easier for us to find by staking out signs pointing Grainger/Smith wedding guests in the direction of the venue, a private beach along Coco Bay's coastline. They even had a separate guest parking lot just off the beach.

I pulled my Jeep up next to a pearl-blue Lexus LX 570 with a Steve Dillon Automart sticker on the lower right corner of the tailgate. The rear window bore a full-size Joseph Ayala Photography decal, making me even *more* confident that we were in the right place.

I hitched my thumb over my shoulder in the direction of the car and looked over at Al. "You like that?"

"It's like I'm looking at Columbo or something," said Al, shaking his head.

I puffed air out my nose. "Oh, come on, Al. Columbo? I think I'm good looking enough to at least be Magnum, don't you?"

Al shrugged. "Grow a mustache and then we'll talk."

I chuckled and got out of the vehicle. Adjusting my sunglasses, I looked out over the beach. Hotel staff were busy setting out rows of white chairs in front of a bare four-posted pergola on the beach. Other workers wove layers of white tulle through the laths atop the pergola and down the four corner posts. "Look, they're still setting up for the wedding."

A slender guy in white linen pants, a blue short-sleeved shirt, and sandals, carrying a camera around his neck, was speaking animatedly with some of the resort staff.

"That looks like our guy." I looked over at Al. "You ready?"

"Ready as I'll ever be."

We walked across the sand, making our way over to who I could only assume was Joseph Ayala. By the time we'd walked all the way over to him, he was done talking to the resort staff and was now down on one knee, holding the camera up to his face.

Approaching him, I cleared my throat. "Mr. Ayala?"

The man's head snapped back to look up at Al and me. "Yes?" He had shoulder-length dark curly hair, olive skin, and a diamond-shaped face with prominent cheekbones, his narrow chin ending in a sleekly manicured goatee.

I smiled at him. "Very good. The woman in your photo studio told us we could find you here."

Al elbowed me in the ribs as the photographer climbed to his feet, dusting sand off of his knees.

"Carlotta?" he asked, his unibrow dropped in surprise.

"Brown-haired woman, long skirt," I said.

"Yes. That's Carlotta. She told you where I was?" He shook his head. "I'm sorry, my staff usually know better than to disclose shoot locations to clients. And as you can see, my schedule is occupied today. If you need to make an appointment, you'll need to speak with Carlotta."

"Well, that's just it. This isn't really something I can speak with Carlotta about. It's more of a private matter."

"A private matter?" he said, glancing up and around at the myriad of hotel resort staff that buzzed around the beach.

"Yes. It won't take but a minute or two of your time," I added.

He looked at me curiously then. "I'm sorry, I didn't catch your name."

I held out a hand to him. "Oh, right. My name is Artie Balladares. I'm the owner of the Seacoast Majestic Resort."

Al swiveled around and stared up at me in surprise.

I looked down at him. "And this is my assistant, Francisco."

Joseph sighed. "I only have a moment, I'm quite busy today."

"Yes, a moment is fine."

He nodded. "I need to go get one of my other lenses out of my vehicle anyway. Let me just finish what I'm doing here, and I'll meet you up in the parking lot in a moment."

"Thank you, Mr. Ayala, we appreciate it."

18

"DRUNK! WHAT IN THE WORLD WERE YOU THINKING BRINGING Artie's name into this mess?" chastised Al while we walked back to the parking lot.

"I was *thinking* that we needed to have a legitimate reason for going to see this guy. It worked, didn't it? Ayala was about to toss us back into Carlotta's unprofessional hands if it wasn't for me throwing some credibility into the ring."

Al shook his head. "Artie's gonna kill you if he finds out about this."

I stopped walking and stared down at him. "Well, there are only two people who know, and I'm not talking. So if he finds out, I know exactly who to blame."

"God?"

"Al."

Al waved a hand in the air and kept walking. "Same thing."

"I'm serious, Al. No mentioning this to Artie. What he doesn't know won't hurt him."

"Yeah, we don't know that, kid. Now listen, I just wanna go on record and say that this is a bad idea."

"Fine. Your complaint is duly noted. I've filed it away in its proper receptacle. The garbage man will be here to see it to its final resting place shortly."

We leaned our backs against my Jeep then and watched Joseph plow his way across the beach towards us with his camera bag slung across his body and his camera hanging around his neck. Wordlessly, he passed right in front of us and went straight to the back of his vehicle.

Al and I followed him.

He opened the tailgate and began to sort through the camera equipment in his trunk. Then he removed the lens from his camera and dug through a bag to grab another. When he was finished exchanging gear, he closed his tailgate and propped his hip up against it. "So. What can I help you with, gentlemen?"

"We were told that you do a lot of work with young models," I began. "I'm looking for someone that can do some work for a new advertising campaign that I'm working on. Something to bring in more of a specific clientele."

He tipped his head to the side curiously. "May I ask you who referred you to me?"

"Yeah, sure. The guys down at Club Cobalt speak very highly of you and your work."

Joseph crossed his arms over his chest and looked down at his feet, kicking a rock out of the way absentmindedly. He looked up again. "Do they?"

"Yes. Of course your showcase of pictures on their wall of fame doesn't hurt at all either."

He frowned. "Yes. I really wish they'd take those down. I'm afraid I won't be able to help you gentlemen; my schedule is booked for the rest of the summer." He rocked to his feet.

"Yes, Carlotta mentioned that. But from what I understand, you're the best in the business at this specific sort of thing."

He frowned and seemed to let down his guard just a bit. "Look, I don't know what you heard, but these days I only do those shoots when I'm required to."

Required to? I wanted to ask him who was requiring him to, but I knew that would tip my hand. "Well, yeah, I understand. If it makes it easier, I've already got the model I want to use in mind."

"Oh yeah?"

I nodded and pulled out a picture of Jordan. I showed it to him, looking closely for any signs of recognition. "She's pretty, huh?"

Joseph lifted a shoulder noncommittally. "Probably not who I would've picked for an advertising campaign, but I suppose she'd work."

"You haven't used her for your shoots in the past?"

He stared at her picture, his eyes blank. He shrugged. I could tell he didn't want to talk about it. I needed to loosen him up a little.

I pointed at his vehicle then. "Hell of a ride you got there."

He glanced sideways at his luxury SUV. "One of a photographer's most important tools."

"Just got mine at Steve Dillon's myself."

He shot a glance over at my ride and gave me a little nod. "Steve's a decent guy."

"Sure is. I just wish those damn tariffs weren't so high. Paid a fortune for it."

Joseph stared at me hard, his dark eyes shining like polished onyx beneath the bright sun. "That shouldn't be too hard for a resort owner to afford."

I shrugged. My heart raced a little. I didn't like the way he was looking at me. I felt the sudden need to backpedal. "No. I mean, of course not. It was a drop in the bucket, really. It still hurts the pocketbook, though. I'm sure yours set you back quite a lot, too."

"Like I said, it's a requirement for the job." He held a hand out then to me. "It was a pleasure speaking with you, Mister..."

"Balladares," I mumbled. From my peripheral vision, I could see Al shooting me a nasty look.

"Right. It was nice meeting you, Mr. Balladares, but I really need to get back to my wedding shoot. The bridal party will be out soon."

I held the picture up. "So you don't recall if you've ever shot this girl before?"

"Take care." He walked away without even looking at the photograph.

Fuck.

"Good going, kid, you chased him away," said Al.

"What the fuck did I say?"

"I told you you shouldn't have told him you were Artie. You really think big resort owners are gonna blink at the price of a Jeep?"

"Shit," I breathed. "I was only trying to loosen him up a little. Get him chatting. Who doesn't like complaining about the prices of shit?"

Al shrugged. "I guess that guy doesn't."

"Ugh. Now what do we do? I feel like that was our last lead."

Al shook his head. "I don't know. Time to regroup, I guess."

19

THAT NIGHT TURNED OUT TO BE AN EXTRAORDINARILY WARM, humid evening. With my windows open as usual, I tossed and turned most of the night, and when my subconscious heard the clickety-clack of Earnestine's claws tap-dancing on my headboard the next morning, I awoke with a start in a soggy pool of sweat.

"Aahh!" I belted from my diaphragm as I was ripped from my paralyzing dreamlike state. Though I couldn't exactly put my finger on what I'd been dreaming about, the ominous feeling of dread gripped my body and clung to me like a burr rolled up in a dog's fur.

"*Morning, stupid, morning, stupid, rawck,*" Earnestine chattered.

"Fuck, Earnestine," I cursed, looking straight up at the bird. My heart raced. Whether it was from my dream or the bird, I wasn't sure, but at that moment I felt like blaming it on Earnestine.

Earnestine looked down at me and let out a whistle.

I pulled my pillow over my head and groaned. My phone rang.

Earnestine mocked the sound of my classic phone ringtone, so she sounded like an echo. Brring. *Brring.* Brring. *Brring.*

I rolled over on my side and reached a hand out to grab my phone from my nightstand. With my eyes closed, I answered it from under my pillow. "Drunk here."

"Danny, it's Frankie."

My eyes popped open. It was not the voice I'd expected to hear, but I had to admit, hearing her voice certainly did something to counteract the tension I felt from Earnestine's wakeup call. "Hey, Frankie. Good morning. How are you?"

"I'm okay, but listen, I've got some news about that girl you were looking for."

My breath caught in my throat. I bolted into an upright position. My free hand went to the top of my hair. "You've got news about Jordan?"

"Well, I'm not one hundred percent sure that it's her, but I think we found her."

I smiled and my shoulders slumped forward in relief. Giselle was going to be thrilled. "No kidding. Is she alright? Where is she?"

There was a pause on the other end.

I looked down at my phone to see if we were still connected. "Frankie? You still there?"

I heard her sigh. "She's dead, Danny. The girl we found is dead."

My heart froze in my chest. "What?"

"I'm sorry to have to tell you. I know this isn't the outcome you were hoping for."

"But if you're not sure that it's her—"

"There's a chance that it's not," she agreed. "I was hoping you could come down here and ID the body."

"How'd it happen?" I asked, climbing out of bed. I pulled some clothes out of my drawer.

"I'd rather not talk about it over the phone. Why don't you

just meet me down at the coroner's office? I'll tell you what I can."

"Yeah. Gimme an hour. I have to shower, round up Al, and get over there."

"Okay. See you in an hour."

"Thanks, Frankie," I said, my heart heavy in my chest.

"I'm sorry, Danny."

"IT'S HER," I said, my head hanging low between my shoulder blades. I swiped a hand in the air and spun around. "*Fuck.*" I couldn't even look at the bloated blue face in the stainless-steel drawer without feeling sick to my stomach. I hadn't thought for a moment that we were going to find Jordan like this. Giselle was going to lose it.

Al walked over to me and put a hand on my back. He gave me a little pat. "Come on. Let's get some fresh air."

Seconds later, we stood outside on the sidewalk beneath a frangipani tree. The soft, fruity scent settled over us, providing me with a sense of calm. It was over. There was no more rush to find the missing girl. She was dead. Now it would just be a question of figuring out what happened to her.

"I'm really sorry, guys. I know this isn't the outcome any of us wanted."

"How did it happen?" asked Al.

"Drowning," said Frankie. "Of course, that's pending the autopsy results."

"Where'd you find her?"

"A fisherman found her. Near a boat launch not too far away from Sandy Bay Beach. It's popular with the younger crowd."

"You think it was accidental?" I asked, running a hand against the back of my neck.

Frankie looked up at me and shrugged. "Until we get the

autopsy results back, I really can't say. It could've been suicide."

"Or foul play?"

She nodded. "Maybe."

"I assume there will be a full investigation?" I asked.

"Unless it's ruled accidental death or suicide."

I shook my head. "I have a hard time believing it was suicide," I said.

"Did you know her personally?"

"No. I didn't, but from everything Giselle's told me about her, I have a hard time believing that."

"Can you tell how long she's been dead?" asked Al.

Frankie shook her head. "We'll know more after the autopsy. I'm sorry, I don't have a lot of answers yet, but I'll let you know if we find anything else out."

"Okay, thanks, Frankie. Hey, can you answer a question for me?"

"I can try."

"Do you know who owns Club Cobalt down in the District?"

Frankie nodded. "That's easy. Kip Dalton. He owns Cobalt and several other bars in the District." She shook her head. "Why?"

"You know anything about him?"

"I've just heard rumblings. He's—uh—" She lifted a shoulder. "I guess you could say he's quite the ladies' man."

Al looked up at me. "Why am I not surprised?"

"So I'm assuming that means he's not married?"

She frowned. "Not as far as I am aware."

"You have any idea where he lives?"

"Not right offhand."

"Think you could find out for me?"

"Yeah, I can probably do that. Care to explain why you want to know?"

"Just something Al and I are working on. I'll let you know if we find anything else out."

Frankie smiled. "Fair enough."

"So are you going to notify Jordan's aunt?" asked Al.

"Yeah, we'll try and get in touch with her now that we know it's Jordan." She looked up at me. "I assume you'll take care of telling her friend that was looking for her?"

I sighed. It was something I knew I had to do, but I wasn't looking forward to it. "I don't want to," I admitted.

"Drunk—" began Al.

"But I will," I finished. "It should come from me."

20

"I GOT YOUR TEXT," SAID GISELLE, STANDING ON MY FRONT porch. "What's up?"

I'd waited to text her until the end of her shift. I didn't want her having to try and go back to work after hearing the news. "I've got news about Jordan," I said, my heart heavy in my chest. I glanced over at Al, who was seated on one of the barstools in my kitchen. His glum face didn't make me feel any better about what I had to do.

Giselle's face lit up. "You found her?"

I gestured towards the living room. "You should sit down. We have some things to talk about."

Doe-eyed, Giselle bobbed her head. "Okay."

When we were both seated on my rattan sofa, I took a deep breath. There was no point in beating around the bush. It didn't matter if I tore the Band-Aid off fast or slow; either way, it was still going to hurt like hell. "Giselle. We did find Jordan."

She sucked in her breath, a huge smile covered her face, lighting up her eyes. "You did? Oh, Drunk! I owe you so much, thank you!" She threw her arms around my neck and squeezed. Then, just as suddenly, she lifted her arms off of me and sat back, her spine straight. "Where is she? Is she at her apartment? I gotta talk to her!"

"Giselle, I hate that I have to tell you this. And there's really no easy way to do it, so I'm just gonna be honest with you. It was the police that found her." I could see it in her eyes. She wanted to rail on me then. She inhaled, preparing to let it out, but before she could, I finished what I'd called her to my cottage to tell her. "She's dead, Giselle. Jordan's dead."

With her mouth agape, Giselle's eyes widened. She froze in place, absorbing the information I'd just laid on her. Seconds later, her head began to shake from side to side. "Nnnooo," she said. "My Jordan's not dead. They found the wrong girl."

"Giselle, Al and I went down there earlier. It's Jordan. I'm sure of it."

"B-but—" Tears sprang up into her eyes.

Al hopped off his barstool and shuffled into the living room. He put a hand on Giselle's shoulder. "I'm really sorry, Giselle. If there's anything we can do, we're here for you."

"This isn't happening," she whispered, as tears began to roll down her cheeks. "How? How did she die?"

"Drowning, from what we understand. A fisherman found her over by the Sandy Bay Beach."

Giselle stopped sobbing long enough to sniffle and look up at me. "Sandy Bay Beach? Drowning?"

"Yeah, they're thinking either accidental drowning or maybe even a suicide. But they're waiting for the autopsy results to come back for a more definitive answer."

Her head shook as she took the tissues Al handed to her. "Why would she have been in the water? Jordan hated the water."

"It might've been accidental."

"How do you *accidentally* get in the water?" asked Giselle, her voice one part hysteria, one part demanding. "She never intentionally went in the water."

"Did you ever go to that beach?"

Wiping her nose, Giselle shrugged. "I mean, yeah, we've been there before. But it wasn't exactly a place we went a lot. If anything, we just laid out, maybe played volleyball. I don't think either one of us *ever* got in the water. But I haven't been there in months. I'm sure Jordan hadn't been there in months either. So I don't know how it could've been accidental."

"Maybe it was suicide."

Giselle's head stopped shaking long enough to look me in the eye firmly. "No. Jordan would *never* commit suicide, Drunk. There's no way. She *loved* life. She was literally *the most* fun-loving, happy-go-lucky girl there was. It's one of the reasons I loved her so much," she whispered before breaking down into a fit of sobs again.

I draped an arm around her shoulders and pulled her in for a hug, letting her cry on my shirt. I patted her hair and did my best to comfort her. Both Al and I felt her misery and pain to our very souls that day.

When Giselle had tired slightly, she sat up. I handed her a wad of paper towels and let her mop up her face. "Drunk, Jordan didn't commit suicide, and I don't believe for a second that she went in the water and accidentally drowned when she literally hates the water."

"Then what do you think happened?" I asked her. While I had some opinions of my own, I wanted to know if there was anything Giselle was keeping from me.

"I think it was them," she whispered.

"Who?"

She glanced over at Al uncomfortably.

"He knows," I said, my voice low.

Giselle nodded and wiped her nose. "I think it was the people that Crystal works for. It has to be, Drunk. This wasn't an accident. I think they killed her."

"Why would they kill her, Giselle? If she just went there to give massages, why would they kill her? I mean, I'll be the first to say that I think what they hired you to do was weird, and really creepy. But I don't think that's against the law."

Giselle's head dropped. "It wasn't just massages," she whispered.

I took a deep breath and let it out. I'd wondered all along if there wasn't more to the story. "Then what was it? Sex?"

Her head bobbed. But then she looked up. "I didn't—"

"No judgment here," I said quietly. "I just want the truth."

She held her hand up as tears continued to roll down her cheeks. "I didn't, I swear! They wanted us to, but they said we didn't have to. They said we'd get an extra two hundred for sex."

"Did Jordan?"

Giselle shook her head. "No, she didn't either. Neither of us did, but—"

"But what?"

"But the guy—" She began to cry again. She put her head in her hands, and her shoulders shook. When she finally got it together, she looked up, but her eyes focused on the television across the room, not me. "The guy, he—he sort of—took care of himself," she explained. "It was disgusting. I never wanted to go back."

"Did Jordan want to go back?" I asked.

"Not at first. At first she said she was creeped out too. But then the next day she kind of got a laugh out of it, like it was funny. But I didn't really want to talk about it anymore. I felt dirty and ashamed that we'd been there to see that. He was this kind of *old* creepy guy. I just didn't think it was funny."

"Did you recognize him?"

She shook her head. "I'd never seen *any* of those people before in my life."

"So eventually you think she went back."

"It's the *only* place she could've gotten that stack of money from."

"Giselle, do you think Jordan would've taken them up on

their offer to make more money by having sex with the clients?"

Giselle's eyes swung down to the ground. Her lips mashed together tightly.

"Giselle?"

"I asked her," she whispered.

"What did she say?"

The tears started again. "She told me it was none of my business. She told me girls were having sex with their boyfriends all the time for free, what difference did it make if she wanted to do it and get paid for it? I told her there was a big difference, but she didn't see it. She didn't *say* she was doing it, but I felt like she kind of implied it."

"Oh man," I sighed, glancing back at Al.

He looked miserable, like he was having a hard time hearing it all and watching Giselle break down.

"Now what?" she asked, looking between the two of us.

"Now, I guess we try and find out if this is what ultimately got her killed."

"Do you think it is?"

"If you honestly don't think she would've taken her own life or gone out on the water voluntarily, I mean, I don't know what else to think."

"I honestly think she wouldn't have killed herself or gone out on the water voluntarily. This was no accident."

My head bobbed slowly. It would have been quite the coincidence if it really was an accident. "Then we make the people who did this to her pay. Al and I are going to start by finding out where they took you that night. What can you tell me about that?"

Giselle frowned and let out a heavy sigh. "Not much. Like I told you before, they put us in a limo and we couldn't see out the windows. Then when we got there, they pulled us directly into the garage. I didn't see the outside of the house at all."

"But it was a big house, right?"

Giselle's head bounced. "Yeah, really big. And there was this old guy there. I guess he was the butler."

"Do you know his name?"

"No. I don't remember anyone saying any names."

"Were there any distinguishing features about the house?"

"Well, the massage room that we were in. That was pretty distinguishing."

"Anything else?"

She shrugged. "I don't know. They didn't exactly give us the grand tour. We literally went from the garage, down a hallway, and to the massage room."

"And there was nothing distinguishing about the hallway? What did the floors look like? What color were the walls? If I were standing in that hallway right now, what would it look like?"

"I don't know. I guess the floors were tile. I couldn't tell you what color the walls were. And there were pictures on the walls." Her voice kind of trailed off.

"Like what kind of pictures?"

"Like models. Girls like me," she whispered. "In lingerie."

I glanced over at Al. That certainly sounded familiar. When I looked back at Giselle, tears were rolling down her cheeks again. She'd had enough for one day, I could tell. I put a hand on her shoulder. "You want me to call your mom and tell her what happened to Jordan?"

"My mom can't know all the details," she whispered. "I don't want her to think badly of Jordan. Or me," she added.

Al chimed in then. "Giselle, this is no time for lies or withholding information. Lies are the enemy of truth. You have to tell your mother everything. You are her daughter. She just wants to be there for you. But she has a right to know the truth."

Giselle stared at Al, her face completely emotionless. Finally, she stood up. "Thank you for everything you've done so far, but I'll take care of telling my mom. Please just take care of finding out who did this to Jordan."

I stood up too. "You have my word, Giselle. We'll do our best."

21

AFTER GISELLE LEFT MY COTTAGE, AL AND I AGREED THAT Jordan's death had to be a cover-up of the child prostitution ring they had going on over at Club Cobalt. And with Kip Dalton's affinity for women and the fact that he *owned* Club Cobalt, it made sense that *he* was the benefactor of such a disgusting business arrangement and the man that we were after.

Frankie phoned not long after Giselle left. She'd managed to score Dalton's number as well as his home address. And after a quick Google Maps search, we discovered that he did, in fact, own a sizable mansion. I felt fairly confident that a search of his house would reveal *the* hallway with the pictures of girls in lingerie as well as the massage room Giselle had described. It was just a matter of finding a way inside so we could have a look around.

The sun had just begun to set when Al and I hoped back into the Wrangler and headed into town.

"So. We gotta figure out how to get inside Dalton's house and have a look around. See if that's where the limo took Giselle and Jordan. Once we know it is, then we can work on tying him to the underage sex ring and maybe even to Jordan's murder."

"Yeah, I suppose that's a start," agreed Al.

I clapped my hands, rubbing them together, anxiously. "So. What's our plan? How are we going to get into the house?"

"We could wait until he leaves, then sneak in," suggested Al.

"Nah, security alarms."

"Plumbers?" he asked with a smile.

"I don't think we can go to that well again."

"Publishers Clearing House? I do a pretty good Ed McMahon. Heeeere's Johnny."

"You sound more like Jack Nicholson."

"Well, hell, kid, why do I always gotta be the brains of this operation?"

"I'm sorry, you'd rather be the ass of the operation?"

Al gave me a perfunctory head bob before turning to stare out the windshield. "You're right. There can only be one of those here. And in reference to your first question, I don't know what the plan is. I can't think with all your yapping."

I shrugged. "Fine, then I guess we'll just drive over there and confront Dalton about his club's connection to an underage prostitution ring. See what he has to say. You know, shake him down."

"But what if he's the one that had the girl killed?" Al shook his head. "Sounds too dangerous to me."

"Yeah? You want me to turn the car around and take you back home to Evie? You can make popcorn and watch *CSI* reruns while I do the dirty work." I put my blinker on.

Al sighed and waved his hand for me to keep driving. "I didn't say I wanted to go home, kid. Jeez. I was just saying that this Dalton guy could be dangerous."

"So's jaywalking. What's your point?"

"My point is, we can't just go in there guns blazing. We need to finesse the guy."

"Okay, well, while you're finessing him, I'll be finding out what he knows about Jordan Lambert."

"I'm serious, kid, we gotta be smarter than that. Think with our heads, not our fists."

"What the hell do you want me to do? Send him a fucking singing telegram?"

"Kid. I got it!"

"SO YOU WANT to pay me to do what exactly?" asked Valentina Carrizo after we'd shuttled her out of the Blue Iguana and into my vehicle later that evening.

I gave a glance in my rearview mirror and pulled away from the curb. "You've heard of a singing telegram?"

Seated shotgun next to me, she nodded. "Yes? But not a singing hookergram. I don't think that's a real thing." She wrinkled her nose.

I glanced over at her and shot her a wink. "Oh, it'll be a real thing tonight."

"But what are *you* going to do?"

"Al and I have some business to take care of in this guy's house. We just need you to keep him busy for a while."

"What kind of business?" she asked.

From the backseat, Al held up a hand. "Sorry, miss. That's on a need-to-know basis."

She turned her torso so she could look back at Al. "Well, I need to know."

I reached over and patted Valentina's leg. "Please, Val. No questions, alright?"

"The less you know, the better for your safety," said Al.

"Is what you're doing legal?"

I lifted a brow. "I could ask you the same thing."

"It is on *thees* island," she said with a giggle. Then she slid over closer to me and rubbed a hand straight down the middle of my crotch. "When I am done here, are we going to go back to your place?"

I glanced up in my rearview mirror again just in time to see Al rolling his eyes. I lifted Valentina's hand from my crotch and placed it on her own leg. "Sorry, love, not tonight. I've got plans." I wanted to add *not any night*, but we needed her technical services for the evening, and I didn't want to risk offending the woman.

She frowned and sat back in her seat in a huff. "You are still going to pay me, right? I want double. Danger equals double."

"Of course you're going to get paid. And fine, double it is. All you have to do is keep him occupied until I text you. It's your choice how far you want to let it get."

"But what if he is not interested?"

"Oh, I have a sneaking suspicion that's not going to be the case."

"But maybe he is not home."

"We already called his home number. He's home alright."

"But maybe I cannot sing very well."

I glanced over at Valentina. She wore a plum off-the-shoulder top that tied in a big knot between her boobs. Her matching figure-hugging skirt barely covered her curvy bottom. "Honestly, Val, looking like that—I don't think he's going to mind if you can't hold a note."

She looked up at me seductively then, batting her eyes and smiling. "Thank you very much. So what should I sing?"

"'Happy Birthday'?"

She frowned. "I don't *theenk* it is going to be his birthday."

I threw my hands up in the air. She was worse than Al. "Fuck, Val. I don't know. Sing the fucking weather forecast, I don't care. Make something up."

She frowned at me. "Do you talk to your mother with that mouth?"

From the backseat, Al chuckled. "I tell him that all the time. Maybe he'll listen to you."

I groaned. "Ugh. Fine. Listen, Val. What song do you know by heart?"

She shrugged. "I don't know. I know the Colombian national anthem."

"That's the only song you know by heart?"

"I don't know any English songs by heart."

"None?"

"I only know 'Happy Birthday.'"

"Then sing him 'Happy Birthday.'"

She nodded. "Okay. I'll sing 'Happy Birthday.'"

PULLING up to Kip Dalton's gated front entrance, we stopped next to a speaker. Al and I cowered down in the backseat while Valentina pressed the button. A man answered, his voice crackling through the speaker. "Yes?"

"Hello." Valentina put on her best smile for the video camera focused on her. "Singing hookergram for *Meester Keep* Dalton."

"Singing what?!"

"Singing hookergram for *Meester Keep* Dalton," Valentina repeated, this time more slowly.

The speaker went dead for an extended moment. Then the voice came back on. "I'm sorry, who sent you?"

"Say Vito sent you," I hissed as quietly as I could from the backseat.

"I am a present from Vito," said Valentina, shimmying slightly to make her breasts bounce enticingly for the camera.

"Vito sent you?" We heard the voice behind the speaker chuckle, and then it went dead again. We waited a long second. Valentina was just about to reach out and push the button again when the gates swung open.

Sweet.

As Valentina pulled ahead, I lifted my head just high

enough to see where we were going. From a distance I noticed that the end of the driveway curved all the way around in a circle. A large stone fountain sat in the middle of it, spewing up random arches and sprays of dancing colored water. I puffed air. "Holy shit. What's he think this place is? The fucking Bellagio?"

"Where do you want me to go?" asked Valentina.

"Park a little ways back from the front door at an angle. Al and I are going to slip out on the driver's side once he's occupied."

She nodded as we passed a detached multiple-stall garage. Six vehicles of different makes, models, and colors all sat out on the pavement beneath a stand of palm trees. The moon reflected off their hoods, and even in the dim haze of the evening, I could see that they'd all just been washed and then polished until they shone.

"You better stay down," she whispered as she pulled the car to a stop. "The front light is on."

"Leave the window open," I whispered. "And be careful. Remember, I'll text you when it's time to go, so keep an eye on your phone."

"Please don't get caught," she hissed back.

"Aww, sweet of you to worry about us," I said, reaching forward to squeeze the back of her elbow.

She yanked her arm away. "I'm not worried about you. I'm worried about *me*! If you get caught, then I get caught."

"Just go," I hissed.

Keeping my head low, I peered up over the seat, and watched her get out of the vehicle. Her heels clicked on the stone driveway and her round bottom sashayed from side to side as she walked up the walk and rang the bell. I kept my eyes glued to the front door, waiting to get a visual on Dalton and praying that he'd take the bait.

"What's she doing?" asked Al, his head still resting on the seat.

"She's screwing him on the front porch," I whispered back.
"Really?"

"No, not really. He hasn't even answered the door yet, Al. I don't think even hookers can work that fast."

"Yes, they can."

I glanced down at him. "You know this from experience?"

"Let's just say I was a different man before Evie polished me up into the gem I am today."

"Al!"

"What? I'm kidding! I can't tell a joke?"

Shaking my head, I looked up at the porch. The door had just swung open. A polished-looking blond man in a tailored, slim-cut grey suit opened the door. The first four or five buttons on his pink button-down shirt were unbuttoned, and he held a tumbler of whiskey in one hand. When he saw Valentina staring back at him, he leaned against the door frame, a broad smile on his face.

"Are you *Meester Keep* Dalton?" we heard her ask in her pronounced Colombian accent.

"I am," he said, a wide smile on his face.

Upon confirmation that she'd found our target, Valentina immediately burst into a sexy rendition of "Happy Birthday."

When she was done, Dalton chuckled. "It's not even my—"

In what I could only assume was an effort to cease any and all conversation regarding her song choice, she sauntered directly up to him and unbuckled his pants.

Al's head poked up next to mine, just in time to see the man's belt come off and smack the air as if it aspired to be Indiana Jones's whip. "See? I told you hookers work fast."

22

THE SECOND THAT VALENTINA DISAPPEARED INSIDE THE HOUSE with Kip Dalton, I pulled my black ski mask down over my face, cracked open the rear driver's-side door, and slid to the ground like a blob of shapeshifting plasmodium slime. Landing in a squatting position next to my Jeep, I held the door open for Al.

"Your turn," I hissed up at him.

Al looked down at me. Only his watery blue eyes were visible under his mask. "I'll break a hip if I slide out like that."

"I'd prefer you didn't. We don't have that much time."

Al rolled onto his stomach and then slid feetfirst out of the vehicle, trying hard to keep his head down.

Duck walking to the end of the Jeep, I turned back towards him. He was standing fully erect. "For fuck's sake, Al. Get down," I whispered.

He shuffled towards me, holding his back. "Are you kidding? I haven't squatted since Reagan was president."

I rolled my eyes. "Just follow me." With my back pressed up against my vehicle, I slipped around the tailgate and into the shadows of the garage. Al shuffled behind me, flat-footed, but with raised shoulders and arms, like he only half-remembered how to tiptoe. Once we were safely ensconced in the shadowed, protective cover between the garage and the house, I felt a little more comfortable about not being seen.

On our way to the back of the garage, we passed between the assorted newly washed luxury cars and SUVs. I pointed at a silver Porsche that still had its dealer plates in the window. "This one doesn't even have its tags yet. Like he really needed another one?" I hissed at Al. "Must be rough." I shook my head. At this point, my only hope of ever being able to afford property and vehicles like Kip Dalton's was for the Cruz brothers to strike it rich. Not that I'd buy all this stuff even if I had the money. I had no problem admitting to my cheapskate lifestyle. As long as my immediate needs were met, I was pretty happy.

We wove through the cars and around to the back of the garage. The plan was to try and find a back door or a back window that was open. But when we got around to the back of the garage, I realized that a ten-foot-tall wrought-iron fence precluded us from getting into the backyard and finding our way inside.

"Shit." I knew I wouldn't have a problem scaling the fence, but even if I could get Al to the top, I was pretty sure he'd break a hip on the way down. I turned and looked at him. "You wait here, I'll climb over and then see if I can find a rope to pull you over or something." Without waiting for a response, I grabbed hold of the bars and began to climb. When I got to the top, I threw one leg over the bars, but when I went to throw my other leg over, the hem of my navy Bermuda shorts caught on one of the spear-tipped points. "Sonovabitch," I breathed, trying to awkwardly hold myself up with one hand and free my pants with my other. One of the spear-tipped points dug into my forearm, making me wince in pain. Then, before I realized what was happening, I lost my grip and fell to the ground, landing on my back.

"Ooof!" I exhaled.

The landing knocked every last breath out of my body.

Fuck.

Rolling around on the ground with my eyes closed, trying to relearn how to breathe, I suddenly felt the presence of someone standing over me. I pinched one eye open and saw a dark figure looming over me. My heart leapt into my throat. I dug the heels of my boat shoes into the ground and extended my legs, pushing myself as far back as I could, trying to put space between me and whatever guard had found me.

But the dark figure followed me.

"You alright, kid?" hissed Al's familiar voice.

My head jerked up to stare at the shadowy figure. "Al?" I whispered.

"Yeah? You break anything?"

"Shit, Al. You scared the fuck outta me," I wheezed.

"You're gonna blame this one on me? You're the one that scaled the fence and fell ten feet instead of just going through the gate like a normal person." He pointed backwards, towards an open gate just down the fence a few yards.

"There was a gate?" I took Al's extended hand and let him help pull me to my feet.

"Of course there was a gate. Where there's a fence, there's always a gate."

"Fabulous." I dusted myself off and tried to regain my pride while simultaneously regaining my breath.

Al nodded.

"Come on." We paced around to Dalton's backyard to find that it sloped down towards its own private beach, which opened out to the sea, facing Isla La Fleur—a neighboring island barely visible on the horizon. A warm island breeze blew in, bringing with it the smell of the briny ocean air and carrying the sweet peachy notes of nearby plumerias. I tapped Al's arm and pointed across the green to the pool, which was adjacent to the main house. A set of French doors had been left wide open. That was our target.

Al nodded and together we crept across the grass beneath the bright light of the moon. We'd gotten about half the distance when we heard the sound of wild barking coming from somewhere between us and the beach.

My eyes widened when I saw the pointed ears of a pair of patrolling Dobermans appear just beneath the hill to the beach. *Fuck.* While I knew I could sprint to the house with my long legs, there was no way Al was making that run. He ran on three speeds—hobble, shuffle, and amble. Without skipping a beat, I turned to face Al, threw him over my shoulder in a fireman's carry, and sprinted towards the open doorway.

The dogs got closer and closer, as did the open doors to the pool. It would be a close race. We hit the concrete just as the dogs did. I ran around a pair of pool recliners. The dogs leapt over the pair on their end. My pulse raced. Who would get to the door first?

I ended up closing the gap first. I slid inside the house and slammed the sliding glass door shut just as the dogs sprang to catch me. They both smashed into the glass and crumpled to the ground, whimpering for only a split second before launching into a full-on bark fest. I bent forward, lowering Al to his feet.

He didn't skip a beat before cupping his chin thoughtfully. "There's an old saying, you know. Before climbing a fence, a wise man must ask himself if the fence is there to keep something out or to keep something in."

I leaned forward on my knees, panting heavily. "Okay, Yoda. You couldn't have pulled that one outta your ass a little earlier in the game?"

Al shrugged. "I have a feeling they aren't there just for show. They're probably Dalton's alarm system. Maybe we ought to find a place to lay low for a minute or two."

"Yeah, I think you're right." With my back pressed up against a wall, I slipped to the nearest doorway and looked inside. It was a bathroom. "In here," I hissed.

Al followed me, and the two of us climbed into the shower, straightening the shower curtain behind us. Within seconds, the light in the little vestibule we'd been in flipped on.

I heard the sound of bare feet slapping on the tile. "What's your problem, Duke?" asked a male voice that I could only assume was Kip Dalton's.

The dog's barked wildly on the other side of the glass.

"Do they always bark like that?" It was Valentina's voice this time.

"They probably just want to come inside. They aren't particularly fond of the dark."

Al looked up at me.

I held a finger up to my ski-mask-covered lips. My heart beat wildly. If he let them in, we were goners. Those dogs would find us in two shakes.

"Oh," said Valentina. "Maybe you should wait to let them in until we finish what we started." She giggled seductively then.

Dalton chuckled. "I like how you think. Now, where were we?" Though overshadowed by the dogs' wild barking, we could still hear the disgusting slurping and moaning sounds of Valentina and Dalton making out.

Valentina giggled again. "I *theenk* they are watching us."

He laughed. "I can promise you that it's nothing they haven't seen before."

"But it's kind of distraction. I can't focus with them barking," she said. "Maybe we should go somewhere that we cannot hear them. I want to be able to focus all of my attention on what I came here to do."

"Oohh," Dalton growled. "Attention to detail. I like it. I can tell you're a professional. Well, then, how about we go somewhere a little more quiet. Upstairs to my room, perhaps?"

Val squealed then, making me wonder if Dalton hadn't scooped her up. Because the next thing I knew, I heard giggles fading deeper into the house. Al and I waited until we couldn't hear any more sounds coming from the pair. The dogs continued barking, but I had a sneaking suspicion that Kip Dalton was going to be too busy to care.

Finally, we emerged from the shower. When we did, Al tugged the mask off of his face. "Oh my gosh, that was close," he whispered, fanning himself with his mask. "I was roasting in there."

"But Val came through," I said. "We'll have to remember to tip her well. She saved our asses."

Al and I walked back into the little tiled room off the pool. The dogs still barked wildly at us, but now I felt a little more in control. I waggled my fingers at them. "It's been real, boys."

"It's never a good idea to taunt a dog," said Al. "Especially dogs that are trained assassins."

"Oh, trust me, Al. I never plan to see those boys again. I don't care if we have to crawl out through a fucking window, we're not going back that way again. Now come on. We've got work to do."

"Now that we're in, what's the plan?"

I shrugged. "I don't know. I guess see if we can't find the room that Giselle told us about."

Al nodded. "You'd think a guy like this has an office somewhere. Maybe you drop me off there and then you can go explore the house."

"Good idea. Come on."

We started moving through the house, and I was instantly surprised at how nicely decorated Dalton's place was. For a bachelor, the guy had a lot of stuff. If I had a place like his, I'd be lucky to have a sofa set and a big-screen TV in the living room, let alone art on the walls and tchotchkes on unnecessary pieces of furniture. But Dalton had it all, right down to the oversized centerpiece on his dining room table. It made me wonder if maybe he *was* married after all, though if he was, I'd yet to see a single framed picture of him and a wife.

Al and I slid from room to room, keeping our eyes peeled

for any of the things Giselle had described. After a few minutes of searching, we finally discovered what had to be Dalton's office.

Inside, I pulled off my mask. "You gonna be alright alone?" I asked uneasily. Leaving Al behind wasn't exactly something I felt good about doing, but I also knew we didn't have a lot of time, and tromping Al through the house sounded painstakingly slow. In truth, his time was better spent in the office rather than touring the house with me.

Al nodded. "I'll call you if something happens," he said, holding up his little flip cell phone.

I would've liked to tell him to text me instead, but Al refused to learn how to text. "Okay. I'll go fast."

Slipping out the office door, I pulled my ski mask back on over my face. I wasn't one hundred percent sure that aside from Val and Kip, we were alone in the house, and I sure as hell didn't want to come face-to-face with anyone.

The house seemed to wrap around in a circle, with another row of rooms on the second floor and double-decker wings jutting off in different directions. The living and dining rooms were situated in the middle of the house with a vaulted ceiling. I poked my head into every room, walked down every hallway, until I ended back where I'd started. Though it sounded dangerous with Dalton's bedroom on the second floor, I went to the stairs anyway. Taking the first hallway to my right, I walked down the hallway, noting the empty hallway walls with the exception of the occasional piece of art. That was when I heard the moans and screams coming from one of the bedrooms.

"Yes! Yes! Yes!" I heard Valentina chanting.

I shook my head. Al was right. Hookers did work fast. Either she was faking or we needed to hurry up, because our distraction was almost over. I finished exploring the upstairs but was unable to find the hallway of pictures like Giselle had described. Nor could I find a massage room either.

As I rushed back down the stairs to reunite with Al, the thought occurred to me that there was also no attached garage as Giselle had described. I frowned. I was starting to feel confident that whatever Giselle and Jordan had been through hadn't occurred in this house.

Back to the drawing board.

Retracing my steps, I made my way back to Dalton's office and slipped inside. I found Al seated on a rolling chair in front of a filing cabinet rifling through a manila folder. "This isn't the place, Al. There's no way that this was where that limo brought those girls. I didn't find a hallway with pictures. I didn't find a massage room. And I didn't find an attached garage."

Al jerked his head to the side, beckoning me over. "Hey, kid. Come here. Check this out."

I rushed eagerly to his side. "Find something about the prostitution ring?"

"Nah, nothing about that. But I did find an interesting invoice on his desk. It's for that new car out in the driveway."

"Yeah?"

Al nodded. "He got it from the same place you bought yours."

"Jeez. Is that literally the only dealership on the island?"

"Seems like it's the most popular, that's for sure," said Al. "And I hate to break it to you, kid, but they cut Dalton one hell of a good deal."

I looked down at the papers he was flipping through. "Yeah? What kind of good deal?"

Al held up the first invoice for me to look at. "Look at that. Not only *didn't* he get charged the tariff, but it also looks like he's paying dealer cost."

"No fucking shit?"

"Read it for yourself."

I lifted the invoice up and stared at it. In one of the corners, it had typing across it that read *Business Owners' Special Pricing*.

My eyes widened. "Holy shit. I bet this was the deal they were trying to give Artie!" I breathed. "Why couldn't they give that to me?"

"Because you don't own a business?" said Al, looking up at me.

"I'm partial owner of a charter boat business."

Al shook his head. "A silent partner. And you weren't partial owner when you bought your vehicle."

"Technicalities! Maybe we'll have to go back to the dealership and see if we can't renegotiate now that I am."

"You're splitting hairs at this point, kid. I think it's too late for renegotiation."

I balked. "It's never too late to save me money."

"It is too late. Now listen. There's more. Seeing that invoice made me curious about what he paid for the rest of the cars out there, so I went through his file cabinet. I found this." Al shuffled all the papers he'd been looking at back into a manila folder and held it up.

I took it and flipped through each one of them to discover that they all had the same *Business Owners' Special Pricing* discount listed and that he'd paid way under book value for each and every vehicle he owned. My jaw dropped. "Get the fuck out of here. This is bullshit!"

"Hey, kid, relax. It ain't the end of the world."

I shook my head. "Al. We're talking *thousands* here. Not just loose change. I'm not as loaded as you are. I gotta make my dollars stretch. I've got half a mind to go down there tomorrow and see if I can't have something done about the price I paid."

Al sighed as he returned the file folder to the file cabinet and stood up. "Whatever. I just thought you might be interested to see that stuff. But unfortunately, I didn't find a single shred of evidence to tie Dalton to what's going on down at Club Cobalt."

I sighed. "I didn't either. Either he's having these girls

shipped somewhere else or he's not involved whatsoever. I don't even know where to look next."

Al patted me on the arm. "Don't worry, kid. We'll figure something out. We always do. Now come on. We need to get back out to the car and call Valentina before she does something she can't undo."

I quirked a smile. "Oh, I think it's a little too late for that."

"Oh, yeah?" asked Al, his shoulders slumping forward.

"Yeah. But don't worry. I can almost guarantee she doesn't mind taking one for the team."

23

"I CAN'T BELIEVE YOU'RE SERIOUSLY GOING OVER THERE. WE'RE IN the middle of a murder investigation."

Gripping the steering wheel tightly, I stared at the road in front of me. "I gotta get it off my chest so I can focus. Besides, I told you, Al. I don't play around when it comes to saving a few bucks. You should understand. You were around for the Great Depression."

Al frowned at me. "I was just a kid back then, thank you very much. And it's not that I don't understand wanting to save some money. I get that. I'm a businessman, after all. It's just kind of embarrassing going back *after* the fact. We already did our negotiating. If a farmer had come back to me after I'd already sold him a tractor and he'd said, 'You know what, Al? I got to thinking about it and I think I paid too much for this tractor. I'd like a discount,' I think I might've laughed him off my property."

I shrugged. "Well, look. If it's so embarrassing, then you can just sit out in the car and wait for me while I go inside."

Al sighed and then let his head drop into the palms of his hands.

I looked over at him. "Fuck, Al. Why you gotta be so

dramatic? It's not that big of a deal." I glanced back at the road again, but not fast enough to notice that I'd drifted off the road a little. My front tire hit a curb and made the vehicle bounce as I steered it back onto the road.

"Jeez, kid, watch where you're going!"

I chuckled. "Curb check. Just checking to see if you were awake."

Al shook his head. "You're gonna wind up wrecking this thing before you can even get back over there to ask for a discount! You put insurance on this thing, right?"

My hand shot out and smacked the top of the steering wheel. "Shit! I knew there was something I was forgetting to do. Remind me to do that later today."

"Come on, Drunk. You gotta be more responsible than that."

My mouth gaped. "In case you hadn't noticed, we've been in the middle of a missing girl investigation, and now it's quite possibly a homicide investigation. I've been a little busy. Cut me some slack, will ya?"

Al's head turned to look out the window. "Just get me there in one piece and then we'll talk slack."

"HEY, how you doing, Steve? Danny Drunk. This is my buddy, Al Becker."

"Mr. Drunk, Mr. Becker, it's a pleasure," said Steve Dillon, a barrel-chested man with narrow hips, smaller-than-average legs, and a bad toupee. His face was pale and shone beneath the fluorescent lighting, only his cheeks were bright pink, like he'd just undergone a chemical peel. "Please, have a seat. What can I help you gentlemen with today?"

"Well, here's the thing, Steve. Can I call you Steve?"

"Only if I can call you Danny." The man across the desk smiled jovially.

I smiled back. "People actually just call me Drunk, if you don't mind."

"That's sure an interesting name. Are you from the States, Drunk?"

I nodded. "I am. I've only been on the island a few months. Are you from the US?"

Steve nodded. "Sure am. Lived in Ohio for the last twenty or more years. I moved out here when the wife left me. Wanted to start all over, you know?"

I grinned. I knew a thing or two about starting over. "I sure do."

"So where in the States are you coming from?"

I pointed at myself. "Kansas City here."

"I'm from a small town north of Omaha," said Al.

"Oh, Nebraska," said Steve, his eyes widening. "I've got a brother in Omaha."

"Huh," said Al, shaking his head. "It's a small world, isn't it?"

"It sure is. Now why don't you fellas tell me what I can do for you? Are you in the market for a new vehicle? If so, you've come to the right place."

I leaned forward, so my elbow rested on Steve's desk. "Well, here's the thing Steve. I actually bought a vehicle from you about a week ago."

"Did you? Is it that Rubicon I noticed you driving in?" he asked.

"It is."

"Great choice. Really great choice. It'll be great on resale value, too. Any of those kinds of Jeeps do well on the island."

"Right," I said before flashing some teeth at him. "Here's the thing. When I bought it, to say that I was taken aback by the sticker price would be an understatement."

Steve sucked air between his gritted teeth and then sat back in his chair, eyebrows raised. "Oh, don't I know it. The prices here aren't what they are back home, now are they?"

"No. They really aren't. But I just realized that when I purchased the vehicle, I forgot to ask for the business owners' special pricing."

Steve's face froze. He cleared his throat, straightened his tie, and sat forward again in his seat. "You, uh—excuse me?"

I nodded and this time sent a wink in his direction. "You know. I'd like my business owner's *special discount*."

"I don't, uh—know what you're talking about," said Steve, lowering his brows and staring hard at me and then at Al.

"Oh, I think you do," I countered, sitting back in my seat and crossing one leg over my knee.

Steve's face was flushed now and the way he messed with his tie made me wonder if it wasn't cutting off circulation to his head. I felt like grabbing the scissors in the cupholder on his desk and reaching out and snipping it at the neckline to save the poor guy. Finally, he spoke. "You own a business?"

I nodded. "I do. I'm partial owner of a charter fishing company." I pulled the check that the Cruz brothers had given me out of my wallet and showed it to Steve. "I invested a tidy sum of money in the company when I got to the island. Granted, they are still slowly making progress towards growing the company, but this is the first return on my investment. I look forward to progressively larger checks, of course."

Steve swallowed hard. "Listen, uh—will you gentlemen excuse me for a moment?"

I glanced over at Al and then back at Steve. "Umm. Yeah, sure. Of course."

"I shouldn't be long." He pointed to a bowl of wrapped candy in a bowl on his desk. "Help yourself to a snack. There's coffee and bottled water out on the showroom floor if you'd like something to drink."

"Thanks, Steve."

He nodded curtly before disappearing out the door.

I clapped my hands together. "Well, what do you think of that, Al? He didn't laugh me out of the building, now did he?"

Al scowled at me. "Don't count him out just yet, kid. This ain't over."

I shrugged and sat back in my seat. At least I'd tried. If he said no, I could go about my business in peace, knowing that I'd done everything I could to save a few grand.

Al stood up and arched his back. He shook out his leg.

"What's the matter?"

"My sciatica is acting up."

"I got this under control if you wanna go take a walk around and loosen things up," I suggested.

Al did a few stretches in front of the door and then shook his head. "Nah. This won't take long. I predict he'll be back in here any second and tell you to take a hike."

I chuckled. "Whatever, Al."

With his hands on his back, Al shook out each leg in turn and then walked back behind Steve's desk to look out his window at the parking lot. When he came back, he paused to look at a bunch of framed pictures on Steve's bookshelf.

I was lost in thought as Al looked on quietly.

"Holy shit," said Al finally, his eyes wide.

"What?"

"You're not gonna believe this. Come here, take a look at this picture." He waved his hand in the air, beckoning me to hurry.

I got up and walked over to take a look at whatever had Al so excited. He pointed at one of the pictures. A silver picture frame held a photograph of a table full of men, all smiles. Between each of the men was a woman in a barely-there bunny costume. But the *really* interesting part was *who* was in the picture.

"That's Kip Dalton," I said, pointing at one of the men in the picture.

Al nodded. "Keep looking. Who else do you see?"

I squinted my eyes and stared harder. One of the men looked familiar but had shorter hair than he had now, but the same caterpillar-like unibrow. "Is that Joseph Ayala the photographer?"

Al's head bobbed. "It sure is. And isn't that the guy that just about smashed your face in the other day?"

Sure enough, there was Vito with his arm slung around one of the bunnies. "Wow. Is this just a coincidence that Dillon's friends with all the guys we've been investigating or is this some kind of cosmic clue?"

Al shrugged. "If you ask me, coincidences don't just happen. Ayala drove one of Steve's vehicles. Dalton drives a handful of them. If I had to guess, Vito drives one too. These guys are obviously connected. We know for sure three of them are connected to Club Cobalt."

I stared hard at the picture. There were two more men facing the camera that I didn't recognize and one with his back to the camera. "What if they're all involved in Jordan's death? If that's the case, we need to identify everyone in the picture. One of them may be the owner of the mansion we're looking for."

"I think we're onto something," said Al. He glanced over his shoulder and started stuffing the framed picture into the front of his cargo shorts.

"What the fuck, Al? You don't think Steve's gonna notice your square boner when we walk outta here?" I hissed, snatching the picture out of his hands and putting it back on the shelf. "This ain't the stone age, Mr. Flintstone." I pulled my phone out of my pocket and took a quick snapshot. No sooner had I slipped it back into my pocket than the door opened and Steve Dillon walked back into the room.

Trying to divert attention away from the fact that I had just been looking at his pictures, I smiled at him and took two steps towards him, my hand extended. "Steve. You're back. So, what do you say? Can we do some kind of retroactive deal on my Jeep?"

Steve frowned at me and kept his arms pinned behind his

back. "Mr. Becker, Mr. Drunk, unfortunately I'm not going to be able to help you."

"But I'm a business owner, I—"

He cut me off. "I don't know what you're talking about. I don't offer business owner specials. Now. I have a lot of work to do this morning. I'm going to have to ask you gentlemen to leave."

I glanced over at Al. The corners of his mouth had just begun to rise. I sensed a lot of *I told you so*s on the horizon. I looked back at Steve. "Oh, come on, Steve. Can't we work something out?"

Al stood up. "Come on, kid. You tried. Let's go."

"But—"

Standing in front of the open doorway, Al tugged on my arm. "Now, Drunk." He looked at Steve. "We appreciate your time, Mr. Dillon. Have a good day."

With nothing else to say, I let Al drag me outside. We both got in the vehicle. "Well. That was sure an interesting visit."

Al nodded. "That it was."

"I may not have gotten the deal I wanted, but we got something." I looked down at the snapshot I'd taken with my phone. "Now, I think we just need to figure out who the other men in this picture are." As I stared at it, my phone began to ring.

"Who is it?" asked Al.

I put the phone to my ear, both eager to hear her voice and dreading what she might share. "Francesca Cruz. Is this a business or pleasure call?"

"Unfortunately, it's business," she sighed.

"Can I at least say it's good to hear your voice?"

"It's good to hear yours too, Danny."

"So, what's going on? Do you have new information to share?"

"I don't know," she said slowly. "I've got something that could be a possible lead."

"Alright. As always, you've got my attention. Let's hear it."

"Well, I decided to do a little digging into some of the other missing girl files. I wanted to see if there was anything connecting them or maybe just a clue that might be able to help us. I found this one case. It was a young girl, she was fifteen. She disappeared under similar circumstances at the beginning of the year and just reappeared a few weeks before Jordan supposedly went missing. I don't know if her disappearance is connected to Jordan's or not, but I thought it might be worth speaking to her. You wouldn't have time to meet me over there later today, would you?"

"Are you kidding? Of course I would. What time are you meeting her?"

"Eleven. Over at her place."

"Yeah, text me the address and I'll be there."

24

"WHERE'S AL?" ASKED FRANKIE WHEN I STEPPED OUT OF MY vehicle at a small house in a run-down neighborhood.

"His sciatica is bothering him," I said. "He decided to stay home." I walked towards Frankie and wrapped my arms around her shoulders. "You're sure a sight for sore eyes."

She laughed and patted my back as I hugged her. "What's the matter, Danny? You sound tired."

I tipped my head backwards so I could feel the warmth of the sun on my face. "I am tired. I haven't been sleeping well. There's a lot I need to fill you in on, regarding Jordan Lambert's disappearance."

Frankie pulled away and looked up at me. "Danny! You were supposed to be keeping me in the loop."

"I just told you there's a lot I need to tell you! I'm going to keep you in the loop. I just haven't had time. Al and I have been following leads all over the island. Trust me, it's a full-time job."

"Plus you *have* a full-time job. How's Artie feel about you doing all this running around?"

I lifted a shoulder. "No worries. I have employees who can

handle the day-to-day stuff. And I check in all the time. I just came from my office, in fact. Senior citizens don't get into a whole lot of trouble over there. Except for the occasional spat over beach loungers, it's pretty slow."

Frankie shaded her eyes with her hand and looked up at me. "Okay, so should we discuss what you know about Jordan before we go interview this girl?"

"It's okay. I'll fill you in after. Are we ready?"

She nodded and began to walk up the front sidewalk. "Yeah. Her name is Heaven Abraham. She's fifteen. Her parents reported her missing in January. She came back about two weeks before Jordan went missing."

"Did she say where she was all that time?"

"Her file says she was with her boyfriend, but she wouldn't tell the cops his name or where they'd been. But that's all I know." She turned, put one hand on her uniformed hip, and knocked on the front door.

We could hear lots of noises inside the house. A baby crying. The TV blaring loudly. People shouting. It took a second series of knocks on the door before a haggard-looking grey-haired woman appeared. "Mrs. Abraham?"

"Yes?"

"I'm Officer Cruz. We spoke on the phone earlier? I'm here to speak with Heaven."

The woman nodded. "You can wait right here. I'll go get her."

"Thank you."

Frankie and I stared at the door. Thoughts about Jordan and the case jumbled through my head, and I suddenly wished that I'd taken the time to go over all of the details with Frankie ahead of time. Maybe then we could've worked through them together and she would've been able to help me ask all the right questions. Now, I kind of felt on my own.

The door opened and a young girl with long, straight black hair that went down to her stomach looked back at us. She was thin, almost to the point of being gaunt. Her eyes looked dark and haunted, and she stared ahead at us like she was afraid.

"Heaven?" Frankie asked kindly.

Heaven's head bobbed.

"Heaven, I'm Officer Cruz. This is my friend Danny. He's kind of like a detective." She looked over at me and gave me a wink.

"It's nice to meet you Heaven," I said, reaching out to shake her hand.

She looked at my hand but looked too afraid to take it.

Pulling my hand back, I smiled at her. "That's alright." I gestured towards a porch swing. "How about we sit?"

She nodded and walked over to the swing. I let Frankie take the seat next to her, and I sat across from them on the porch's short railing.

I glanced at the door. "Is your mom going to join us?"

Heaven's eyes widened, and her head shook rapidly. "No," she whispered. "I didn't want her to."

"That's okay," said Frankie, giving the girl a reassuring smile. "Heaven, the reason we are here today is actually because of another case that we're working on."

Heaven looked interested then and slightly less afraid, like she knew she wasn't in trouble.

Frankie nodded and continued. "There's this other girl that disappeared kind of like you did. No word to her family or friends for quite a while."

Heaven stared at Frankie, wide-eyed.

"You told the police when you came back home that you were with your boyfriend. Is that where you really were, Heaven?" asked Frankie.

Heaven's head kind of bobbed slowly, but it was obvious she wasn't fully committed to that answer.

"Where did you and your boyfriend hide for all that time?" asked Frankie.

Heaven shrugged.

"Was it on the island?"

The girl nodded.

"Was it at your boyfriend's house?"

Heaven shrugged again.

"You know, we're really worried that something bad is happening to this other girl," I said. "I bet your parents were really worried about you when you were gone."

She looked down at her hands.

"I promised this other girl's family that I would help find her and try and keep her safe."

Heaven looked up at me. For a brief moment, it almost looked like she wanted to talk, but then she pressed her lips together between her teeth.

So I decided to continue. "This other girl. She got involved in something she might've regretted. Do you ever regret leaving your family?"

Heaven nodded.

"Yeah. Sometimes things don't work out the way you wanted them to. This girl that we're looking for, things didn't work out the way she thought they were going to either. She met some people that didn't exactly do what they'd promised her."

I heard Heaven's breath catch in the back of her throat.

"You know, anything you tell us, we'll keep to ourselves," I said. "We'll only use it to help find this other girl."

"He's right," added Frankie, holding up her hands. "I'm not here trying to get you in trouble or anything. I'm just here to figure out if maybe you and this other girl were involved in some of the same things. So we can bring her home."

Frankie and I were both quiet then. We wanted to give Heaven a turn to speak. The girl swallowed hard. "He wasn't actually my boyfriend," she whispered.

Frankie's eyes darted up to look at me for just a split second. Then she looked at Heaven again. "Oh, who was he?"

"He was kind of my boss," she whispered.

"Were you being paid while you were gone?" I asked her.

She looked up at me, a little surprised, and nodded.

"This other girl that disappeared, she was being paid too," I divulged.

Frankie glanced over at me but kept her cool.

"They told her she could be a model," I added.

The girl's eyes grew really large then. "M-me too."

"Did you get to do any modeling while you were away from your family?"

Her eyes swung down to the porch and her head shook. "Huh-uh."

"Is that why you came home?" asked Frankie.

She lifted a shoulder. "Sorta."

"You didn't like what they were paying you to do?" I asked calmly.

Her head bobbed and tears began to roll down her cheeks. She bit her bottom lip.

Frankie put her arm over the girl's shoulder. "It's okay. We just want to help this other girl, but we don't know where she is."

"I don't know where it is either," she whispered.

"Well, how did you get there?" asked Frankie, lowering her brows in confusion.

"In a limo?" I asked knowingly.

Heaven nodded. "And the windows were blacked out."

"Were you at the same place the whole time you were gone?" I asked.

She nodded.

"Then you probably know a lot about the house. About the people you met. Maybe even some of their names?" I asked.

Heaven sucked in her breath and clamped her mouth shut tightly. Her head shook as if she was suddenly scared again.

I held a hand out calmly. "It's okay, I already know some of the stuff. I know they told you they'd hurt you if you ever told anyone about where you'd been or went to the cops."

"Yeah," she whispered. "They really wanted me to stay. They threatened me."

I lowered my brows. "Then how were you able to get home?"

"The butler," she said quietly. "He liked me. We were kind of friends, and he knew I wanted to go home to my family. And one day when the boss was gone, he put me in the limo and dropped me off downtown. I took a bus home with some of the money I'd earned."

"You've been home all this time and they haven't come after you," I said quietly.

Tears fell down her cheeks again. "I don't sleep very well anymore."

"You're scared they'll come and get you?"

She nodded.

"Then help us, Heaven. Other girls shouldn't have to go through what you went through," said Frankie.

"I can't. They said they'd find me if I talked to the cops."

"They're never going to know we were here," said Frankie. "I swear to you."

"Please, Heaven. Just tell us about this house they took you to."

She was quiet for several long moments, no doubt contemplating what she felt comfortable sharing. "It was on the beach," she whispered.

"Was it a big house?"

Her head went up and down, her eyes wide.

"A really big house, huh?"

"Yeah. He had a butler and a limo. It was big."

"Were there more girls there than just you?"

"Yes. Some girls stayed there. But some of the older girls came and went. They had their own cars and their own bedrooms," she said. "They got the cars from the boss for doing a good job and being trustworthy. That's what he said. He said if I stayed long enough and became trustworthy enough, I'd get my own car too someday. And he said he'd help me go to college when I graduated from high school."

"Wow. That all sounds nice."

She shrugged as her eyes welled up again. "I just couldn't keep doing what I was doing," she whispered. "It all felt so wrong. I wasn't raised like that. I just got started because I thought I could earn money doing modeling. I thought the other stuff wouldn't be as bad as it was. But eventually I realized that it would take years to be a model. If I could ever be one at all."

"Smart girl," said Frankie, patting the girl's hair gently.

Heaven looked up at her then. A police officer had just called her a smart girl. I could tell that it made her feel good.

"If you could only tell us anything about the people that kept you—"

"The butler's name was Fernando. He was really nice to me."

"Did he ever—participate in—"

Heaven was quick to shut that notion down. "No. Never. He was nice to all of us."

"Do you know his last name?"

"No," she whispered.

"How about his boss's name?"

She swallowed hard. I could tell she knew it. Whether or not she wanted to tell was a different story.

"Please, Heaven," said Frankie. "You might be saving other girls from what you went through."

"It wasn't all bad," she said quietly with a little shrug. "They fed us well, and we got to swim in his pool and go to the beach when he wasn't having parties."

"What happened when he was having parties?"

"Then we had to work," she said. "We each had our own room. And they'd bring in different guys, for—uh, massages. At least, that was always how it started."

"But they wanted you to do more?" asked Frankie.

She bit her lip and nodded. She couldn't look either of us in the eyes.

"Did you know or recognize any of the men they brought in?"

"No," she whispered.

"Were they always different?"

She shrugged. "Sometimes they were different. Sometimes it was someone I remembered."

As we talked, a little girl of about five stuck her pigtailed head out the door.

"Go inside, Josie," snapped Heaven.

"Whatcha doing?" asked the little girl.

"None of your business. Go inside." When the little girl didn't budge from her place, Heaven lifted her brows. "I'll call Mom out here."

Josie sighed. "Oh, fine." She wiggled her fingers at Frankie and me, giggled and ran back inside, slamming the door behind her.

"Your little sister?" asked Frankie.

Heaven nodded.

"Look, Heaven. Guys like the man you dealt with need to get taken off of this island. Think about it. Whoever he is, if he's still doing business in a couple of years when Josie's your age and he gets his claws into her, how would you feel about her doing what you did?" I asked.

Her eyes filled with tears again.

"Do you want that to happen?"

She shook her head and tears rolled down her cheeks. "No."

"Then you have to help us take this guy off the streets."

She was quiet.

"What's his name, Heaven?" asked Frankie. "All we want is a name."

Another few seconds passed. Finally, Heaven closed her eyes and sighed. Then she opened them and looked at me. "Harvey. His name was Harvey."

25

"Miss me already, Danny?"

I chuckled into the phone and put on my turn signal. "All the time, Frankie."

She laughed too. "So what's up? Think of some *other* important detail you forgot to share with me?"

I was driving away from the park where Frankie and I had gone after interviewing Heaven. I'd shared as much of the pertinent details of the case as I felt comfortable sharing. Of course, I'd left out the parts about sneaking into Kip Dalton's house and embarrassing myself at Steve Dillon's Automart. Some things were better left on closed lips, even if it meant not being able to show her the picture I'd taken.

"No, nothing else to share. I'm just jazzed about the fact that we have a name now. I wish we had a last name to go with it."

"Well, you're gonna have to be patient. I told you. As soon as I get back to the station, I'll work on it."

"I know. I just wanted to thank you for continuing to dig on Jordan's case. And I really appreciate you letting me in on that interview with Heaven. She really blew this whole case wide open."

"Yeah, well," she said with a sigh, "I had no idea about the underage prostitution ring going on on the island. So you blew that wide open for me, too."

I smiled. It felt good being able to share some information with Frankie, instead of it only being the other way around. "Good. How's the saying go? I rub your back, you rub mine?"

Her hearty laugh warmed my heart. "It's I scratch your back, you scratch mine, Danny."

"Meh. I'd prefer to rub yours. Maybe we could throw in some massage oil and a few drinks." The thought of a topless Francesca Cruz lying on my bed awaiting a body rub-down made my pulse accelerate.

"Umm, how exactly did we veer this far off topic?" I could hear the smile in her voice.

"Are we off topic?"

"We are."

"What was the topic again?"

"The case we're working on? Jordan Lambert ring a bell?"

I chuckled. "Right. Anyway, I just wanted to call and thank you for everything."

"Oh. That's sweet of you. Well, you're welcome. We work well together."

"I completely agree. And I'll call you if I get any new information. You'll do the same?"

"I will."

"Great. Hopefully we'll talk soon, then."

"Sounds good. Bye, Danny."

She hung up before I could even tell her goodbye, but I didn't care. Something about spending the afternoon with Frankie Cruz had buoyed my spirits. It was exactly what I'd needed. I didn't know if it was the new information we'd gotten, including the name Heaven had given us, or if it was simply getting to sit across a picnic table from the woman at the park for an hour. Regardless, I was flying high when I happened to glance in my rearview mirror and saw flashing lights behind me.

I glanced down at my speedometer. I was under the speed limit, an odd habit of mine—when I was tired or lost in thought, my feet seemed to have helium balloons tied to it. I pulled to the side of the road, thinking the lights must have been for someone else. But when the squad car pulled over to the shoulder with me, I groaned.

Shit.

I wondered if I had a light out or something. Though that seemed unlikely, considering I was driving a new vehicle. Maybe it was because I only had dealer plates or something. As I pulled my wallet out of my back pocket to retrieve my license, I shot a glance in my rearview mirror. My eyes nearly popped out of my head when I saw none other than Sergeant Gibson.

My head fell back against the headrest. "Ugh," I groaned. "Fuck." Maybe it was my imagination, but it seemed as if the man had had it in for me since I came to the island.

I rolled down my window. "Sergeant Gibson."

"Officer Drunk."

I hated it when he called me that. It was almost as if he was rubbing it in my face that I'd been a cop in the States but that amounted to nothing on his island. "Really, Sarge, just Drunk is fine. So, to what do I owe this fine pleasure?"

Standing with his feet spread shoulder-width apart, he had his hands propped up on his hip—one hand dangerously close to his piece. Even though I maintained eye contact with him, I kept a close watch on that hand. "Is this your vehicle?"

"It is. I just got it. What do you think? Do you approve?"

He looked it over and then turned his coal eyes back on me. "Does this mean that you are staying on my island?"

I lifted my brows. "Well. I have a job here. My own place. I've made some friends. And now I have a car. So, yeah. I think

I'll stay. I kinda like island living." I smiled at him. "You wanna hang out sometime? I just got Bloodborne on the PS4. You're welcome to come over and check it out if you haven't already. I'm personally kinda digging it."

"If you are planning to stay on my island, then I think we need to get a few things straightened out now, before you create too much of a problem."

I frowned. "Problem? What kind of problem?"

"I have had some complaints about you recently."

My head jerked back. "About me? From who?"

"On several different occasions, I have had business owners in the community call me to tell me that you have been harassing them in their places of business."

"Is that right? Like who?"

"Steve Dillon was the most recent call. He said he almost had to get security to toss you out."

My eyes bulged. "He said that?"

Sergeant Gibson's head moved up and down slowly. "He did."

I couldn't believe he'd tattled on me. *What an asshole.* "Look, Sarge, I just went over there to speak to him because I felt like I got overcharged for my new vehicle. I didn't cause any trouble, and he certainly didn't have to get security."

"I am just telling you what he said. This would not have been an issue, but I also got a call the other day from a well-regarded photographer on the island. He said that you showed up to a wedding he was shooting and harassed him as well. I told him I had not had any other reports of you causing problems, so there was little that I could do. But now, hearing similar complaints from Mr. Dillon, I felt I should say something."

I shook my head. Fucking pussies. Couldn't handle me getting too close to the fire, so they had to tell on me? "Look, Gibson. I had legitimate reasons for speaking with both of them. I certainly didn't harass either one of them, and I left when the conversation was over. They're obviously exaggerating."

"I am not here to debate that fact with you, Officer Drunk. I am merely here to tell you that you are starting off residency on this island on a bad foot."

"Bad foot?! I've nabbed several criminals while I've been on the island. That's hardly starting off on a bad foot, if you ask me."

"Exactly. Criminals seem to follow you wherever you go. Why is that, Officer Drunk?"

My face burned. I was getting heated. "I don't know, Sergeant Gibson. As a member of law enforcement, the same could be said about you. Now couldn't it?"

Sergeant Gibson's eyes narrowed. He leaned forward. "I am warning you. Stay away from island business owners. It is in everyone's best interest. Otherwise, you shall get yourself in over your head."

"I appreciate your concern, Sergeant Gibson. I do. But I haven't done anything wrong, and I certainly am not afraid of your island business owners."

"Officer Drunk, have you heard the saying 'A wise man follows the customs of the land in which his feet reside'?"

I quirked a brow. "Hmm. Is that Tolstoy?"

He frowned at me. "Suit yourself. But do not say that you had not been warned."

I threw my hands up, palms flat. "Hey. You did your job. No shame there. Thanks for the chat, SG."

He pivoted on his heel.

I stuck my head out the window and watched as he walked back to his car. "Don't forget we're gonna hang out sometime. Have a few brewskis. Play some cards or something. I'll put it on my calendar."

His door slammed shut.

I pulled my head back in and sighed as he drove away. I grinned to myself. Somebody out there was shaking in his boots. We were getting closer to the big boss, and he didn't like it one little bit.

26

After my impromptu meeting on the side of the road with Sergeant Gibson, I returned to the Seacoast Majestic surer than ever that we were on the right path to bringing down the head of the underage prostitution ring. All we had to do was figure out who this Harvey character was, find his lair, and then turn in the evidence and show Gibson just what kind of a bad foot I'd really gotten off on.

I'd no sooner returned my Jeep to my cottage, gone inside and cracked open a refreshing bottle of Dr Pepper than my phone rang. "Drunk here."

"Drunk, it's Al. I'm down at the clubhouse playing cards with the fellas. What time are you headed back to the resort?"

"I just got back. I was just gonna make myself a sandwich. Why?"

"I was just talking to the guys, and Big Eddie and Ralph thought they could help us out with identifying the people in that picture you took. Why don't you come on down? You can grab something to eat at the snack bar."

"Yeah, alright. I gotta stop in my office and see if I have any messages, and then I'll be down in a few."

THE LINE to the snack bar was about eight guests and a dozen or so seagulls long, so instead of waiting it out there, I swung by the swim-up bar to say hey to Manny the bartender, a good friend of mine.

"'Sup, Manny? What's shakin'?"

"Your choice, Drunk. I got a mai tai, a martini, and a beachcomber."

I smiled at him. Though I hadn't really been in the market for a drink while I waited, I'd been offered. And what had Sergeant Gibson said to me just a short hour ago? Something similar to "when in Rome"? "You don't put coconut in a beach-comber, do you?"

Manny chuckled. "I forgot about your irrational disdain for our national fruit. No, man, you're safe. No coconut in those."

I pounded my fist on his bar top agreeably. "Sold!"

"One beachcomber coming up."

As Manny set about making my drink, I slid my butt onto a barstool. "Busy today?"

"Surprisingly, yes."

I nodded. The line to the snack bar had been a dead give-away. "Occupancy is up right now."

"Yeah. That's what one of the cleaning girls said this morning. That's gotta put a smile on Artie's face."

"Oh, for sure."

Done pouring the rum, triple sec and fruit juices into the shaker, Manny put the lid on and began to shake. "I haven't seen much of you the last few days. What's going on with you?"

"Oh. Kind of a long story."

Manny leaned forward kind of conspiratorially then. "Hey, man, you got something going on with Giselle?"

My eyes widened. "You mean Mari's daughter?"

Manny had a wide smile on his face. "Yeah."

"Dude. She's seventeen years old!"

Manny shrugged. "One of the girls said they saw her sneaking over to your place the other day. And I was sure I saw you down here talking to her all secret like not that long ago."

My shoulders crumpled inward and I let my head fall to the bar. The *last* thing I needed was this horrific rumor making its way back to Mariposa's overly judgmental ears. She'd have my nuts in a sling. I lifted my head. "No, man. I'm just helping her out with something."

Manny nodded his head like he knew what I was helping her out with.

"Ugh. Not like that, Manny. I swear. It's just something she can't go to her mom about. I told her I'd help her out. Like an uncle or something." I held up two flattened palms. "Completely innocent, I swear." I nodded towards the clubhouse. "Al's in on it too. He's helping me out."

"Yeah?"

I nodded. "I'm on my way over there now. Big Eddie and the Weaz are gonna help us with our project."

"Anything you can share?"

I took the drink he slid me. "Nah. Not yet. Gotta keep things on the DL until we know a little more. I promised Giselle." I took a big swig of the mildly fruity concoction. It hit the spot on the beautifully warm day, with the sound of the surf breaking at my back, the palm trees swaying overhead, and the dry, gritty feel of sand gathered between my toes. With the exception of the case I was working on, living in Paradise was—well, for lack of a better word, paradise.

"Yeah, yeah. No problem."

"But hey, do me a favor, Manny?"

"Anything for you, Drunk."

"Shut down any more rumors you hear about me and Giselle. Alright? That shit is so far from the truth it's almost laughable."

"Oh yeah. No problemo."

"Thanks, Manny." I stood up then. The line to the snack bar had gone down. "I'm gonna go get some lunch. I'll talk to ya later, man."

"*Hasta luego*, Drunk."

As usual, Al's posse was seated out back of the clubhouse, playing cards. A warm ocean breeze blew through the back porch, bringing enough air movement to keep the shaded area from being stiflingly hot but not enough to disrupt the cards on the table.

"Hey, guys," I said, coming through the main dining room carrying a cheeseburger and fries basket.

Big Eddie was seated to Al's right, Gary the Gunslinger to his left, and the rest of the guys rounded out the table. Everyone turned to look at me when I came in.

"Drunk!" cheered Tony, a big guy wearing a blue bucket hat. He was seated in a motorized scooter driven all the way up to the table.

"Hey, Tone-Lōc, what's happening?"

"We were just talking about you," said Gary.

"Yeah?" I quirked a brow at Al. I hoped he hadn't been shooting his mouth off about this case. I really wanted to keep it under wraps as long as possible.

Gary nodded. "Yeah. Al said you guys got yourself another doozy of a case."

"Did he?" I sent a scathing look in Al's direction.

He waved his hand in the air and scooted his chair back. "Oh, don't go getting your knickers in a knot, kid. I didn't tell them anything good."

"That's because we don't know anything good."

"Yeah, yeah," he said. "Whatever." He had to rock back and forth in his chair to give himself enough momentum to get out of it. When he was on his feet, he looked down at Eddie. "You and Ralph wanna follow me and the kid?"

The Weaz stood up and motioned for me to follow him. "Let's go to the computer room, Drunk. I think Eddie and I can help you out with your picture problem."

Word around the resort was that in a former life, Ralph the Weasel had been a coconspirator of a mob hit on a couple jewelry stores on the East Coast. In some kind of plea deal, he'd become an FBI informant and had ratted out his bosses for a string of murders. Some breach in the government's computer system had resulted in the inadvertent release of Ralph's personal records, leading to a not-so-subtle attempt on his and his wife's lives. Because of that breach, he'd sued the government and walked away with a hefty twenty-six-million-dollar settlement. Once he'd pocketed the funds, he and his wife had changed their names, left the US, and gone to hide out on Paradise Isle, where they planned to spend the rest of their days safe from the fear of having their throats slit in their sleep.

Apparently, he'd shared the story with one of the guys when he'd first gotten to the island, and they'd jokingly given him the nickname of Ralph the Weasel as a result. Considering he didn't look much like any Ralphs I'd ever known, I preferred referring to him as simply the Weaz. I found it more fitting.

"So Al didn't tell you any of the good stuff, but he told you about the picture?"

Ralph looked back at me as he walked into the clubhouse. "He didn't say what the picture was about. I work on a need-to-know basis. I've learned it's better that way. He just said you had a photograph and you needed the guys in the photo ID'd."

I sighed. "Okay, fine. So you think you can help us with that?"

"We can sure try."

Al and Big Eddie followed Ralph and me back to the resort's public computer room. Big Eddie pointed at a scanner in the corner of the room. "You can just put the picture on there."

I pulled my phone out of my pocket. "It's on here." I scrolled until I found the picture I'd taken. I showed it to Eddie. "It's actually a photo of a photo."

Eddie frowned. "Ohhh."

"Is that bad?" I looked over at Ralph.

"It's not good. That's for sure. You couldn't get your hands on the original?"

Al crossed his arms and looked up at me.

"Not without getting caught," I said, locking eyes with him.

Ralph nodded and held up his palms. "Say no more. We'll make this work. You got your charging cable so we can hook it up to the computer?"

"I don't."

Al pointed at Ralph. "Tony might have one. He always carries that stuff in his bag."

Ralph nodded. "I'll be right back."

He disappeared.

Big Eddie looked down at my phone. "You need to know who all these guys are?"

I pointed at the faces of the guys I didn't know. One was a forty-something white guy with a receding hairline and perfect teeth, and the other was a young, good-looking olive-skinned fellow with long dreadlocks and aviator glasses. The third guy was seated at the table with his back to the camera, the only thing I could tell about him was that his arm was black. "Just those two." I pointed at the third guy. "And it would be nice to know who that is, but you can't see his face. I doubt there's anything you can do about that."

Eddie smiled at me. "I certainly can't make him stand up and turn around, if that's what you're getting at."

I chuckled. "You've been hanging around Al too long."

Ralph reappeared with a phone charger in hand. "Will this one fit your phone?"

I looked down at the end of it. "Yup. Same as mine."

"Good deal," said Al.

Ralph and Eddie took the phone and the charger over to a computer and sat down. They set to work, hooking my phone up to it with the USB cord and downloading the photo to the computer's hard drive. Then they set about trying to use Google's facial recognition software on the picture first.

While they worked, Al and I pulled up chairs. "Is it gonna work?" I finally asked after they were quiet for a while.

"It's too early to tell," said Ralph.

Eddie nodded. "And if this doesn't work, I have a friend in the States that I can send it to. He's got some better software available to him."

I nodded and sat back to eat my burger. With a mouthful of food, I looked over at Al. "You're never gonna guess what happened to me on the way back here."

"You got pulled over?"

I nearly choked on my bite of burger as I sat up, coughing. When I could breathe again normally, I looked over at Al, my eyes watering. "How'd you know?"

"What else is gonna happen to you while you're driving, kid? It's called logic."

"I could've had an accident."

Al shook his head. "If you'd had an accident on the way home with no insurance on your vehicle, I'm pretty sure I would've heard about it already."

I shoved a couple fries in my mouth. He had a point. "Okay, fine. So you're a good guesser. You know, I think my vehicle might be a little too flashy, Al. Maybe next time I buy a new car, I'll go for something a little more subtle."

"Subtle, huh? Wow. I'm proud of you, kid."

I frowned at him. "You ever gonna stop calling me kid, Al?"

Al tapped a crooked finger on his chin. "I tell you what. I'll stop calling you kid when the difference in our ages changes. How's that?"

I rolled my eyes and stuck another fry in my mouth. "Care to guess *who* pulled me over?"

Al sat quietly for a moment, his face expressionless. Finally he shrugged. "Gibson?"

"Shit, Al. What the fuck? Are you a mind reader or something?" I narrowed my eyes at him. "Or do you have an in at the police department?"

"You know exactly *two* of the people at the station. Officer Cruz and Sergeant Gibson. You just left your meeting with Cruz, so process of elimination tells me it was Gibson."

"Well, shit. You just blew my mind."

"And let me tell you, fellas, it was the easiest thing I've ever done, too," said Al, patting Eddie on the shoulder. He looked over at me. "So. What did he want?"

"How'd you know he wanted something?"

"I have a feeling Sergeant Gibson isn't exactly pulling people over for speeding these days. That's a little below his pay grade."

"No," I sighed. "You're right. He wanted to have a talk with me."

"About what?"

"You mean you don't have a guess?"

"I'm not in the mood for twenty questions, kid, just tell me what he wanted."

I glanced over at Eddie and the Weaz.

Al swiped his hand across the air. "Oh, don't worry about these two. They aren't gonna say anything to anybody."

I stared at Ralph the Weasel. I wasn't particularly worried about Eddie; he was scared of his own shadow. But Ralph, he had a reputation for snitching.

Ralph looked over at me. "What? Who am I gonna tell?"

"I don't know. The guys. The bartenders. The snack bar girl. Your wife? Take your pick."

"Look, I don't have a dog in this fight. I got no reason to open my mouth, Drunk."

I pursed my lips. "I find out you shared any of this information and..."

Ralph narrowed his eyes and leaned closer to me. "And what?"

I lifted a brow. Did I really wanna threaten a former mobster? "And... well... let's just say Al won't let you win at miniature golf anymore."

Ralph sat back in his chair and laughed, letting his arms fall down by his sides. "Oh, please. Al doesn't have to *let me win*. I win all on my own merit."

"You just keep telling yourself that, Ralph," said Al.

"I do!"

"Anyway, you swear you won't tell, Weaz?"

"Yeah, yeah, kid. Your secret is my secret."

"Fine. Gibson pulled me over because Steve Dillon and Joseph Ayala told him I was harassing them in their places of business."

Al frowned. "Get outta here?"

"I'm serious. Dillon told Gibson he practically had to have security toss me out."

"Well, that's a downright lie."

"That's what I told Gibson."

"He believe you?"

"He didn't seem to. I don't think he cared, actually. Anything to get me off his island."

Al shook his head. "Where's he get off thinking it's his island anyway?"

"Fuck if I know." I sighed. "How's it coming on that picture, Eddie?"

He shook his head. "Google's software didn't pull anything up. I'm gonna send it to my contact in the States."

"Ugh," I groaned, letting my head fall backwards. "How long is that gonna take?"

Eddie shrugged his skinny shoulders. "Depends on how busy he is. I couldn't tell you. Could be a couple hours. Could be a couple days."

"How about you convince him to make it the former rather than the later?"

"I'll do my best, Drunk."

"Thanks, Eddie. Thanks, Weaz."

"No problem, kid. You always bring the excitement."

27

WITH LITTLE ELSE TO DO UNTIL BIG EDDIE'S CONTACT IN THE US got back to us, I decided to go back to my office and catch up on some resort work. I spent a couple hours buried in purchase orders and safety inspections before Al shuffled into my office looking rather salty.

"Make any money down there?" I asked, looking up from my work.

He frowned and swatted the air with one gnarled hand. "Nah. Today wasn't my day."

"They can't all be."

"Yeah, I know."

"Eddie hear anything back from his friend?"

"Not yet." He lowered himself slowly into one of the chairs in front of my desk. "So, you gonna fill me in on what you learned from that interview, or do I gotta buy you dinner and drinks first?"

"Dinner and drinks? What, no flowers?" I asked, dropping my pen to my desk.

"Come on, kid. What's the story?"

I sighed. Al was never in a very good mood after losing money at cards. I leaned back in my seat and steepled my fingers over my chest. "Well, the short version is the girl that we interviewed went through the same thing that Jordan did. She took the same blacked-out limo from Club Cobalt. Was taken to the same house and asked to do the same things. Except she decided to stay for a few months. And when she decided she'd had enough and wanted to go home, they threatened her so she'd stay."

"How'd she get away, then?"

"The butler. A guy she called Fernando."

"So did she know where the house was?"

"No. He dropped her off downtown and she took a bus home."

Al swatted the chair's armrest with the palm of his hand. "Dang it. So is that all the info you got out of her?"

"No, that's not everything." I ran a hand against the back of my neck. "She was scared to talk, especially at first. They told her if she went to the cops or told anyone else where she'd been, they'd find her. But she's got a little sister she didn't want to see get involved in this eventually. So in the end, she gave us the boss's name."

Al's eyes lit up. "Did she? What's the name?"

I smiled. "Harvey."

"No last name?"

I shook my head.

"A first name's better than nothing."

"Oh, absolutely. You know, I came straight back here to get some work done. I haven't even taken any time to do a search on Harveys on the island." I sat up straighter and rolled my chair up closer to my computer. Giving my mouse a wiggle, I woke it up and opened my internet browser.

"Has Francesca ever heard of this Harvey fellow?"

"Nope," I said while hunt-and-pecking the letters into my computer. When I'd run the search, I scrolled down the list of options, clicking on a white pages list. "There are at least a dozen Harveys on the island—and another dozen or so with the last name Harvey. Who woulda thunk it?"

"Anyone look promising?"

I stared at the screen, randomly clicking links. "I mean—where do I start?"

"We could get a list of all the Harveys on the island and all their addresses and drive around trying to figure out which one has a limo and a big house?" suggested Al.

I curled my lip. "Once again, Fred Flintstone, it's called technology. Ever heard of Google Maps?"

Al's arms bounced up off of his lap in an exaggerated shrug. "Technology's not my go-to, kid. Back in my day, if you wanted to spy on someone, you drove over to their house and peeked through the window like a normal person."

I looked at him. "Like a normal person? Fuck, Al."

"It was just an idea." He scooted his chair forward. "Hey, how about you gimme another look at that photo? Maybe we'll be able to see where it was taken or something."

I pulled out my phone, found the picture, and handed it to him while I kept searching on the computer. "There are like three Harvey Smiths alone," I said in a sigh.

Al handed me the phone back. "Can you print it and make the picture any bigger or something?"

I showed him how to use his fingers to blow it up on the touchscreen. He frowned and nodded. "Nice."

"Yeah. Maybe if you feel like joining the modern world, you'll upgrade that flip phone to a smartphone."

Patting the phone case attached to his belt, Al shook his head. "Oh no. I'm perfectly satisfied with my flip phone, thank you very much. I'll just leave that new technology to you youngsters."

"Suit yourself."

We were both quiet for a few minutes, each lost in thought. Finally, Al leaned forward. "Look at this." He held the phone across the desk and pointed at one of the men's zoomed-in hands. "See this?"

"What? His wrist?"

"His cufflink."

"Oh. Yeah?"

Al nodded. Then he slid and readjusted the picture to show me another guy's wrist. "Look. Same cufflinks. As far as I can tell, they all have the exact same cufflinks. But I can't make out what's on them."

I took the phone from him and held it up closer to my face. And that was when I noticed it. "PGC," I said, handing the phone back to Al. "I found those same exact cufflinks in Vito's desk drawer when we were at Club Cobalt fixing their plumbing."

Al frowned. "I wonder what it stands for."

"I don't—"

The phone on Al's hip rang. Al glanced down at his waist-line. "Evie must be ready to go to supper."

I looked at the time on my Fitbit. It was only four o'clock.

Al looked at his phone in surprise. "Oh. It's not Evie. It's Eddie. Hey, Eddie. What's the word?"

I scooted my chair closer to the desk and stared at Al.

There was a really long pause and then finally Al nodded. "Oh.... Is that right?... No, no. Thank you.... Yeah, tell him thanks too. Alright then. Hey what time are you and the fellas going to supper?... Yeah, okay. Evie and I will see you then." He hung up the phone.

"Well? Did he hear back from his contact?"

"He did. He said the guy could only get one facial recognition match. A guy by the name of Ziggy Thomas."

"Ziggy Thomas? Now there's a name." I turned to look at the computer. "I bet there aren't a hundred Ziggy Thomases on the island."

Al pushed himself up into a standing position and came around my desk to watch my search. "I'd suppose not."

"You know, Ziggy sounds like a nickname. Maybe he's actually this Harvey character. I guess we'll find out." I googled the name and got a ton of hits, all for the same guy. Ziggy Thomas, we discovered, was the owner of a helicopter tour company on the island. In picture after picture, we saw a younger guy with dreadlocks and a soul patch, and he wore aviator glasses in most of the pictures. "That's him alright."

"He looks like a hippie."

"Kinda." I scanned the headlines on each of the articles, many of them from the *Paradise Isle News*. From what I gathered, not only was he rather well known among islanders, but he was also well liked by the female population. Picture after picture featured Ziggy with a different woman on his arm. "He's a ladies' man, that's for sure."

"I'd say." Al tapped his chest. "Kinda like me back in the day."

I stifled a laugh and looked over my shoulder at him. "I'm sorry. Was that before or after Geico stopped selling horse and buggy insurance?"

"Funny, kid. One of these days you're gonna be old too. Then the jokes won't be so funny."

I smiled and went back to the computer. "Yeah. But then I'll be old, and I won't care." I chuckled as I scrolled through all the websites that mentioned Ziggy Thomas's name. Pretty soon, a trend kind of emerged. His name appeared in numerous results from what appeared to be a celebrity blogger's website. I clicked on one of the links and was sent promptly to a picture of Ziggy on the arm of a stunning brunette. I read the caption beneath the picture aloud. "*Ziggy Thomas spotted out and about with model Harlow Anderson for the third weekend in a row. Ladies, has Paradise Isle's most eligible bachelor finally been taken off the market?*"

I clicked the blog's homepage button. Splashed across the top of the screen, a sparkling GIF read *Paradise Eyes* above a pair of heavily glittered, eye-shadowed eyes. Just beneath the eyes in slightly smaller print, it read *Paradise Isle's most up-to-date celebrity sighting news blog*. I scrolled through the most recent month of entries and found Ziggy Thomas's name mentioned in at least four different articles.

"I wonder why that guy's so famous," said Al.

I quirked a smile and looked up at Al. "Well, for starters, he owns a helicopter company. So he's gotta be loaded. And I'm secure enough in my manhood to say that not only is he rich, but he looks like that. I mean, look at the guy. He looks like a freaking Calvin Klein model." I rubbed the scruff on my chin. "I mean hell, he's *almost* as good looking as me."

Al put a hand on my shoulder. "Hey, kid. All that stuff about us getting married earlier—that was all just for show, right? You're not really... you know, sweet on me, are ya?" He chuckled.

I rolled my eyes and turned back towards my computer. "Well, shit, now I'm curious to find out exactly how Ziggy got his start in the first place. He seems pretty young to own his own helicopter company."

I ran a search from within the blog and clicked on the oldest blog entry about Ziggy Thomas that I could find. The article was just over five years old. *"A relative newcomer to the island, twenty-four-year-old Ziggy Thomas has purchased the Hidden Beaches Aerial Tours company from previous owner Arlan Jamison. His financial backing to make such a large purchase comes from an unnamed silent partner. Thomas, an Australian native, says he's always had an affinity for helicopters and looks forward to providing not only tours to those visiting the island but also charter services, aerial photography, and utility and jungle inspections. Ladies, prepare yourself—this sexy Aussie hunk is not only single and ready to mingle, but my prediction is he will quickly become Paradise Isle's biggest attraction. Where do we sign up?"*

"Why didn't I get a write-up when I moved to the island?" I grunted, clicking back to the homepage.

"Maybe because you don't own a helicopter charter company."

"No, but I'm partial owner of a fishing charter company."

"You're gonna milk that for all it's worth, aren't you, kid?"

My head bobbed. "Damn straight. There's gotta be *some* perks." I clicked on one of the blogs from almost a month prior and scrolled down. My jaw dropped. I almost couldn't believe what I saw. "Al. Get a load of this."

Al stood up again and stooped over my shoulder, peering at my computer screen. He adjusted his glasses and then pointed at one of the people in the picture I was looking at. "Is that one of the other guys in that picture you took?"

I smiled up at him. "Not only is it one of the other guys, but his name happens to be Harvey."

"Get out."

I nodded. "Harvey Markovitz to be exact." I pointed at the caption beneath a picture. *"It's splitsville for Ziggy Thomas and Harlow Anderson as Thomas attends one of Harvey Markovitz's famed beach parties on the arm of socialite Elise Sawyer."*

Al shook his head. "Well that's some A-plus detective work, kid. You found our guy!"

"We found our guy. Without the name Ziggy Thomas, we could've spun our wheels for weeks. I didn't even *see* the name Harvey Markovitz on that list of Harveys I pulled up earlier. That was all you."

Al nodded like he couldn't agree more. He pointed at the screen. "Now we have a real name to look up. Why don't you see what the interwebs think about this Markovitz fella?"

I googled him and was surprised to see a Wikipedia page pop up. "Harvey Markovitz is an American film producer. He and his close friend Peter Economopoulos cofounded the entertainment company Celestial Body Entertainment." The article went on to list many of the movies attributed to his and his friend's production company. I scanned through the article. "His first wife left him in the nineties. His second wife left him in 2002. It says he splits his time between Los Angeles and the Caribbean."

"Huh. So he comes out here, has his way with young girls, and then goes back to his day job in California?"

I nodded. "Sounds about right."

"So. How do we nab the guy?"

"I think for Gibson to believe anything we have to say, we're gonna need some serious proof."

"You think that girl you interviewed would be willing to come forward and tell her story to him?"

"Definitely not. She was barely willing to tell it to Frankie and me." I shook my head. "No. We need to come up with some hard evidence to tie him to not only this underage prostitution ring, but also Jordan's murder."

Al nodded and looked down at his watch. "Look, Drunk. I'd love to stay and chat, but I gotta meet Evie and the gang for supper. We'll come up with a plan after. Alright?"

"Yeah. Go ahead. I need some time to think anyway."

28

I SPENT THE REST OF THE AFTERNOON INTO THE EARLY-EVENING hours in my office working on resort business and thinking about the connection between Harvey Markovitz, Ziggy Thomas, Joseph Ayala, Kip Dalton, Vito, and Steve Dillon—all the guys in the picture we'd found in Steve Dillon's office. Vito ran Club Cobalt. Kip *owned* the club. They found these underage girls and shipped them over to Harvey Markovitz's place, but why? Why would they risk their own necks to help Markovitz satisfy his desire for young girls? And why would Ziggy Thomas, a guy that seemed to have it all, want to hang out with a pedophile like Markovitz? It just didn't make any sense. And then there was Joseph Ayala, running a lucrative photography studio. Why would he want to take pictures of these young girls, quite possibly jeopardizing his reputation? None of it made much sense. Was it just that they were all perverts like Markovitz?

One thing did stand out to me, though: the photograph. It had clearly been taken at some sort of party. And the fact that that celebrity blogger had said that Ziggy was at one of Harvey's famed parties made me wonder if that wasn't where the picture had been taken—Harvey's place.

I was sure the sun had already begun to set when Artie stuck his head into my office. "You're sure burning the midnight oil."

"Hey, Artie." I poked my head around my computer.

"I gotta say, Drunk. I'm impressed with the changes you've made to your work ethic."

I puffed air out my mouth. "Thanks, Artie, but this place pretty much runs itself. It's like a well-oiled machine."

"I like to think so. But if things are running so smoothly, what's up with being cooped up in here when you could be keeping an eye on things down at the clubhouse?"

"Well, I'm actually working on something else more or less personal."

"Oh yeah? Anything I can help you with?"

I shrugged. "I'm really not at liberty to say."

Artie lumbered into my office and took a seat on the chair in front of my desk. "Oh, come on, Drunk. Who am I gonna tell? If it involves my resort, don't you think I should know?"

"Who said it involved your resort?"

"Oh, I just assumed."

I sighed. Then I pushed myself away from the computer and looked at Artie. "Oh, what the hell. You can't breathe a word of this to anyone."

Artie made a cross against his chest. "I swear on my late wife's grave."

"You know Mari's daughter, Giselle?"

Artie's head rolled forward. He caught it with one hand. "Oh no, Drunk. Tell me you didn't."

"Fuck, Artie. I didn't. Jeez. What's with all you guys? I *am* able to practice a little self-control."

Artie let out a breath of relief. "Oh, thank God. Mari would've taken your man parts if you'd gone after her daughter."

"You don't think I know that? Hell no, I'd never go there.

Not even if it was someone else's daughter. That's just too young for me."

"Good." Artie's head bobbed. "So, then what's this got to do with Giselle?"

"One of her friends went missing and she asked for my help to find her."

"And you're having a hard time finding her?"

"Actually, we found her."

"Good for you."

"Not good for me. The cops found her drowned over at the Sandy Bay Beach. She was dead."

"Oh shit."

I nodded. "Yeah, oh shit. It's led to all kinds of stuff I wish I'd never found out about. But mostly, it's led me to this guy who lives on the island part-time. His name is Harvey Markovitz. He's from the States. Ever heard of him?"

Artie's lips swished over to the side. "Mmmm. The name rings a bell. I might've heard it before. Of course I don't get off the resort property a whole lot, so I don't know him personally or anything."

"Yeah," I said with a sigh.

"So you've got a name. What's the problem?"

"Well, the problem is that Sergeant Gibson isn't exactly my biggest fan. There's no way he's gonna believe me if I go to him without any kind of evidence to link Harvey to this girl's death."

"So get some evidence."

"Thanks," I puffed. "Never would've thought of it."

Artie chuckled. "Okay, okay, maybe that was too obvious."

"I guess Al and I just need to find out where he lives and sneak in somehow."

Artie winced. "Sounds dangerous. Do me a favor, will ya? Leave your partner behind when you do that assignment."

"Hey, don't underestimate Al. You'd be surprised at the amount of heart that guy still has left in him."

"I never said anything about his heart. I'm more concerned about his legs. I'm not sure how good they are at running anymore," sighed Artie.

"Don't worry. I can handle the running part for both of us. From what I understand, this guy Markovitz throws these like big beach parties. Maybe I need to find out when the next one is and see if I can't get an invite."

"There you go. Sneak in right under his nose."

And then a thought hit me. "Hey, Artie. You remember Steve Dillon was willing to give you a discount on a new car on his lot?"

Artie lowered a brow and looked at me curiously. "Yeah?"

"It recently came to our attention that Steve Dillon is a friend of Markovitz's. We were in his office the other day, and Al found a picture of the two of them together. I'm not much of a betting man, but if I were, I'd put money on the fact that the picture was taken at one of Markovitz's parties. Think there's any way you could call Steve and try and get an invite?"

Artie's eyes widened. "Oh, *that's* the party you're talking about?"

I frowned. "What do you mean?"

Artie pulled a handkerchief out of the breast pocket of his white linen suit and sopped up the sweat that glistened on his face. "A couple times a month, I get an email inviting me to a beach party. It's invite-only. And from what I understand, the invites only go to notable business owners on the island. I think it's kind of like a who's who in Paradise."

"And you think it's the same party I'm talking about?"

"It sounds like it, doesn't it? Steve's name is always in the contacts list."

"Does the email come from Harvey Markovitz himself?"

Artie frowned as he thought about it. "No. I've never seen that name before. I believe the invitation comes from Kip Dalton. I think he owns a couple clubs on the island."

I couldn't help the smile that poured across my face. It *had* to be the same party. "I can't believe it, Artie. *You* get invited to Harvey's parties?"

"You don't have to sound so surprised."

I gave him a half shrug. "Sorry, man, you just don't seem like much of a party guy to me."

"Well," he said before clearing his throat. His face reddened. "I've never actually *gone* to one of the parties. But that doesn't mean I don't have connections. You seem to be forgetting that I own a major resort on the island, Drunk. You don't own something like the Seacoast Majestic without getting to know a few people. As a matter of fact, last year I happen to have rubbed elbows with the new governor of the island."

"No way. You know the governor? Like personally?"

Artie's head bobbed. "I do. Governor Bustamante invited me to a luncheon when I first moved to the island last year. He invited all of the other resort owners so I could get to know my peers. Very down-to-earth guy—real salt of the Earth. I really appreciated him taking the time out of his busy schedule to welcome me like that."

"Huh," I said, shaking my head. "I never would have guessed. So you and Steve are buddies too, then?"

Artie kind of chuckled. "Steve's a different story. I only know *of* the guy. Governor Bustamante's office keeps a master email list of all business owners on the island. I assume that's how he got my address."

"So are you trying to tell me that you *can* get us an invite to the next party?"

Artie shook his head. "No. What I'm trying to tell you is that I don't need to get you an invite, Drunk. I've already got one."

I grinned widely and my hands shot out wide. "Fuck! Artie! I love you, man!"

Al came tottering around the corner just then. He raised his eyebrows at me. "Oh, am I interrupting something, fellas? Do you need another minute?" He pointed at the door. "I can come back."

Artie laughed. "Come on in, Al. Have a seat."

"Yeah, Al. You are *never* going to believe what Artie just said."

"Lemme guess—that he's in love with you too?"

I chuckled. "Better." I spent the next couple minutes explaining to Al about the parties Artie had been invited to and how I thought those had to be the ones that Harvey was known for throwing. "Artie, you know offhand when the next party is?"

"Yeah, there's one this Saturday night."

I looked over at Al. "Better dust off your dancing shoes, Al."

Al shook his head. "I think not, kid. If Steve Dillon's at that party, he'll blow the whistle on us for sure."

I leaned back in my seat. "Shit. You're right. And if Ayala's there, he'll recognize us for sure too. Plus there's Vito. He might get smart and put two and two together and realize we were the plumbers and were really snooping around in his office. We gotta get some legit business owner into that party and find out why they're inviting island big-wigs."

Al and I both stared at Artie.

Artie's dark eyes widened. He held up his dimpled hands in protest. "Oh no, fellas. Don't look at me."

"Oh, come on, Artie. We *need* you!"

"Yeah, Artie. Come on. The kid and I saved your ass, you know that. You owe us one."

Artie sponged off his forehead again. "I already gave Drunk a job. What more do I need to do?"

"Go to this party and find out why you got an invitation. Al and I will handle the rest. Look, Artie. I know you like to live vicariously through me and Al's stories. Don't you want to be a *part* of one for a change?"

Artie's face flushed redder than usual. His eyebrows were both raised as he shook his head. "No, not really."

"Oh, come on, Artie—"

"I can't, guys. Come on. I'm not great in social situations. There's no way I could go in there all alone."

"This is about a date?" I practically hollered. "Shit, Artie. Why didn't you just say so? I can find you a date."

29

"So. Are you gonna explain to me what we're doing here?" Frankie asked me the next day.

We were standing in the middle of a ritzy boutique in the downtown touristy area of the island. I'd called and asked Frankie to meet me down here the night before, but I'd told her I'd explain everything when we saw each other in person.

"You're gonna love me," I said, shooting her a wide smile while browsing through the rack of cocktail dresses.

"Yeah? Why's that?"

"Because *I* figured out who our guy Harvey is."

"I did a little digging too," admitted Frankie.

"Did you figure it out?"

"No, but I think I was getting close. I had a list of Harveys I was combing through."

I smiled. She didn't need to know that if we hadn't gotten a lead on that picture I'd taken, we'd be combing over the same list. "What do you think of this one?" I asked, holding a little black dress on a hanger up to my chin.

"Looks a little small for you."

"Well, obviously I won't be the one wearing it."

"You gonna tell me about this Harvey guy, or do I need to beat it out of you?"

I raised my eyebrows and smiled at her. "Oooh. I think I prefer option two."

Smiling, she elbowed me in the ribs. "Be serious, Danny. I have to get back to work. What do you know? Fill me in."

"Okay. Here's what I found out. Have you ever heard of Ziggy Thomas?"

"Of course I have. He owns the helicopter tour company on the island. He's kind of like a local celebrity."

"Okay, well, Ziggy is buddies with our guy Harvey, whose last name is Markovitz. Ever heard of him?"

Frankie frowned. "Mmm. Sounds familiar, but it's not coming to me right offhand." She tipped her head sideways. "Now, how exactly did you figure this out?"

I winced. I didn't really feel like telling her about my visit to Steve Dillon's yet. "It's kind of a long story, but trust me. I have a picture of him at a party with our guy Markovitz, Steve Dillon of Steve Dillon's Automart, Joseph Ayala the photographer, Kip Dalton, and the guy who runs Club Cobalt, Vito something."

"Vito D'Angelo. He's kind of a shady character. He's been in a bit of trouble here and there. Mostly assault charges."

"Okay. Yeah. Why does that not surprise me?" I said, rubbing my stomach. I could almost feel the punch in the gut once again.

I put the little black dress back on the rack and pulled out another one. This one had a shorter hemline. I thought that might work better for my needs. "Anyway, so Markovitz seems to have these parties at his place like every couple of weeks. And all these guys seem to party over there with him. So, the plan is really quite simple. We go to the party. Get some evidence on this underage prostitution ring. And take it to your boss. Easy peasy."

Frankie's brows shot up. "Easy peasy? Danny, are you out

of your mind? That's a major sting operation. That's not just something where we waltz in and have a look around."

"Why not?"

"Why not? Danny, that's dangerous. I just got done telling you that Vito's a dangerous guy. You really think he's just going to let us in the front door to bust up whatever's going on over there?"

"Well, no. I didn't exactly figure it was going to happen like that."

"I think we need to get Sergeant Gibson involved at this point. Let him handle the investigation from here on out. We've got a name and I assume an address. We've done a huge part of the work."

I shook my head. "No, Frankie. There's no way we can go to Gibson yet. I didn't tell you that he pulled me over after our interview yesterday."

Her mouth gaped open. "Gibson pulled you over?"

"Yup."

"For what?"

"To warn me, basically."

"Warn you? Warn you about what?"

"Well, it certainly wasn't about global warming, I'll tell you that."

"Danny. What did he warn you about?" She looked concerned now.

I rubbed the pads of my hand against my forehead. Even though I really didn't want to, maybe it was time to come clean with Frankie. I sighed. "The other day, I went to see Steve Dillon about my new vehicle. I was concerned about the price I'd paid for it."

"Why?"

"Because Al and I sort of found out that Kip Dalton isn't paying the tariff on his vehicles."

"How'd you find that out?"

I shrugged. "Let's just say I happened to see a couple of the invoices. We discovered that he's getting some kind of business owner's special."

"Okay?"

"Well, now that your brothers have cut me into the business, I thought maybe I would be eligible for that discount too, and I wanted to talk to Steve about it. And he basically kicked me out after asking."

"Hey, the boys said something about bringing you in on the business. That's awesome," said Frankie with a wide smile. "Congratulations. I guess you're part of the family now?"

I laughed and held up my hands. "No. Definitely not part of the family. Let's not get any funny ideas. We are most *definitely* not related."

"I don't know about that. Solo said you're like an honorary brother now."

I rolled my eyes. "Did he?"

"Yeah. He was pretty direct about it, too."

I shook my head. I'd deal with all of that later. For now, we needed to keep our focus. "Anyway, Al and I also paid a visit to Joseph Ayala regarding some pictures that he took of some of the underage girls I thought Harvey had been assaulting. When I started asking him questions, he basically clammed up and walked away. Both of those douche canoes reported me to Gibson."

"Danny, you have to be careful. There are some dangerous people on this island. Everything on Paradise isn't all palm trees, beaches, and mai tais. There's a darker side too."

"Oh, you don't have to tell me. I've gotten very exposed to it over the last couple weeks. And I'll admit that I don't exactly like what I see, but I promised Giselle I'd get justice for Jordan and that's exactly what I plan to do."

"It's very noble of you. I just want you to be careful while you're doing it."

I gave her a tight smile. "Thanks, Frankie." I sighed. "Now.

Which one of these two dresses do you like better?" I held two black dresses up.

She quirked a brow. "Danny, I sure hope you don't think you're going to get me in one of those dresses."

I laughed. "As much as I would *die* to see you in one of these little numbers, no, they aren't intended for you."

"Well, then, who are they—"

"Oooh, hellooo, Drunk! Over here!" sang Valentina Carrizo, standing in the doorway of the boutique. "I was so *excited* to get your call!" She ran at me, her clunky plastic-wedged shoes clomping loudly on the travertine tile. She wore a bursting-at-the-seams pink sequined tube top and matching sequined skirt. She threw her arms over my shoulders and made a show of hugging me. "Oooh, I missed you!"

"You know this woman?" asked Frankie, quirking a brow.

I cleared my throat and tried to suppress my smile. Frankie almost looked jealous. In a weird kind of way, I found it to be sexy. "Oh. Yeah, I do. Frankie, this is Valentina Carrizo." I unhooked Val's arms from my shoulders and spun her around to face Frankie. Val curled into my side, hugging me around the waist.

"Val, this is Officer Francesca Cruz. She's a friend of mine."

Val refused to let go of my waist but did extend the fingers of one well-manicured hand to Frankie. "Hello," she said shortly, like she didn't like me being friends with Frankie.

Frankie barely took Val's hands, giving her fingers only a light squeeze before dropping them and wiping her hands on her uniform pants. "Hey." She looked up at me. "So, what's going on, Danny?"

"Ooh, your first name *ees* Danny? Can I call you Danny too?" She squeezed her arms tighter around my waist and looked up at me, her long fake lashes fluttering at me.

"Mmm. Let's just stick with Drunk, shall we, Val?" I tried to unlatch the woman from my waist before Frankie got the wrong idea about us. "Umm, Val is here because she's going to help us out tomorrow."

"Just like I help you out the other night, no?" Holding me around the waist again, she winked up at me then reached down and grabbed my beef right in front of Frankie.

Val! Fuck!

Frankie stared at Val's hand before blowing out a puff of air. "Well. I better get back to work. You two have fun shopping for new slut apparel." She pivoted on her heel and began to leave.

I yanked Val's hand off my crotch, wiggled out of her vise-like grip, and rushed towards Frankie. "Frankie, wait!"

But she kept walking and was out the front door before I could grab hold of her.

"Frankie!" I started to chase after her, but Val hollered at me.

"Wait! Where are you going? Aren't we going to look at new dresses for the party?"

"Yes, we are," I said firmly. I held out my hands palms up as if Val were an easily spooked animal. "Stay right there. I will be *right back*. I need to go talk to my friend."

Val's eyes swung downward and she pouted out her bottom lip. "You like her better than me?"

"Val, don't do that. Please? I swear. I'll be right back. I need my friend's help tonight at the party. Okay?"

Val sighed.

I pointed at a rack of shoes. "While we're getting you a new dress, how about we get shoes too?"

That perked her up. "Oooh, new choos?"

"Yeah," I agreed, smiling ear to ear. "New choos. Go crazy. It's on me."

"Yay!" she squealed, excitedly clapping her hands.

I pointed at the sales lady. "Can you help her? She needs a dress for a party. Get her whatever she wants, okay? I'll be right back."

The sales lady's eyes widened as her head bobbed up and down. "Sure thing."

I rushed out to the sidewalk after Frankie. She was already all the way over to her squad car. "Frankie, wait!"

"Danny, I really don't have time for these games you play with crazy women."

"Games I play with crazy women? What are you talking about?!"

She gestured towards the boutique. "Are you telling me that one isn't crazy?"

"Who, Val? I mean, she's a little—umm—out there, I'll give you that, but I wouldn't call her crazy."

"Okay, well, then there was Mack."

I nodded. "Okay. You're right. *She* was crazy."

"And Nico."

My mind went back to the throat punch that had kicked off my trip to Paradise Isle. "Oh yeah. She was *definitely* crazy."

"Okay. See? You seem to gravitate towards crazy women." She shook her head. "Honestly, it kind of makes me feel a little crazy for being your friend."

I sighed. "Frankie, don't feel like that. You're not crazy. Yeah, I'll admit, I don't always attract the best people in the world, but *you* are the exception. You're the best woman I've *ever* attracted. *Ever*." I reached out and tugged on her hand.

She pouted at me. "Who said I'm attracted to you?"

I flashed a smile at her, trying to coax one out of her in return. "Oh, come on. You know I'm sexy."

She didn't let go of my hand, but she turned her head. "I know no such thing."

"I think *you're* sexy," I said in a low voice.

She turned her head and smiled at me then, rolling her eyes dramatically. "Well, duh. That's because I *am* sexy."

Staring at the way her cheeks dimpled when she smiled, I chuckled. "You have the *best* smile. I much prefer seeing you smile over being mad at me."

"I'm not *mad* at you, Danny. I'm just—frustrated. You frustrate me sometimes."

"I'm sorry that I frustrate you. I don't try to. Honest." I squeezed her hand. "Val and I don't have anything going on between us. I swear. I met her at the Blue Iguana a few weeks ago. She's a professional escort, and she tried to put the moves on me." My hands went up. "But I didn't touch her, I swear. I did call her to help Al and me out on something related to the case."

"Related to the case? What could she possibly—"

I sighed. I hadn't wanted to tell her everything, but now I felt like I had no choice. "We sort of broke into Kip Dalton's place. I thought that was the house where they were taking the girls."

"You did what?! Danny! I can't believe you!" She put a hand on either side of her head, covering her ears. "You shouldn't be telling me any of this!"

"I'm sorry. I know. I didn't want to. I just don't want you thinking that Val and I ever—you know—"

"Well, what did she have to do with *that*?"

"She was sort of our distraction. Like a decoy."

"A decoy? What are you talking about? How?"

I rubbed my fingers against my sweaty brow. "We, uh, sent Kip a singing hookergram."

Frankie's brows shot up. "Danny! You didn't!"

"Well, we needed to keep him busy for a little while we looked around his place. And it worked. That's how we found those invoices for the cars, which led us to Steve Dillon, and on and on." I smiled sweetly at her. "And Val promised she'd help us again. I need to get Artie into that party."

"Artie?! I thought *we* were going in?"

"We *are* going in." I smiled sheepishly at her. "Just not through the front door."

"Well, then, why even have Artie come at all? He could get hurt."

"It's a risk I'm willing to take," I said with a little laugh.

"Danny, be serious for once. You don't want Artie getting hurt. Or Al. Please tell me we're not taking Al along too?"

I stared at her blankly.

"Danny," she whispered, shaking her head.

"What?! He wants to go."

"This kind of stuff isn't a joke."

"Look, I've learned where Al's concerned, you can't tell him what he can or cannot do. Only Evie can do that."

"Well, then, tell Evie not to let Al go."

I shook my head. "I can't do that. I've learned my lesson the hard way. My nose does not belong in their marriage."

"So, what's Val's job in all of this?"

"She's Artie's date. He needs someone who knows how to work a crowd."

Frankie's brows shot up. "Oh, I have no doubt that woman knows how to work a crowd alright. Explain to me again why we even *need* Artie to go in through the front."

"I want to know *why* they're inviting all these business owners. What do Kip Dalton, Ziggy Thomas, Joseph Ayala, and Steve Dillon all have to do with Harvey Markovitz's weird obsession with underage girls? If we go in through the back, we're only getting a small picture of what's really going on over there. I want to understand the whole operation."

She nodded and let out a little sigh. "Yeah, alright, I get it."

From behind us, Valentina's voice called out. "Drunk, what do you *theenk* of *thees* one?" She was standing on the sidewalk in front of the boutique, wearing black straps of strategically placed fabric around her body. The sales lady stood next to her, apparently afraid she was going to make a break for it in what I only could assume was some designer's idea of a dress. Valentina threw her arms up and toddled around in a circle on the pavement.

Frankie put her hands on her hips and looked at me curiously. "Yeah, *Drunk*, what do you *theenk* of her dress?"

"Be nice," I whispered with a laugh. "She's a sweet girl. A little boisterous, but sweet."

"Uh-huh."

I turned to look at Val. I tipped my head sideways and called out, "Umm. Are you sure you don't have that on backwards?"

Val looked down at her dress and then back up at me. Her bottom lip plumped out. She looked at the sales clerk and shrugged.

"Okay, well—maybe we'll try on a different one. Oh, and by the way, do you guys provide hair and makeup services?" Before either of them could respond, I crossed my hands in the air and shook my head. "Never mind, we'll talk about it in a minute. Go back inside and I'll be right there, I promise." I smiled at Val and the sales lady before turning around to look at Frankie.

"Look. Call me when you get off work and we'll work out all the details for the party? Okay?"

Frankie shook her head at me. "Ugh. The things I do for you, Danny."

"You love me and you know it." I leaned forward and brushed a kiss against her cheek. Then I backed up towards the boutique and pointed at her. "I gotta go. I'll talk to you later." I shot her a wink, then held two fingers to my lips, kissed them, and blew the kiss in her direction.

She rolled her eyes and got in her squad car, refusing to give me so much as a wave before driving away.

Women.

30

"Artie, Valentina. Valentina, this is Artie." I stood back and smiled as Artie's eyes nearly popped out of his head.

Valentina wore the new little black dress and heels we'd picked out for her. She'd gotten her hair done and toned down the makeup considerably. Though her dress was tight and her neckline plunging, she still managed to straddle the line between classy and slutty perfectly in my opinion.

Artie wiped his meaty grips on the black tuxedo pants he wore and extended his hand to Val. "I-it's nice to meet you, Valentina."

"Hello," she cooed back. "It *ees* so nice to meet you."

"Artie's my boss at the Seacoast Majestic," I explained.

Valentina's face lit up. "Ohhh, you are the boss?"

His face was red as he kind of nodded. "Well, actually I own the place. It's my resort."

That bit of information seemed to pull Val's lever. Dollar signs registered in her eyes. There might as well have been flashing lights over her head, blinking *Jackpot Jackpot Jackpot*. "Ohhh, you *own* the place? Isn't that niiiice?" She clung to his arm.

"Valentina, you remember Al?"

"Good to see you again," she said, shaking Al's hand and gracing him with one of her flirty smiles.

"And of course you met my friend Officer Cruz. She'll be working with us tonight."

Valentina looked Frankie up and down. Giving her a frown, she nodded. "Yes. Hello again." Then she turned to look at me. "So what are you guys gonna do while me and Artie are at the party?"

"Al, Officer Cruz and I will be posing as caterers for the event." It had only taken me calls to six local caterers to find out which one was working the party. I'd told each of them that I needed to make a change to the menu for the Kip Dalton party. The sixth one had taken the bait. Once we knew who was catering, a quick look at pictures on their website told us exactly what the uniform looked like. Black dress pants and shoes, a white button-down shirt with a black tie, and a burgundy apron.

"And what are Val and I supposed to do?" asked Artie, all tuxedo'd up and staring at Val. His face seemed to melt a little more than usual.

I tossed him the bar towel I'd brought as part of my props. "For fuck's sake, Artie. Can you turn off the waterworks for one night?"

He stuck a finger in his collar and tugged. "Like I can control it? I'm roasting in this penguin suit. Are you sure I don't look ridiculous in this?"

"I think you look very handsome," said Val, cuddling up to Artie's side. "Like a *beeg* teddy bear."

Artie cleared this throat. "Oh, well, uh. Thank you. You look very nice as well. Very, uh-hum, pretty."

"Ooh," she squealed. "Thank you so much."

"Okay, look, Artie. All you and Val have to do is get in. Okay? Then play it cool. Go with the flow, you know? Something's going on over there. Keep your ear to the ground and see what you can't figure out."

Artie nodded. "Okay. We can do that, right, Val?"

"Of course we can," said Val with a smile. Clinging to his arm, she rubbed his chest seductively. "You are in very capable hands, you know."

Artie blotted his face once again while Frankie and I exchanged looks.

Al pointed at Artie. "You printed out your invitation?"

He patted his breast pocket. "Got it right here."

"Did you ask Desi to drive you?" Al asked.

"I, uh, rented a limo, actually. You know, since I don't go out very often, I thought maybe I'd splurge a little."

Val's eyes lit up. Her hand rubbed up and down Artie's chest again. "Oooh. A limo! Artie, that's so sweet of you."

Artie sucked in a deep breath, making a little wheezing sound. I silently wondered if he'd thought to bring along an inhaler. I didn't want him to pass out on the way to the party or anything.

"Okay. Well, you've got your phone. If you see or hear anything suspicious, just call. Okay?"

Artie nodded and then crooked his arm for Val to take. "Shall we, m'lady?"

She giggled excitedly. "Ohh, so romantic." As they began to walk away, she turned around to wiggle her fingers at us. "Bye-bye."

"Have fun," said Al.

"Don't do anything I wouldn't do, Artie," I hollered after them.

Artie laughed as he turned to face me. "So pretty much everything's on the table, then, eh, Drunk?"

Val's hand slipped down to squeeze Artie's ass. "Oh, yes, *everything*."

AFTER ARTIE AND VAL LEFT, Frankie, Al, and I hopped in the

van we'd borrowed from the Cruz brothers once again and headed to the address listed on Artie's invitation. Harvey Markovitz's beachfront mansion was located at the very tip of the Avalonian Peninsula. The line of cars waiting to be approved for entry was long, and we sat with the windows rolled down, trying to air the fishy smell out of the vehicle to keep from vomiting.

When it was finally our turn to be approved at the guard shack, I held my breath from the back. Frankie drove and Al rode shotgun.

"I'm sorry, this is an invitation-only event," said the guard to Frankie.

Frankie hitched her thumb towards the back of the vehicle. "The caterers ran low on crab. They placed a last-minute order. We're just delivering."

The guard sighed. "There's a service entrance for deliveries around back."

"Oh. Is there? They didn't mention it. Can't we just come in through here?"

"They're the ones with the lists over there. I only have the guest list here."

Frankie groaned. "Look. We just waited twenty minutes in this line. If we have to go around and wait in another line, we're just gonna bounce. We were doing *you* a favor by rushing over here, *after hours* because someone in there doesn't know what the hell they're doing. You know lack of planning on your part does not constitute an emergency on *our part*." Frankie sighed and I felt the vehicle lurch slightly as she took it out of park. "We're just gonna go, and *you* can explain to your boss why his guests ran out of crab."

The vehicle began to roll forward.

"Wait. Wait," shouted the guard. He let out a little grunt and then mumbled, "Fine."

The van stopped rolling.

"Ugh. But next time you have to go through the delivery entrance. See that lane over there? That's where you go."

We were in.

Yes! Good job, Frankie!

"Thank you," she said curtly, taking her foot off the brakes once again.

"Oh. But before you take off, since you don't have an invitation, I do have to inspect what's in the back of the vehicle."

My eyes widened.

"Oh, uh, yeah. No problem," said Frankie.

I pulled the tarp that was draped over my head tighter and held my breath as I heard the back doors of the van open up. With my other hand, I clutched the handle of the 9mm Glock 43 I'd purchased after the incident with Pam's abduction. The boxes of crab meat we'd brought along were all the way down at the tail end of the van. I could hear the guard open one of the boxes. My heart pounded wildly, hoping they wouldn't ask to see what was under the tarp.

The doors slammed shut and I heard him pound the side of the van. "Good to go," he hollered at Frankie.

I let out a breath of relief.

"You okay, kid?" asked Al.

I uncovered my head and looked up at Al. "Yeah. It smells like shit back here, though."

"Toughen up a little, Danny. We'll be there in a second."

"Easy for you to say. You're sitting next to an open window. I've got a fishy tarp locking in the odors. It's like a fish Dutch oven under here." I felt the van rolling around for what seemed like several minutes but was probably only thirty seconds or so. Then it came to a stop and the gentle rattling of the engine stopped.

"We're here. You can take the tarp off now, I think we're safe," said Frankie.

I tossed the tarp off my head. Stale, tepid air washed over me, cooling the sweat on my brow but bringing a whole new wave of dead fish smell to my nostrils. "Ugh, I gotta get out of this van before I hurl."

"I'll let you out," said Frankie, hopping out of the van and slamming her door.

She pulled open the back van door and I burst out. "Oh sweet Jesus, air!" I whispered with my arms spread wide open and my eyes closed and looking heavenward.

"Dramatic much?" asked Frankie.

I opened one eye and looked over at her. "Next time we'll hide you in the back of a fish van under a smelly fish tarp and see how dramatic you are. Deal?"

She pressed her lips together and raised her brows. "Mmmkay. You done now?"

I smoothed my black slacks and shirt and ran a hand through my hair. Taking one last deep breath, I nodded. "Yes."

"Good. Let's go. We have work to do." She grabbed one of the boxes of crab out of the back of the van and I grabbed the other and then walked around to the front door of the van and opened it for Al.

"Ready, Al? It's go time."

Al nodded and tried to climb out.

I leaned against the van and watched him struggle to slide down to his feet. Artie's concerns replayed through my mind. "You sure you don't just want to stay out here? It'll be safer."

"And miss all the action?"

I shrugged. "I'll fill you in when we get back."

Al shook his head and slid out of the vehicle. It was dark out and we were parked in an employee parking lot behind the house. Al hobbled around in circles, holding his lower back.

"You alright?"

"It's just my sciatica again. I gotta walk it off and loosen up a little."

"Maybe you should do some stretching and stuff. You know, bend over and touch your toes."

Al looked at me like I was crazy. "Look, kid, if God wanted me to touch my toes, he woulda put 'em on my knees."

I chuckled. "Alright, then. Bend over and touch your knees."

Al wagged his finger in the air. "See, there you go again with your lines." He shook his head. "You can just keep that line between you and your lady friends."

Fighting a laugh, I rolled my eyes. "Line? It's not a line, Al." I shook my head at him. "Look, I think it's best for all of us if you stay in the van."

"I agree," said Frankie, walking around the vehicle to check on us. "We aren't gonna have a lot of time in there. And if something were to go wrong, we're gonna need you out here waiting for us with the car at the ready."

Al pressed his fingers against his chest. "Lemme get this straight. You wanna reduce me to being the getaway driver?"

"Yes. That's exactly what she's telling you, Al. Remember, there are no small parts, only small actors. Besides, Evie would be thankful. Come on. Whaddaya say?"

Al straightened, then caught a sharp pain somewhere in his body and winced. Rubbing the kink out, Al nodded. "Fine. But only because I'm not moving very fast today."

I fought a smile. "Today, right—"

Frankie didn't want to wait around. She gave him a curt nod. "Keep an eye on your phone. We'll call if we need you to bring the van around. Be ready, alright?"

"Yeah, okay." He frowned. I could tell he wasn't very happy about getting left behind, but I also knew he was hurting and didn't have much choice.

I put a hand on his shoulder. "This is for the best, Al."

"Yeah, yeah. Just don't be a hero, kid."

I gave him a tight smile. "Thanks, Al. You be safe too."

31

THE STAFF ENTRANCE OF HARVEY MARKOVITZ'S MANSION BUZZED louder than a refrigerator with a busted compressor. People in all sorts of uniforms raced around, some with trays of empty champagne flutes and others with newly restocked hors d'oeuvre trays. Chefs hollered orders while others cooked or washed dishes. So when Frankie and I walked in carrying our boxes of crab, we blended in easily.

We'd made it about a dozen steps towards what appeared to be the exit when someone in a chef's cap spotted us and hollered, "You over there, let's get that refrigerated, ASAP."

I glanced sideways at Frankie.

She nodded at the man. "Just lookin' for the cooler, boss."

He cocked his head backwards. "Over there. Once you get that done, hurry back. The buffet needs restocking already."

"Sure thing, boss," she said, giving him a nod.

The two of us did as instructed. We delivered the boxes of crab meat to the cooler and then returned and got new orders. Chef Frederick, as his name tag read, handed each of us a chafing dish. Frankie's was full of steamed shrimp and mine was a pasta dish that smelled of heaven, but I felt myself holding my breath as I followed Frankie out to the party floor.

Between Ayala, Dalton, Steve Dillon, and Vito, I worried that showing my face could jeopardize our mission, and then not only would our sting be over, but I might be arrested for trespassing, and Frankie would likely be out of a job. But, following her confident lead, I kept my head down and held my stainless-steel chafing dish up high as we cut through the crowd of partygoers. As soon as we replaced the nearly emptied trays of food with the full ones and began to walk away with the empty ones, a woman in a matching maroon apron clicked her tongue at us.

"Didn't they train you how to do this?" she hissed at us.

Frankie looked down at the tray of food she carried. "Excuse me?"

"Look at how much food you're wasting. You are supposed to combine the old food with the new food."

Several guests at a nearby table looked over their shoulders at us, getting chewed out like small children. Ignoring her speech, I lifted my chin slightly to get a view of the room for the first time and noticed Val and Artie circulating around the room. Val clung to Artie's arm, but still managed to put on quite the show, grinning and laughing, enjoying every man's attention over her. For his part, Artie didn't seem to mind having such a well-admired date. In fact, his chest seemed more puffed out than I'd ever seen him before.

Good for you, Artie, I thought as the woman named Brenda in the maroon apron continued to rail on Frankie and me.

"Now, do it properly," she finally commanded.

Frankie sighed. "Come on."

We went back to the table and I began to scoop the rest of the pasta out of my chafing dish and into the new pan when I heard a familiar voice in line next to me.

"So then I told the guy, not if I have anything to do about it!"

Raucous laughter filled the air around me. Keeping my chin to my chest, I allowed only my eyes to glance up. It was

Vito, chatting with Kip Dalton. My eyes widened. I was literally two steps away from Vito and across the buffet table from Kip. I shot a glance further down the buffet line and was surprised that I recognized another face. It was Monica Arndt, the realtor Al and I had met with earlier in the week. An older man was chatting with someone next to him, and he had his arm draped around her shoulder. Keeping my head down, I quickly unloaded the rest of my tray and raced back to the kitchen with Frankie hot on my heels.

Brenda nodded as we passed her by. "Better. Now fill up the sides. We're running low."

"Yes, ma'am," I whispered, just anxious to get out of there.

Frankie and I rushed back to the kitchen, unloaded our empty trays, and then, careful not to let Ms. Snippy Pants see us, took a left instead of a right to head back towards the party floor. Out there, we took the first hallway we saw and began our exploration, poking our head into each and every room we encountered. It didn't take long before we realized what an enormous mansion it was and how difficult it would be to search through every room without getting caught.

I whispered at Frankie, "Giselle told me that they came in off the garage and went down a hallway that had a bunch of girls' pictures. I think we need to find that hallway first and make sure we're even in the right house to begin with."

Frankie stopped walking and looked around. "How are we supposed to find the garage?"

"I don't know, but if I had to guess, it's not going to be right by the service entrance. I bet it's on the other side of the house."

Frankie frowned. "Well, then, why did we come this way?"

"Because Sergeant Snippy Pants was going to make a scene if we came back without our trays."

"Ugh," groaned Frankie. "Okay. We'll have to sneak back across the party to the other wing of the house."

"Be careful, because I saw Vito D'Angelo out there earlier.

He knows what I look like. We sorta had a run-in not that long ago."

I was thankful when Frankie didn't make me explain. "Okay. Come on."

We walked back through the hallway and peered into the party. It was in full swing now with people laughing and drinking. I noticed Artie talking to a balding blond man with wire-rimmed glasses and a relaxed grey suit.

"Hey, Frankie, I think that's our guy," I hissed. I could only see a side profile of the man, but I felt confident that it was the same guy in the pictures we'd seen.

"I wonder what he and Artie are talking about," she whispered back.

"I don't know. We'll find out when we get back to the resort. For now, how are we supposed to get across the room without the boss or Vito seeing us?"

Frankie picked up a huge feathered centerpiece off a side table and held it front of her face. "Follow me."

The two of us skimmed across the room, darting between guests and the waitstaff. When we were finally on the other side of the massive room, Frankie put the plant back down on another table, and we slipped into the hallway on that side.

"Nice going," I said, shooting her a smile.

She grinned back at me, flexing her dimples. "Thanks. Now come on—before we get busted."

We set about exploring that wing of the house, looking for a hallway that led to an oversized garage that could fit a limousine, when we finally discovered exactly what we were looking for. The hallways were long, like a hotel's, and the music from downstairs blared, making it easier to feel inconspicuous.

Finally, we turned a corner and my breath caught in the back of my throat when I saw the pictures on the wall. "Frankie. This is it! These are the same kinds of pictures that

Al and I saw at Club Cobalt. We're in the right place! This was where Jordan Lambert and Giselle were taken."

"Now we just have to find some hard evidence that we can take to Gibson," said Frankie.

"There's gotta be an underage girl around here or something," I said, opening doors and peeking inside.

"You wouldn't think he's got them down here during the party. That's too risky. Someone might see what's going on."

I shook my head. "Giselle said they came in off the garage and went into a room where they changed clothes, and then they were led to another nearby room that had a massage table in it, and that's where it happened. Those rooms have to be around here somewhere."

We opened several doors in the hallway but found nothing like Giselle had described. Finally, we came to a locked one. I wiggled the handle and then knocked, wondering if there was someone in there. I waited a few long moments with my ear pressed to the door. Finally, I stepped back. "No one's in there." I patted the top of my head. "Ugh, and of all times, I didn't bring my hat," I whispered to Frankie.

"You use a hat to open locked doors?"

I rolled my eyes. "You're funny. I've got bobby pins in the hat band."

Frankie reached around and pulled some pins out of her hair. "Funny, I keep my bobby pins in my hair, not in my hat." She handed them to me.

I beamed at her. "I could just kiss you."

"Oh, come on, Danny. Save something for the honeymoon."

With the pins between my teeth, I shook my head. "Don't tempt me, Frankie. I mean it." I bit down on the pins, bending them as Nico had taught me, and then squatted down and got right to work picking the lock while Frankie kept watch. It didn't take long for the lock to spring. Either the locks were getting easier, or I was getting better. I had to assume it was the latter.

"You ready?" she whispered.

Nodding, I held my breath. My heart raced. I pushed open the door to discover the room was empty, with the exception of a few chairs and a massage table. "Hah!" I said, pointing at the limited furniture. "Just as Giselle said it would be!"

Frankie frowned.

"Why are you frowning? This is exactly what we needed to see!"

"Danny, you said it yourself. We already knew this was where all the girls were taken. I mean, yeah, the extra proof is nice to have. But this still gives us nothing to go to Gibson with. We need solid evidence. *Proof* to hand to him."

I tossed my hands up. "Okay, well, we're in the right house to find proof. I say we keep looking. We'll find something. Come on."

We poked our heads into another couple of rooms on the first floor, discovering nothing, before we came to a set of stairs. Making sure that the coast was clear, we crept up them and then slid against the wall at the top of the stairs. I put a hand on the first doorknob I saw and turned it.

"It's locked," I whispered to Frankie before immediately squatting once again to spring it. "Come on."

We opened the door and slid inside, shutting out the blaring sound of the party's music behind us. Monitors hung on the wall with a single desk below them. A keyboard and a mouse sat on the desk. I gave the mouse a wiggle, and all the monitors fired up, showing screens from all around the house. It was obvious—Harvey had cameras everywhere in his house.

Frankie sucked in her breath. "I should've known. He's got us on video, Danny."

"We'll edit out parts of the video," I said with a nod. Then I pointed to one of the rooms on the monitor. "Frankie, look. It's the massage room downstairs."

Frankie nodded. "Yup." She reached back and grabbed my arm then. "Omigosh, Danny, the door's opening! Look, someone's going in there."

32

THE DOOR SWUNG OPEN, AND ARTIE BALLADARES OF ALL PEOPLE
was led inside. Trailing him were Harvey Markovitz and Kip
Dalton. Val was nowhere to be seen.

"Artie!" I breathed, my eyes springing open wide. "Fuck,
this can't be good." With my hand on my gun, which was
fitted in my appendix holster, I started to move towards the
door, but Frankie held my arm.

"You asked him to get the intel. Maybe that's what he's
doing. Give him a minute."

Though she was right, I couldn't help but worry about
Artie. I stared at the screen hard, ready to make a move if
anything went awry.

As I kept a close watch on Artie, Frankie scanned the rest of
the monitors. She pointed at one of them. "Danny, look. Look
at this one."

My eyes followed her finger to see a bedroom with two
girls of maybe fifteen or sixteen lying on a pair of twin beds,
talking. They were both wearing almost nothing, just a nightie
of some sort. "Two of his victims," she said, shaking her head.

"Fucking scumbags!" I couldn't believe what I was seeing.
My eyes darted back and forth between screens, watching

Artie and then the girls. "Frankie, we gotta get them out of here."

"First we need to see if there are any more." She pressed a key, and the screen with the two girls disappeared and another set of bedrooms popped up. Several of them were empty, but two of them had girls in them. She was just about to switch to another set of cameras when I noticed the door opening at the bottom of the screen.

"Wait! Look!"

A man entered the room. He said something to the girl and she looked up at him. Without volume, we couldn't tell what they were talking about, but he nodded towards the door, and the girl got up and followed him out into the hallway.

"I've got a really bad feeling about that," I said, staring at Artie's room on the screen.

It didn't take long before, sure enough, Artie's room opened and the girl was deposited inside. Harvey and Kip left the room.

I rubbed the pads of my fingers on my forehead. "Oh fuck."

Frankie sighed. "This is bad."

I put my eyes back on the camera again. "Artie isn't going to do anything inappropriate, but he's not going to be happy to have been put in that position. We gotta get him out of there."

"Artie's not an idiot, Danny. He can handle himself. Right now we need to erase ourselves from the security footage, and then we need to see what else is on this computer. I have a feeling this is the proof we need to show Gibson about the operation that's going on over here." She clicked through to the computer's hard drive. Within seconds, we were both staring at a treasure trove of evidence. They were hundreds of saved video recordings. Several of the video files were named with the last names of business owners, followed by dates. Ayala. James. Dillon. On and on the files went. There were names on the list that I'd never heard of before.

"Open one," I said. Though I was fairly confident I knew what would be on the video, I had to know that it was what I thought it was.

Frankie double-clicked the first file in the list. Ayala. It began just as it had gone with Artie. Joseph Ayala was led into the massage room to a waiting girl. When the girl began to undress completely, I couldn't watch any longer. Just knowing what was happening made my stomach turn. "Shut it off, Frankie."

And just like that, we'd found what we'd come for. All the proof we needed to take to Gibson.

"Holy shit," I breathed. I couldn't help but feel disgusted.

Frankie's head shook slowly as she scrolled through the list of files. "Look at this, Danny. File after file of Paradise businessmen. This is huge. It's sickening."

I nodded. "And some of them have multiple recordings."

She stood up straight and stuck her hand in her pocket, pulling out a thumb drive. She stuck it in the computer's USB port.

I stared at her. "You brought a flash drive with you?"

As she clicked through on the computer system, she nodded. "You should know me by now. I always come prepared. What kind of evidence did you think we'd find? Used condoms?"

I made a face. "Eww. No. I guess I... I wasn't really thinking about it."

Pressing another key, she stood upright. "You gotta always be two steps ahead of the bad guy, Danny. Especially when you're the underdogs, like we are." She pointed at the computer. "I'm copying the hard drive. Then I'll delete any traces of us being here."

"Frankie, that's gonna take forever. Harvey and Kip—those guys could come in here any second."

She shrugged. "We don't have a choice. We need the evidence."

"But we have to get those girls out too."

"Then you go get them out. I'll wait until these files finish downloading."

I shook my head. "No way, Frankie. I'm not leaving you alone in here. If Harvey comes in here, things could get bad for you."

Frankie patted the gun she wore behind her apron. "Don't worry about me. I can handle myself with Harvey. You just find the girls."

I shook my head staunchly. "I'm serious. I'm not going anywhere without you."

We both looked at the screen. The files were downloading, but there was still a ways to go. "I'll be okay. By the time you find the girls and get them out of their rooms, the files will be done. Now go. We don't have much time." She went to the door and held it open for me. "Hurry."

Feeling conflicted, I stepped out into the hallway, and the door promptly shut behind me. I could only hope I'd find the girls in the video footage. With the music still blaring downstairs, I raced down the hallway, opening every door I came into contact with and sticking my head inside the rooms. I'd gone about half of the length of the hallway when I found my first locked room. I gave a little knock on it. When no one answered, I squatted, preparing to pick the lock. But it opened before I could even get the pins out of my pocket. A young girl with blond hair wearing a white teddy opened the door. My eyes widened.

She stared back at me, confusion shining in her blue eyes. "Who are you?"

"I'm here to help you," I whispered.

"Help me? Help me do what? Are you a cop?"

"Well, I'm like a security officer."

She wrinkled her nose. "You mean like a mall cop?"

"No, not like a mall cop."

A girl's voice behind her hollered, "Who is it, Becca?"

"I don't know," she said over her shoulder. "Some mall cop."

"I told you, I'm not a mall cop."

The second girl came to the door, wearing a similarly revealing outfit. She looked to be almost the same age but had a darker skin tone and brown hair. "Who are you?"

"Look, I don't have time for a lot of questions. My name is Danny, and I'm here to get you out of here. Are you being held here against your will?"

The blond girl looked unimpressed. She shrugged. "Not really. They pay really well."

"Speak for yourself," said the darker-haired girl, pushing her out of the way. "I told them I wanted to go back to my family and they told me that I couldn't go yet. Not until I'd proven my loyalty to them."

"Look, I can get you out of here. I have a vehicle out back by the kitchen. Come with me?"

The girl looked down at her dress. "I can't go dressed like this," she said. "Harvey's having a party tonight."

"Fine. You have one minute to put something else on while I go look for the rest of the girls. Now go!" She disappeared back inside the room. I looked at the blond. "How many of you are there?"

"Right now? Four."

"Okay, your name is Becca, right?" I asked. "What are the names of the other girls?"

"She's Kayla, and the other two are April and Sonia."

"Was Jordan Lambert ever here?"

Becca looked down at her feet. "She was."

"Do you know what happened to her?"

She wouldn't respond or make eye contact with me.

"Becca, please. Do you know what happened to her?"

When she finally looked up at me, her eyes were glossy.

"They said she went home, but I don't know what really happened."

"What do you mean you don't know?"

"She kept begging to go home, and they always told her no. Just like Kayla said. They don't want us to leave. They're scared we're gonna talk to the cops about what goes on over here."

"Which is exactly why I need you to come with me. I hate to break this to you, Becca, but Jordan never made it home. They found her body floating in a bay."

Becca's mouth fell open. "Floating in a—you mean like dead?"

"They said it was suicide or an accident, but I don't believe it," I said.

She shook her head in disbelief. "Yeah, I don't think Jordan would kill herself."

"I think they killed her, Becca. These are dangerous people. They could kill you too. You have to come with me."

Kayla showed up then, dressed in shorts and a tank top and Converse sneakers and carrying a duffle bag over her shoulder. "I'm ready."

"Becca. Come with us. Please?" I begged, shooting a backwards glance down the hallway.

"Yeah, come on, Bec. You don't wanna stay here either."

"But they said they'd find me if I left before they said I could. I've been here long enough, they said pretty soon I'll get to start doing some modeling."

I sighed. "There just luring you with that. There isn't some big modeling contract at the end of all of this." I looked backwards down the hallway again. "Now, come on. We don't have time to talk about all this right now. Someone could come up here any second. We have to go."

"We have to get April and Sonia too," said Kayla.

"One of them is downstairs in the massage room," I said. "I saw her on the surveillance video."

"That's probably Sonia. She's new. They usually put the new girls down there."

"Okay, you go get April. I'll get Sonia," I said. "I have a van parked back by the kitchen. Can you all meet me down there?"

Kayla nodded. "I think I can sneak down there without anyone seeing me."

"Okay. Becca, I really hope you'll be down there when I get there." I wished I could throw her over my shoulder and force her to come with me, but I was afraid she might make a scene and ruin the mission for everyone. I turned to leave the girls to hash it out and went straight to the surveillance room. I gave two knocks on the door. "Frankie, it's me. Lemme in."

The door cracked open and Frankie peered out.

"Is it done?"

She rushed back to the computer. "In a few seconds. Did you find the girls?"

"Two of them. They're gonna get the other girl upstairs. I gotta get the one with Artie. They're gonna meet us out back by the van."

"Okay, one more sec..." Frankie watched as the download strip went to one hundred percent. "There. Done." She pulled the USB out of the computer and stuck it in her pocket. Then she went to the security system's software and erased the last two hours of footage and stopped all the cameras from recording anymore. Smiling, she stood up straight. "We were never here. Now, let's go."

We rushed for the hallway. The girls were nowhere to be seen. The coast looked clear, so we raced down the stairs and back down the hallway towards Artie's room. No sooner had I knocked on the door than I heard someone behind us. Frankie and I turned around to see a couple security guards standing behind us.

"You two can't be back here," one of them said.

"Oh, I'm, uh, looking for the bathroom," I said to the guard.

"The staff bathrooms are off the kitchen."

"Oh, yeah, I know." I shot him a wink. "Her and I were looking for something a little more, uh, *private* if you catch my drift." With my heart racing wildly, I waggled my eyebrows at him.

The guard was just about to say something when the door behind us opened. Artie stuck his head out into the hallway, took one look at Frankie and me, and furrowed his brows. "Drunk, what are you doing over here?"

I closed my eyes.

Fuck.

"You know this man?" asked the guard.

Artie's eyes widened when he realized there were two guards behind us. "This guy? Oh, uh, no?"

But it was too late. The guards didn't buy it for a second. The bigger of the two of them grabbed me the back of the shirt. "You're coming with us."

I glanced over at Frankie. This was not going to be good.

33

"I FOUND 'EM SNEAKING INTO THE NEW RECRUIT ROOM," SAID THE guard, who'd manhandled me all the way back up the corridors before passing me off to Harvey Markovitz just inside the front door of his mansion's grand foyer.

Harvey put his drink down on a side table and looked Frankie and me up and down. "Who the hell are you?"

"Look, this is all just a big mistake," said Frankie. "We're on the catering team."

"Yeah. We were just looking for a private room to use, if you catch what I'm throwing," I said, shooting a glance over his shoulder at Val, who'd just poked her head out into the foyer. And then, just as quickly as she'd appeared, she disappeared, leaving us alone with Markovitz and his goons once again.

The guard behind me shook his head. "I don't believe him," he said, his voice incredibly deep. "They were trying to get into the new recruit room. Your guest in there seemed to know him. He called him Drunk."

Recognition brightened Harvey's eyes. His head tipped sideways as he moved closer to look me dead in the eye. "So *you're* this Drunk character that I've been hearing about?"

"My reputation proceeds me?" I grinned at him.

"You're the one that's been going around the island harassing my friends."

"Huh," I said, pretending to think. "Tell me who your friends are, and I'll tell you if I've harassed them."

"Danny," whispered Francesca. "Now's not the time."

"I'd have to agree with your girlfriend here." He walked over to Frankie and rubbed his hand down the length of her cheek. "And what's your name, dollface?"

Heat from somewhere deep inside me boiled the blood in my veins. "Her name is take your fucking filthy hand off of her or I'll break it," I snarled, taking a step towards the disgusting excuse for a human being. But before I could get close enough to make a move, one of his guards grabbed me in a double chicken wing and they wrenched my wrist in up between my shoulder blades, forcing a wince out of me.

Harvey laughed. "Oh, is that right? You really think you can tell me what to do in *my* house at *my* party?"

"I'm shutting your party down. I know what you're doing."

He chuckled. "Oh, really now. And just what exactly am I doing?"

"You know damn good and well. You're running a sex trafficking ring, and it ends tonight. You're disgusting."

"Sex trafficking? I have no idea what you're talking about."

"You know exactly what I'm talking about. And I'm bringing you down, Markovitz."

"Is that right?"

"It is."

He shrugged. "I'm sorry to burst your delusional bubble, Mr. Drunk, but it's going to be kind of hard bringing me down when you're dead." He chuckled and then gave a little nod to his crew. "Take them outside, fellas. Make 'em disappear. Now, if you'll excuse me, I have guests waiting for me."

"You heard him, let's go," grunted the guard who still had

ahold of my arms. He kneed me in the back, forcing me out the front door behind Frankie and her guard.

My mind raced as we were shoved towards the door. But with both my arms in an armlock, I couldn't get a hand on my weapon, and the guard holding Frankie had her in the same hold. It was beginning to look hopeless.

We'd no sooner walked out onto the sidewalk in front of Markovitz's house than from out of nowhere, the sound of tires screeching tore apart the air. Turning towards the sound, I saw a white van barreling towards us. I was relieved that it was none other than my better half, Al Becker, behind the wheel!

Hallelujah!

The van flew right at us. The guards simultaneously released us and shoved off as they tried to get out of the way. Al jerked the wheel, just narrowly missing Frankie and me, but slamming directly into them and catapulting them through the air. They landed with a thud just in front of the shrubbery and rolled lifelessly to the pavement just as Al brought the van to a screeching halt.

"Woohoo! That'll leave a mark!" Al hollered through the open window. "Get in the van!"

"Come on, Frankie!" I screamed, jumping into the van. Breathless, I turned to Al. "What happened to 'don't be a hero,' eh, Al?"

"Did I say that?" He shook his head. "My memory ain't what it used to be."

Just as Frankie got in, Al started to pull away. But shouts coming from the front door made him slow down. I glanced out my window to see Artie and Val waving us down.

"It's Artie!"

Al slammed on the brakes, causing my head to lurch forward and nearly hit the glass. He threw the vehicle into reverse and snaked backwards out of control, almost hitting Artie and Val. He slammed on the brakes again.

"Fuck, Al. Watch the brakes!"

"Sorry."

I stuck my head out the window. "Get in the back!"

Artie waddled as fast as he could towards the back of the vehicle. Frankie jumped over the seat to open the door for them from the inside. That was when I noticed the two girls huddled in the back of the van together. It was Kayla and April.

"Where's Becca?" I hollered as Frankie helped Artie and Val in.

"She wouldn't come with us," cried Kayla, cradling a sobbing April in her arms.

I didn't have time to dwell on the fact that we'd left two girls behind as a second later, Frankie was hollering.

"All in! Go, go, go!"

"Step on the gas, Al!" I hollered, my adrenaline racing. The two guards Al had hit had just begun to stagger to their feet when the van moved again. We'd just rounded the top of the circle driveway when shots rang out, peppering the side of the van. As we came back around the driveway to head in the other direction, I leaned over Al's lap and returned fire, making one of the guards double over.

"I got one!" I hollered. "Go, go, go!"

Al tore down the driveway. The guard at the guard shack tried to stop us from exiting, but Al gunned the engine, forcing the guard to either become roadkill or jump out of the way. He chose the latter, landing in a thorny bush on the side of the road.

"Go, Al, go!" cheered Val from the back of the van.

My heart raced as I watched the rearview mirror, waiting to see if anyone was going to give chase. But after several long seconds of watching, it looked like we were in the clear. I sat back in my seat and let out the breath I'd been holding. "Thanks, Al, that was a close one!"

"You can thank the girls. They saw you get hauled out to the front door."

I looked over my shoulder at the girls. "Thanks, girls."

Val frowned. "Drunk, that man that you pay me to sing for the other day?"

"Dalton?"

She nodded. "He recognize me tonight," she said, her eyes wide. "I *theenk* he figure it out that his friend did not send me. I hear them talking about it while Artie was gone."

I smiled. "Well, then it was a good thing Al came when he did." I looked back at the girls. "Are you two alright?"

They both nodded. April was still crying on Kayla's shoulder.

"What about Sonia and Becca?" asked Kayla.

"We've got the evidence we need now. We'll get the cops and go back there and get them. I promise."

Their heads bounced. I looked at Artie. "You alright, Artie?"

Sitting on the floor in the back of the van, he lifted a shoulder. "I'll be honest, this was not how I expected this evening to go, Drunk."

"Yeah, I know, Artie. I'm really sorry about that."

"And you got another vehicle shot up."

I sighed. Frankie's brothers weren't going to like that one little bit, but I'd worry about that another day. "Yeah, it is what it is. Nothing I can do about it now."

He scrubbed his face with his hands. "Ugh. All I want right now is to get back to my place and get out of this penguin suit and relax."

Frankie's eyes met mine. She shook her head.

Wincing, I sucked air through my gritted teeth. "Yeah. About that—look, I hate to tell you this, Artie, but there's no way we can take you back to the resort now. Not yet, anyway. Not until we get these guys behind bars, because now they know where you live and work. They might realize what you were up to and come try and kill you."

Val's eyes grew large. "Omigosh," she whispered. "They are going to kill me too?"

"You're not safe, either, Val. We'll have to find a place to store the four of you until we can get this whole thing resolved."

"You mean we can't go home?" asked Kayla, her eyes wide.

"Sorry, girls," said Frankie. "Not yet. You're witnesses. You can't go home until we get Harvey and his guys behind bars. But don't worry. We have enough on him and his operation to put him away for a very long time."

"So then where are we supposed to go?"

"We'll go to another resort," said Artie. "I have a lot of friends in the industry. They'll put us up." He pulled his cell phone out of his suit's breast pocket. "I just need to make a few calls."

"Me too?" purred Val, snuggling close to Artie.

Artie nodded, his cheeks flushed. "Absolutely. I got you, Val. No worries."

She latched onto his arm. "Oooh, Artie, you make me feel so safe."

Letting out a little guttural sound, I turned back around and slumped back against my seat. I looked over at Al. "I suddenly feel less special now."

Al leaned over and said out of the side of his mouth, "Be thankful, kid. I have a feeling that was the most expensive buck twenty-five you ever lost."

34

AFTER GETTING KAYLA AND APRIL TUCKED INTO THEIR ROOM WITH strict instructions not to leave, call, or talk to anyone until further notice, the five of us piled into the penthouse suite that Artie had procured from a fellow resort owner friend of his.

The penthouse suite at the Marimont Resort blew the cottages at the Seacoast Majestic out of the water. Everything was brand-new and luxury, from the generously sized kitchen's marble waterfall island and stainless-steel appliances to the six-person jetted hot tub on the balcony overlooking the ocean. The living room had an L-shaped grey leather sofa in front of a large flat-screen TV mounted to the wall above a built-in fireplace. There was a full-sized dining room table with eight lavishly upholstered chairs, and the suite had two bedrooms, each with its own king-sized bed and attached private bathroom.

"Oooh, this place is sooo niiiice," purred Val, cozying up to Artie's side after running from room to room to check the place out.

Artie tossed the room key down on the side table by the door. "Val, I'm afraid you're stuck here with me until Drunk,

Al, and Officer Cruz can get everything sorted out. So make yourself at home. Take your pick of the bedrooms."

Val clung to his arm. "I don't care. Which one do you want?"

He pointed at the one nearest the door. "I guess I'll take that one, then."

"Okay, then I'll take that one too." Running a hand around Artie's wide waistline, she let out a husky laugh, causing Artie's cheeks to flame a brighter red than usual. The smile on his face told me everything I needed to know.

The second we left, Artie was getting lucky.

Frankie rolled her eyes. "Before we get out of here and leave you two alone, Artie, can we do a little debriefing? Go over what went down at the party?"

I walked over to the dining table and took a seat. "Yeah, Artie. Let's get the scoop."

Val pointed at the bathroom. "Do you mind if I take a bath?"

"No, not at all," said Artie.

"Thank you," said Val, heading for the bedroom. A second later, she was back in the main room. She plucked a bottle of champagne out of the ice bucket it was chilling in and walked over to Artie. Caressing the side of his face with her hand, she leaned over to whisper in his ear loud enough that we could all hear. "Oh, Artie, feel free to join me when you are done with your meeting," she sang.

Glancing back and forth between Al and me, Artie cleared his throat uncomfortably. "Oh, uh, thank you for the offer."

When Val disappeared back in the bedroom, I reached over and slugged Artie in the shoulder. "She wants you, man."

Frankie rolled her eyes. "She wants *something* alright." She let out a little disgusted puff of air.

Wagging a finger at his buddy, Al nodded in agreement. "Francesca's right. You better be careful, Artie. A woman like that is out for only one thing. And it's in your wallet."

I nodded. "Al's got a point. You got a condom in there, right?"

Exhaling a deep breath of air, Artie shook his head and then looked up at us. "Listen, gentlemen, how about we talk about business here and leave my sex life to *my* imagination, not yours?" His voice was more confident once again, as if with Val out of the room, he could resume his usual commanding presence.

I chuckled. "Okay, Artie. Let's get down to business. What did Harvey have to say?"

Artie sucked in a deep breath as his eyes darted around the table. "Well, for starters, the second we walked in the door, one of his buddies recognized Val."

I glanced over at Al. He had to be talking about Dalton. "You know who it was?"

"I don't recall the guy's name, but Harvey introduced him as a club owner. That's why it really didn't surprise me that he recognized Val, since you'd met her at a club downtown."

"Yeah, that's Kip Dalton," I said assuredly. I grinned. "We were hoping he'd recognize her."

"Oh yeah, why's that?" asked Artie.

I smiled. "Let's just say Dalton's *vividly* aware of Val's career choice."

"And considering the kind of operation they've got going on over there, the kid thought we needed to establish you as kind of a playboy," added Al.

"In other words, we thought you needed a little street cred, Artie."

Frankie quirked a brow. "So you decided to give him street cred by hanging a prostitute on his arm?"

I nodded. "He was too squeaky-clean. We had to rough him up a little. They had to believe he'd be down for anything. Right?"

"I suppose," she relented.

Satisfied that Al and I had made our case, I looked over at Artie. "So. Then what happened?"

Artie blotted his face with his handkerchief. "Right from the get-go, they rolled out the red carpet for us, immediately plying us with food and booze. Lots and lots of booze. The second my glass was empty, they had someone out there bringing me another. I think Harvey wanted me loose."

I quirked a brow. "You don't seem very loose."

Artie chuckled. "He probably wasn't expecting someone of my stature. It takes a lot more than a few drinks to make *me* loose." Artie smiled. "But I'm a good actor."

"Okay, so he plied you with liquor. What else happened?"

"Well, like I said, they kept the drinks flowing. They introduced me around. I finally met Steve Dillon. Some guy with dreadlocks that owns a helicopter company. And that guy that knew Val. What was his name again? Dalton?"

I nodded. "Yeah, Dalton."

"Yeah, so at one point after I'd had quite a lot of drinks, Harvey and Dalton pulled me aside and asked if I'd be interested in joining a gentlemen's club."

Al looked surprised. "A gentlemen's club?"

Artie's head dipped. "They called it PGC. Paradise Gentlemen's Club. They said it was sort of like an island fraternity."

"Ahhh, PGC," I said, looking at Al and nodding. "I found a pair of engraved cufflinks in Vito D'Angelo's desk that said PGC, and in the picture Steve Dillon had in his office, we could tell a couple of the guys were wearing the same cufflinks."

With her hands clasped, Frankie leaned forward on the table. "So did they explain what this gentlemen's club was all about?"

"To some extent. He outlined the main perks, which were pretty impressive, to be honest." Artie looked kind of sheepish admitting it. "Private helicopter use. Private beach parties. Major discounts on just about anything I want on the island. Harvey said almost anything I need to grow my business. The members do whatever they can to help the other members. He said that PGC business owners have the most lucrative and well-known businesses on the island."

I frowned. "What do you have to do to be a member?"

Artie shrugged. "It wasn't really clear. He said that members of PGC all scratch each other's back. He said when the time came that they needed something from me, they'd let me know."

"He give you any more details?"

Artie shook his head. "Not really. He said I'd learn more about the perks once I decided whether or not I was interested in joining PGC and then after I'd been inducted."

I tipped my head. "Inducted? What's that about?"

"There were a lot of holes they didn't seem very interested in filling in. Instead of answers, they just kept insisting I relax and enjoy myself and not worry about the trivial details. They wanted me to have a great evening so I could see what kind of great parties they threw."

"So, did you give them any indication that you were interested in joining PGC?" asked Frankie.

Artie nodded. "Of course. I mean, that was the whole reason I was there, wasn't it? To infiltrate their circle. Find out everything I could."

I stared at Artie, wondering where this sudden bravery had come from. "You said you wanted to join?"

Artie frowned. "Isn't that what you wanted me to do?"

"No, yeah, of course it is. I'm just a little surprised, to be honest. But you did good, Artie. You got them to trust you." I patted him on the back.

Al nodded. "The kid's right. You did a great job, Artie. So was that it? Was that all that happened?"

My eyes darted over to look at Frankie.

Without moving her head, her eyes caught mine. She was thinking the same thing that I was. There was more to the story. We'd *seen* Artie go into that room.

Artie sucked in a deep breath and held it for a second. Then he pushed it all out in one giant breath. "No. I wish that was all." He glanced over at me, shaking his head. "This is the part I'd have liked to have had a little warning about."

I looked down at my hands. I felt bad for keeping him in the dark, but at Frankie's insistence, I'd agreed that we had no other choice. Everything had to look real. "Yeah, sorry, Artie. We thought if we told you what might happen, then your reaction wouldn't have been authentic. We were doing it to protect you."

Al looked between us. "What are you talking about?"

I sighed. "They took Artie to the room that Giselle and Jordan were taken to, Al."

"And they brought a girl in to see him," added Frankie.

Artie wrinkled his nose. "It was so uncomfortable. Her name was Sonia. She couldn't have been more than fifteen or sixteen."

"What did they say to you about it?" asked Frankie.

Artie lifted a shoulder. "Harvey said that they keep massage girls on staff, and that anytime I wanted to come over for that little 'perk,' I was welcome to." He shook his head. "And then he took me to the 'massage room,' as he called it. I was shocked when Sonia came in. I thought it was going to be like an adult woman, but it was this young sliver of a thing. I was shocked."

"Did they say anything to her?"

"No. She seemed to know what she was supposed to do. Harvey said I could ask for anything. And by the way he said *anything*, it was obvious he wasn't referring to my choice of aromatherapy oils."

Frankie sighed. "Yeah. That's what I assumed. That's how they're running this whole thing. They catch prominent businessmen on camera doing inappropriate things to underage girls, and then they blackmail them into doing their bidding.

Once you're in the PGC, you're not getting out. They've got hours upon hours of footage on their computer."

Wincing, Al shook his head. "You didn't do anything you'd be ashamed of getting out, did you Artie?"

Artie shuddered as if the memory of being back in that room haunted him. "I didn't know *what* to do. I felt obliged to play along so they wouldn't think anything was suspicious."

"Artie!" breathed Al.

Artie's hands splayed open on the table in front of him again. "What?!" he said with a shrug. "What was I supposed to do? I blame you three. You could have told me what to expect. I didn't know what to do, so once Harvey left us alone, I lied and told the girl I had psoriasis and I refused to take my shirt off. In the end we spent the time talking about her needing a full-time job because she was living on her own after her mom died of a drug overdose. I felt bad for the girl, so I told her she could come work for me at the resort if she didn't like what she was doing for Harvey."

Frankie reached across the table and patted Artie's hands. "Thank you, Artie. You did a great job tonight. You found out what we needed to know, and you distracted all of them so we could get the evidence we needed to show Gibson." Frankie pulled out the flash drive.

"You found proof of what he's doing over there?" asked Artie, his eyes wide with hope.

Frankie nodded. "We did. And with your testimony and the testimony of the girls we saved, I think we've got more than enough to put Harvey Markovitz and all of his PGC pals away for a very long time." She put her hands on the table and pushed herself up. "We better get going. We need to get this over to Sergeant Gibson before something happens to those girls."

"Yeah, I agree." I nodded. "It's time to shut this operation down. But before we do, don't you think it would be a good idea if we went over that USB drive with a fine-tooth comb, so we could show Gibson a list of who's all in PGC?"

"I mean, yeah, that would be nice, but our backs are up against a wall here. Sonia and Becca are still over there. Who knows what those monsters are going to do to them if we don't get a team in there immediately and get them out of there?"

Al nodded. "I think you're both right. Look. How about this? I think we need to divide and conquer. First of all, I need to go home. I can't leave Evie all alone at the cottage. Just in case they're able to figure out who drove the getaway vehicle—"

"Al, they aren't—"

Al held up a hand. "You don't know what they know, kid. Now listen. Before you go get the troops rounded up to save those girls, drop me off and I'll have Big Eddie make a quick copy of the flash drive. I'll have him and Ralph go over it and make a list for you. That way you've got the initial information you can give to the police. Once he's compiled a list of the members of PGC, I'll have him go over it a little more thoroughly and see what else we can find that might be of help. Alright? This way you don't get slowed down."

I nodded. "Yeah. That's sounds like a great idea, Al. What do you think, Frankie?"

Frankie nodded. "Fine. That'll work. I just want to get those other two girls out of there before something bad happens to them."

Al nodded. "We all do." He stood up. "Now come on. We've got work to do."

35

AFTER HAVING BIG EDDIE MAKE US A COPY OF THE USB DRIVE TO give to Sergeant Gibson, we dropped Al off at his place, and then Frankie and I headed over to the King's Bay Marina to drop off her brothers' van. I had a niggling feeling of regret about the bullet holes that Markovitz's goons had strewn across the side of the vehicle. It didn't compare, though, to the feeling I had about getting their boat blown to bits. At least this time, I felt like I had partial ownership of the van. So hopefully they couldn't get *too* butt-hurt about the condition I'd returned it in.

After parking the van, Frankie and I each got back into our personal vehicles and drove separately over to the police station, where Sergeant Gibson had agreed to meet with us. I was excited to share the information we had, not only so that we could bring down Harvey Markovitz's whole loathsome operation and relieve the stress from *my* shoulders, but also because I looked forward to showing Sergeant Gibson once again that I wasn't the menace to society that he liked to make me out to be.

"You ready?" I asked Frankie when we were reunited and

standing in the darkness on the sidewalk in front of the building.

She raised her brows and let out a breath. "Ready as ever."

I took her hand and gave it a squeeze. "You know, if Gibson doesn't give you the respect you deserve after making a bust like this, I think you really need to start looking at getting a different job."

She gave me a tight, sad little smile. "Law enforcement is all I know, Danny."

"Yeah, but you don't deserve to be relegated to being Gibson's secretary. You're a great cop, Frankie. If he doesn't see it after all this, he's an idiot."

"Thanks, Danny. You're a great cop too."

"Oh no." I chuckled, swiping my hands in the air as we crossed the street. "No, no, no. I'm not a cop. And I gotta say, I like it so much better this way."

She laughed too. "To each their own." She led us inside the building and straight to Gibson's office. When Frankie had called him, he'd already been home in bed, but when she told him we had an emergency situation on our hands, he'd agreed to come in and meet us despite the late hour.

"This had better be good, Cruz," said Sergeant Gibson the second we walked in the door.

Frankie nodded and cast a furtive glance towards me. "Oh, it is. It's big, boss. Really, really big." Taking a seat at the chair in front of his desk, she looked up at him again.

"And what are you doing here, *Officer* Drunk?"

What an asshole. I closed my eyes and silently prayed for patience. I opened them and thrust my hand towards him. "I'm fine, thanks, Gibby. How you doin'?"

Frankie rubbed the back of her neck. "Danny—" she whisper-hissed.

"What? I'm just greeting the sarge, Frankie."

Sergeant Gibson seethed in my direction. I could tell he

didn't like being called Gibby anymore than I liked being called *Officer* Drunk. "Can we get on with this?" he growled.

"Yes, please." Frankie sighed. "Sergeant Gibson, earlier this week, Drunk was approached by a young woman he works with, a teenager by the name of Giselle Marrero. She said she thought her best friend, Jordan Lambert had gone missing."

Sergeant Gibson frowned. "Jordan Lambert—she's the girl the fisherman found along the Sandy Bay Beach?"

"Yes."

"I don't recall seeing a missing person's report for Jordan Lambert prior to her body being discovered," said Sergeant Gibson, frowning.

I raised a hand to cut into the conversation. "That would be on me. I didn't file a police report. Ms. Marrero asked me not to. She wanted help finding her friend, but she didn't want to advance it to becoming a police matter. So, I went to Frankie— err, *Officer Cruz,* and asked her if she could just do a little digging on her end."

Frankie shot me a look that said I probably didn't need to have shared that bit of information with her boss. "He just wanted to know if perhaps she'd been arrested. I was able to confirm that we had not arrested a Jordan Lambert." She took a deep breath and continued. "But then, as you know, several days later, her body was discovered."

Sergeant Gibson's head bobbed then.

"Her death prompted us to keep searching for answers regarding the truth about her death."

"The coroner's office ruled it an accidental drowning," said Sergeant Gibson.

Frankie looked surprised. "They did? I hadn't heard that."

He nodded. "The report came back earlier today."

"Well, we have evidence to suggest otherwise," I said. "We believe Jordan Lambert was murdered, and we think we know who might be responsible."

Sergeant Gibson's eyes widened. "You have proof?"

"We have proof of a sex trafficking ring that's going on on the island," I said. "We think the head of the operation had Jordan killed to keep her from talking."

He frowned and shook his head as if his ears were plugged and he'd had trouble hearing us. "I'm sorry. You have proof of what?!"

Frankie and I spent the next twenty minutes explaining in detail everything that we knew about Harvey Markovitz and his operation, including those associated with him that were known participants in PGC. When we were done, Sergeant Gibson sat back in his chair and steepled his fingers over his stomach.

"This is all quite a lot of information. How am I to believe such a far-fetched story? You say you have evidence, but you haven't shown me a single strand of it."

Frankie pulled the USB drive from her pocket. "We have proof. When we were at the party tonight, I made a copy of Markovitz's hard drive. He's got notable island business owners on video engaging in sexual relations with minors." She handed Sergeant Gibson the drive. "It's all right there. You can see for yourself."

Sergeant Gibson wasted no time in inserting the USB into his computer and opening the files. He double-clicked on the first file. Joseph Ayala. As Frankie and I had done, he watched the video until things became overtly sexual and then shut it off. "Are all of the videos on here the same?"

Frankie swallowed hard. "I believe so. I didn't open any more of the files. We were pressed for time and believed that Markovitz and his men might discover our presence in the surveillance room at any moment, so we simply made a copy of the hard drive and basically came straight here with it."

Sergeant Gibson nodded. "I see."

"Markovitz's men did try and kill us, though," I added. "When he finally discovered us, he did instruct his men to *handle* us."

"Handle you?"

"Kill us. They took us outside to kill us. Thankfully we were able to get away with a couple of the girls who they'd been holding."

"And where are they? I'd like to speak with them and hear in their words what happened."

"They're holed away somewhere safe," said Frankie. "We didn't want Markovitz's men coming for them. Once we've got Markovitz and his PGC pals behind bars, the girls will speak with you. But the priority right now is getting the other two girls out of there before those people there can hurt them."

Sergeant Gibson sat up straight. "No, no. I completely agree with that." He pressed a button on his phone and lifted the receiver. "Ames. Call Jones in. I want the two of you in my office in ten minutes. We've got a situation." He hung up the phone. "I must say, I'm impressed with the work that you did on this, Cruz." He nodded at Frankie.

Frankie smiled at him. "Thank you, Sergeant."

"You've done a lot of good work lately. You're really changing my mind about you."

His words seemed to make her sit up a little straighter in her seat. "Thank you very much. I appreciate that, sir."

He nodded and then looked at me. "And you've been a surprising asset too, Drunk. Maybe I was wrong about you."

I shot a glance at Frankie. Had I heard him correctly? Had he actually just paid me a *compliment*?! My head bobbed. "Well, it took you a while to come to that conclusion, but I accept your apology."

Sergeant Gibson's mouth opened to say something and then promptly snapped shut. He nodded. "Well. I've got Ames and Jones headed over here now. We'll assemble a team and come up with a plan and we'll go get those other two girls. Don't you worry about it."

Frankie smiled. "Can I be a part of the team that brings them in, Sergeant?"

He sat back in his seat and seemed to mull it over in his head. Then he nodded. "I tell you what. You've had a long night. Why don't you go home? Get some rest. Come in first thing in the morning, and I'll add you to the team."

Frankie's face brightened as she glanced over at me. "Are you serious?"

"Absolutely. Without your work, this case wouldn't even be on our radar."

Frankie's head bobbed. "Well, thank you, Sergeant. I promise, you will not regret that decision."

"I hope not. Now, I hope that I can count on the two of you to keep this whole situation between the three of us until we can get it resolved appropriately?"

"Yes, of course," said Frankie, nodding somberly.

I didn't really feel like sharing that we'd already involved Al, Artie, and Val. I was too tired. So, I pushed myself into a standing position.

"Oh, you've got nothing to worry about there. My lips are sealed. Now if you don't mind, since Frankie's going home, I think I will too. This has been a very stressful week, and I'm incredibly thankful to get this all off my shoulders and onto the professional's shoulders."

Sergeant Gibson stood up and offered me a handshake. "Absolutely, Drunk. You've done an outstanding job on this case, but you're right. I think it's best to let the professionals take it from here."

36

"I can't believe how easy it was to persuade Gibson to help," said Frankie as she crawled into her Suzuki Samurai only minutes after walking out of the station.

I slammed her door shut and leaned in through the window. "I'm a little shocked too. It was way easier than I expected. But I'm certainly not gonna complain. I am literally *beat*. Today—this week—it all wore me out. I'm gonna go home and sleep until next Tuesday."

Frankie smiled at me. "Well, you can't exactly go home. Markovitz and his guys could easily find you there."

"Yeah, I know. I think I'm gonna see if Artie'll let me sleep on his penthouse sofa."

"Seriously, Danny? You wanna get in the middle of Artie's alone time with Val?"

I leaned back and laughed. "Says *you*, the one who's so *not* a fan of Val?"

Frankie shrugged. "Artie's different."

"Different," I said with a puff of air. "How's he different?"

Frankie looked at me and then looked away. "I don't know. I guess I just didn't like her when she was flirting with *you*." She couldn't look me in the face then, but beneath the dim glow of the streetlamps above us, I thought I could see Frankie blushing.

Though she wasn't looking at me, I smiled. "Yeah," I said quietly. Still hanging on to the side of her car, I looked down at my feet. "Well, I suppose you're right. Artie needs his privacy tonight. I really don't want to go over to Al's. My vehicle's like a flashing neon light for the bad guys. I'll just bring them to his place, and that's the last thing I want."

Frankie turned to look at me then. "You could stay at my place tonight. We'll park your vehicle around back."

The blood in my body immediately began to run faster. "Your place, huh?"

She gave me a little smile. "I mean, you know—only if you want to."

Our eyes locked. "I suppose I might sleep better knowing you're safe and sound with me there," I said quietly. "You sure you don't mind?"

"No, I don't mind. I've got plenty of space."

My head bobbed gently. "Yeah, alright. Your place sounds good. I'll meet you over there."

"Okay. I'm gonna run through a drive-thru on my way," said Frankie. "I'm starved. You want something?"

"Yeah. Just get me two of whatever you're having."

"Okay. If you get there before me, I've got a key hidden in the fire extinguisher box between my door and the apartment door next to mine."

"Oh, that sounds totally safe," I said with a grin.

She laughed. "It is. Okay. I'll see you soon."

I stuck my head into her window then and brushed my lips against her cheekbone. With one hand cupping the side of her head, I moved my mouth to her ear.

"Don't be long, I'm starving," I whispered before pulling my head out of the vehicle. Our eyes met one last time before I turned around and strode across the parking lot to my vehicle.

I almost couldn't get to Frankie's house fast enough. When

AC/DC's "You Shook Me All Night Long" came on the radio, I cranked the volume. It started innocently enough with my thumbs drumming on the steering wheel, and the next thing I knew, my whole body was into it, jamming out behind the steering wheel. Whether it was the fact that Frankie and I had handed Jordan Lambert's killer to the cops on a silver platter or if it was the look in Frankie's eyes that had me floating on top of the world, I wasn't sure, but I was so busy testing out the springs in my Rubicon's driver's seat that I almost didn't notice the red-and-blue lights behind me.

When I finally did notice them, my first instinct was to glance down at my speedometer. I was going under the speed limit. My eyes flicked back and forth between my rearview mirror and my side mirrors. Was that Gibson again? Had he thought of additional questions he needed answered about Markovitz's operation? I assumed he could find my phone number if he didn't already have it, but I wasn't entirely sure.

I sighed. I really didn't want to have to stop and waste time dealing with more questions when I could be on my way to Frankie's place. I'd planned to use the couple of minutes before she got there to sort through her wax melt collection and find the perfect fragrance to set the mood for the evening. That and get reacquainted with Hugo, her Shetland-pony-sized Great Dane.

But now the red and blues were in my rearview, seemingly impatient that I'd yet to pull over.

"*Fuck*," I grumbled.

I put on my blinker and pulled to the side of the road, then sat back, watching my side mirror and waiting to see Sergeant Gibson's stocky form emerge. Instead, both sides of the car opened and two dark, shadowy figures got out. Neither of them were built anything like Sergeant Gibson. The one on the driver's side was slender, with narrow shoulders and a stiff gait. The one on the passenger's side was much larger in comparison. His thickness borderlined on obesity, and from the way the moonlight shone off his scalp, it looked as if he was bald.

I tipped my head to the side as I watched them stalk their way towards my vehicle with their hands resting on their weapons as if in quick-draw mode. A gnawing in the pit of my stomach told me that something about the situation wasn't right. If they were there simply to ask a few more questions about Jordan Lambert's case, why did they seem like they were being cautious about approaching my vehicle? I held my breath as I waited for them to get a little closer. In retrospect, I suppose I should've just pressed on the gas and made them eat my road raisins. But sitting there, watching them approach, I couldn't help but wonder what they wanted.

You know what they say.

Curiosity killed the cat.

It was when the fellow on the driver's side of the vehicle was just a half a step away from my door that I noticed the light of the moon reflect off a knife blade in his left hand. I realized the gnawing in my stomach was warranted and shit was about to hit the fan.

Adrenaline raced through my body. I shoved the door open just as he raised the knife and began to pivot towards my open window. The door swung in front of his body, slamming into his arm, sending the knife flying out of his hand and clattering out onto the darkened road.

I jumped out of my vehicle, and the man shot a weak left hook at my head. I ducked down and came back quickly, drilling a hybrid left hook/uppercut into his liver. I heard his breath leave his body in an involuntary groan just before he crumpled to the ground in a fetal position.

Slender man was going to need a minute.

I spun around to find that the other officer had come around the front of my vehicle. I drop-stepped towards him for a takedown just as a shot rang out in the darkness. It missed, but by its sound, I was sure it had come precariously close to hitting me. Burying my shoulder into the officer's stomach, I ran through him, driving him into the ground. We landed with a thud.

I grabbed his wrist and pinned it down with my knee, making it easier to wrench the gun from his hand. With one hand on his throat, my other hand aimed the gun at his head. "Who sent you, you fuck twat?" I hollered. "Markovitz?"

The cop held his free hand against the back of his head, making a face like it'd hurt when his skull had slammed into the concrete. "You were speeding, you asshole. Are you some kind of psychopath?" He lowered his hand to his side.

I tightened my grip on this throat and gave him a shake. "Bullshit. I wasn't even going the speed limit. Who sent you?" I shook him again. "Who sent you?"

"We—we—"

"Spit it out. Who sent you?"

He glanced behind me. Concerned that the other guy had managed to get to his feet and was creeping up on me, I cast a backwards glance over my shoulder to see that the driver was still locked in the fetal position. That was when I felt a sharp, stinging punch to the ribs. I dropped my elbow towards the pain. My fist involuntarily clenched, engaging my trigger finger and accidentally causing me to fire a shot into the night. The officer beneath me grabbed my wrist and shoved the gun away from him, and it went flying into the ditch.

As he rolled me off him, I felt an intense tingling, burning sensation in my side. That was when I realized I'd taken a knife to the ribs. Warmth oozed down my side.

Then he was on top of me.

He rained blow after blow down on me. I did my best to deflect the punches and swing from the bottom, but he landed a clean shot that drove my head into the concrete. Stars burst in my periphery and tunnel vision set in.

I took several more clean blows.

Two loud pops filled the air.

The man on top of me flinched. He hollered out something unintelligible, jumped off me, and disappeared.

When he was gone, I struggled to get up. My head throbbed, my limbs didn't seem to function properly, and I felt faint. I couldn't keep my eyes open. The lights faded out, and darkness settled around me like a heavy blanket lulling me to sleep.

37

BEEP BEEP BEEP BEEP...

Where in the hell is that noise coming from? I wondered with my eyes closed. *Did Earnestine learn to mimic a new sound?*

I smacked my mouth. It was so dry, like I was sucking on dried grass, or worse, one of those little wheat squares someone put in a box and called cereal. I gagged a little.

"Danny? Oh my God, you're awake!"

Was that Frankie's voice I heard? Had she stayed over at my place last night? Had I gotten lucky? Why didn't I remember getting lucky? My eyelids fluttered. A narrow sliver of light made it past my locked lashes.

Fuck!

I flinched. Why was it so bright in my bedroom?

"Danny? Can you hear me?"

"Frankie?" I mumbled. My words were slurred. We must've been drinking. My brain was foggy. I didn't remember sitting at a bar. In fact, I didn't remember drinking at all.

"Yeah, Danny, it's me. Oh, thank God, you're alright!"

I smacked my mouth again. "Need water," I whispered.

"Water. Yes. Coming up."

The next thing I knew, a straw was in my mouth. I gave it a

little tug, and cool refreshing water poured into my mouth. I took several long draws and then relaxed. My eyelids fluttered again as I tried to get my eyes to open. Finally, my lids parted and I saw Frankie staring down over me. Her eyes were full of something. Concern, maybe. Fear?

I looked around. I wasn't in my bedroom.

"Where am I?"

"You're in the hospital. You were attacked," she whispered. "They stabbed you."

"What? Stabbed?" The words jarred my memory into action, causing the events of the night to come flooding back. I'd been pulled over by a pair of cops. "They tried to kill me," I whispered.

"I know. I know. I saw them attacking you," she agreed. "I was on my way home and I saw your Jeep on the side of the road with a cop car behind it. So I got out to see what was going on, and I saw Jones on top of you. He stabbed you."

And then I remembered feeling a warm substance seeping out of my side. My hands slid across the bedsheets to the spot on my ribs where I'd felt the knife plunge in. My ribs felt tender, and I felt a thick layer of gauze covering the site. I looked up at Frankie. "Why'd he stab me?"

"I don't know. I have some ideas, but I don't want to say just yet. First I want to make sure you're okay. How do you feel?"

"Everything hurts," I whispered. "Head hurts."

"Yeah. You got pretty beat up. The doctor said you've got a concussion. I'll see if they can give you something for the pain."

"Stab wound?" I whispered.

"It was superficial," she said. "You were lucky. It was just a pocket knife; the blade glanced off a rib. You got a few stitches, but you're gonna be okay."

I looked up at Frankie. Her head was right in front of my face. The bright hospital lights shone behind her, casting a halo of light around her head, making her look like an angel. My angel. "You saved me."

"I did. I'm thankful I was passing by when I did. If I hadn't, you'd be dead."

"Where are they?"

"I don't know," said Frankie with a sigh. "I had a choice. I could chase after them, or I could save you. I chose to save you."

"Good choice," I whispered weakly.

"I thought so." She shot me one of her dimpled smiles.

And then the memory that I'd been rushing over to Frankie's house came back to me. I hated the fact that our evening had been interrupted. "When can I go home?"

"Tomorrow. They want to keep you overnight for observations. Because of the concussion."

"I think I'm okay to go home," I said, trying to sit up. The shooting pain in my head made me wince, and I stopped moving.

"No. You're staying here tonight. I'll stay here with you, though." She sighed. "Danny, I'm so sorry you're hurt. As soon as you're out of here, I'm going after those two."

"They did it on Gibson's command, didn't they?" I whispered knowingly.

Frankie leaned over me on my bed. "Maybe. I'll find out."

"They did," I whispered. I was sure of it. As sure as I was that Gibson was out to get me. I'd never felt good about the Paradise Isle Royal Police Force sergeant. He'd always rubbed me the wrong way. Whether it was because he didn't treat Frankie right or because he seemed to think I was a piece of shit based solely on the fact that I was an American, I wasn't sure. But I'd always had my suspicions about the man.

Always trust your gut, T. My old buddy Mikey had consistently imparted that nugget to me when I'd gone through the academy. I should've known. But truth be told, I think I *did* know. I'd just chosen to believe Gibson could change.

And then that picture of the PGC came to me in my foggy, hazed mind. Dillon, Ayala, Ziggy, Markovitz, Dalton, Vito, and that black man that had his back to the camera. My body went rigid and my breath caught in my throat. Had that been Gibson?

I heard a phone ringing then.

"I think that's your phone, Danny." Frankie got up and strode over to a plastic bag sitting on a counter in my room. She dug through the bag filled with my clothes to pull my phone out of my pants. She looked down at it. "It's Al."

"Have you spoken to him? Does he know what happened?" I asked, suddenly worried about my partner.

"No. I didn't have his number, and I didn't want to worry him until I knew more."

"Answer it."

Frankie nodded and put the phone on speaker. "Hi, Al. It's Francesca."

"Francesca? Put Drunk on the phone, I've got some big news."

"Danny's kind of tied up at the moment," she said, glancing over at me.

Once again I tried to pull myself into more of an upright position. My side burned and my head throbbed. Wincing, I fought through the severe discomfort and managed to pull myself into more of an upright position. Giving Frankie a flick of two fingers, I whispered, "Lemme talk to him."

"Okay. He's here. Hang on a second."

She handed me the phone. "Hey, Al," I croaked.

"Drunk? Whatsamatter? You sound like hell."

"Oh, well, I had a little run-in with Gibson's guys," I admitted.

"Gibson? Hey, kid, listen to me. Don't trust that Gibson character. He's in on all of this," said Al.

I ran a hand through my hair, letting it settle on top of my head. "Yeah. I sorta figured that out on my own."

"You alright?"

"I will be."

"Where are you?" asked Al.

"Just in town. I'm gonna stay over at Frankie's tonight," I lied. Al didn't need to worry about me.

"Look, kid. There's a lot I gotta tell you about what Big Eddie and Ralph found on that computer stick of yours."

"More than just Gibson being on Markovitz's payroll?"

"That's just it. Gibson isn't on Markovitz's payroll, because Markovitz isn't the one running the show."

Frankie looked down at my phone curiously. "So what are you saying? Gibson's the one in charge?"

"No. Gibson's being blackmailed just like the rest of them. Someone else is in charge."

"You're kidding? Who?"

"I'm not sure," said Al hesitantly.

"Well, then, how do you know?" I asked.

"That computer stick had some financial stuff on it too. Ralph said we needed to follow the money," explained Al. "So we did some digging, and we found out that PGC is being funded by someone, but it isn't Markovitz. Markovitz is being paid through PGC."

"Well, then, who's funding PGC?"

"Like I said, I don't know yet. I got Ralph and Eddie working on it."

"Alright, well, we're not going to be able to go after the boss until we know who the boss is," I said.

"I know. The guys and I are on it. I'll call you if we figure anything out."

"Hey, Al," I said, adjusting myself on my hospital bed to get a little more comfortable. "You and Evie probably ought to stay over at Gary's place tonight just to be on the safe side."

"Yeah, way ahead of you. Evie's staying with one of her girlfriends. I'll stay with Eddie or Ralph. Don't worry about me. You just keep yourself safe."

"Will do. Call me when you get new information."

"Count on it."

Al hung up before I could say goodbye. It was a habit I'd noticed about him—hanging up before a conversation was over. Maybe I was a little OCD, but I had to say goodbye to the empty airwaves. "Talk to you later, Al."

38

I WOKE UP SEVERAL HOURS LATER, FEELING A LITTLE MORE HUMAN than I had earlier. The throbbing headache I'd initially had when I'd first woken up in the hospital had reduced in intensity from an eleven to a three and was now only a slight dull ache behind my skull. The lights were off in my room, and the monitors behind me beeped steadily, reminding me to be thankful that I was alive. Frankie was asleep in a chair next to me. Her head was cranked back at an awkward angle and her mouth had fallen open. She still wore the white blouse and black dress pants we'd worn to the party at Harvey Markovitz's, but now her top buttons were all undone and her shirt was partially untucked.

I stared at her.

She looked so vulnerable like that. Possibly the most vulnerable I'd ever seen her. Usually Frankie was a kickass police chick. Fierce. Intelligent. Sweet. Adorable. And sexy. All the traits of a perfect woman, rolled into one gorgeously toned package. But now here she was, letting out the softest of snores. Her face was relaxed. One arm rested in her lap, and the other dangled off the side of the chair. A tiny bit of drool glistened near the side of her mouth, threatening to run down the side of her face.

For the first time since I'd met Francesca Cruz, she looked unabashedly human. And it made me appreciate her that much more.

"Hey, Frankie," I whisper-hissed in her direction.

Her mouth snapped shut, but her eyes didn't budge.

"Frankie," I said again. This time I leaned over and got a hand around the chair's wooden arm rest and pulled her towards me. The wood against the tile floor made a hoarse scratching rolled *r* sound, *trrrrrrr*.

Frankie's whole body flinched. Her eyes opened and she sat up in her chair, looking around. "Danny? What's the matter? Is everything okay?"

"No. You look uncomfortable." I scooted towards the outside edge of my twin-sized hospital bed. My stab wound smarted, but I refused to show it in my face. "Come lay with me. I've got plenty of room."

"Danny, I—"

"Lay with me." The words came out as a bit of a whine. Admittedly, I wasn't above whining.

She smiled. "Okay. Scooch over."

I slid over until my back rested up against the plastic railing on my bed. "That's all I've got to give."

Frankie crawled in bed next to me. She lay on her side and propped her bent arm underneath her head. "This okay?"

I smiled at her. Her white blouse had popped open slightly, revealing a tiny morsel of the white lace bra she wore beneath it. "Better than okay."

"How's your wound?"

"Can't even feel it. How are you feeling?"

Frankie's dark eyes stared back at me for a second before she shrugged. "Frustrated."

"Yeah? About Gibson?"

She let out a little sigh. "Yeah, Gibson. Gibson and the

whole police force. I've been working for them for years and have never gotten anywhere in my career there. For *years* I thought it was *me*. I thought it was because I was a woman. I thought it had something to do with me living in America for a while. I thought maybe I'd done something in my early days to piss the sergeant off. I just—" Looking down at the bed, she shook her head. Then she swallowed hard and looked up at me. Her eyes were glossy. "I doubted myself, Danny. Gibson and all the other guys like Jones and Ames made me doubt myself. And now to find out that the *reason* I never got anywhere *close* to making inspector was because Gibson and Jones and Ames and who knows who else were the bad guys? It's just—ugh." She rolled back a little and covered her face with her hand.

I gave her a tight smile. "Yeah, I get it. It feels like you've wasted all that time?"

"Well, yeah, that. But mostly they made me feel insecure about myself. I'm not an insecure person, Danny."

"Yeah, I know you're not. I've never seen you once act insecure."

"That's because *you* don't make me feel that way. With you I feel like an equal. But it's never been like that at the PIRPF. And now I find out it's all been a lie? It's just—I don't know— kind of overwhelming to be honest."

"And now we have to figure out how to bring Gibson and his cronies down."

"Oh, I know. Before I fell asleep, it's all I could think about. Who do you go to when the person you're supposed to go to is in on the corruption?"

I sighed. I felt exactly the same way. Where did we go from here? We were both quiet for several seconds, each of us lost in thought. Finally, I spoke. "You know, I have my own insecurities too."

"Yeah? Danny Drunk, the cockiest guy I know, is insecure? What could you possibly be insecure about?"

"Crazy, right?" I chuckled. The movement made me grunt a little as a shooting pain surged through my side.

She raised her head, her face filled with concern. "You okay?"

I nodded. "Yeah, I'm good." I shot her a smile. "You know, I don't know if I mentioned this to you or not, but my goal since Pam left the island has been to become a better person. To become the person everyone else seems to think I can be. To become decent and trustworthy."

"You mentioned you were working on those things," she said softly. "I think you're doing a good job."

I leaned backwards against the railing and covered my face with my free hand. "I don't. I feel—defeated. Like no matter what I do, I just can't win. I can't save everyone."

"You don't have to save everyone to be a good person, Danny."

"I feel like I do, because I have so much to make up for. Like the only way I'm going to prove myself is to be better than my best." I sighed. The pressure to be perfect tightened the invisible noose around my neck, making it difficult to breathe. I forced a deep breath of rigid air into my lungs. "And now Gibson's in on all this. The one guy we thought we'd be able to go to to take it from here, and he's working against us. Like what do we do now, Frankie?" I ground the pads of my fingers into my eyes.

Frankie reached a hand out and touched the side of my face.

Her soft touch caught me off guard. I moved my hand from my eyes and looked at her.

"This isn't all on you, Danny. I'm here too. We're doing this together," she said, her voice low. Her fingers trailed from the top of my cheekbone down to the stubble on my jaw.

When they got to my chin, I reached out and caught hold of them. I pulled her hand into my mouth and pressed my lips against the top of it. Her hand felt soft and cool against my lips.

"Thanks, Frankie," I whispered, letting go of her hand.

Our eyes locked and I suddenly wished that we weren't in a hospital bed, but rather alone in Frankie's apartment like we were supposed to be. My eyes moved to her lips. Craving the taste of them, my mouth watered. I stared at the plump pair long and hard, finding myself torn between wanting to devour her and being afraid that the pain meds I was on were clouding my judgment.

She sucked her bottom lip between her teeth and bit down gently.

Desire surged through my veins.

Ahh, fuck it.

In one fluid motion, I reached a hand out and snaked my fingers into her hair and around the back of her head, pulling her towards me. Our eyes closed in unison as my lips introduced themselves to hers for the very first time. She tasted sweet, like the strawberry Jell-O we'd had as a snack earlier.

Focusing my attention on her deliciously soft, pillowy lips, I stopped short of invading her mouth with my tongue. I wanted to take it slowly with Frankie; I wanted our first kiss to last forever, and at the same time, I wanted to give Frankie time to back out of it if that was what she wanted. But when I felt her hands in my hair, I knew this was where she wanted to be too.

And yet something seemed to be holding *me* back. "Frankie," I whispered.

Her eyelids fluttered open. "Yeah?" Her chest heaved up and down.

"Maybe this isn't the right thing for us?"

The fog cleared from her dark eyes right in front of me. She pulled back a little. "You don't want to kiss me?" Veiled hurt curled the edge of her question.

"No, no, Frankie. I've been dying to kiss you. I don't

wanna stop."

She smiled. "Well, then, why did you stop, dummy?"

I groaned. "Because I promised myself I wouldn't go after you until I felt worthy. I don't feel worthy yet."

"Danny, I'm not some goddess that you have to be perfect for. I'm just a woman. And you're just a man. We're both flawed."

Emotion that I didn't know was inside of me erupted. Tears burned the back of my eyes. "But I couldn't save her, Frankie," I whispered. "What kind of man am I that I couldn't save a sixteen-year-old girl?"

Frankie looked at me for a split second, and then before I knew what was happening, her arms were around my head. She scooted herself up and closer to me, so that my head was nestled between her arms, snug up against her breasts. She hugged my head tightly. "It's not your fault that Jordan died, Danny."

"But what if they killed her because I started looking for her? What if it was my fault?"

"You were trying to save her. You didn't know what was going on. You can't blame yourself. You not being able to save her doesn't make you a bad man, Danny. It doesn't make you unworthy."

"It doesn't make me a good man either," I whispered, wrapping my arms around Frankie.

"Chasing after the bad guys makes you a good man. A worthy man. We're going to make the men who did this to her pay. I promise you. We're going to take them all down. Every last one of them. And then you'll see. People *can* count on you." She patted my hair softly. "Then you'll *know* you're a good man, worthy of good things."

Whether it was the warmth of Frankie's embrace or the pain medicine I'd been given or the release of the emotions I'd held back, I felt my body shudder, and then slowly, I drifted off.

39

THE NEXT MORNING, FRANKIE AND I PULLED OUR VEHICLES UP TO my cottage at the Seacoast Majestic. My head still ached and I felt a little off-balance, but the medicine the doctors had me on kept the pain mostly at bay, so much so that I couldn't even feel the pain from my flesh wound. We'd gotten a few hours of sleep and by ten a.m. I'd been discharged. Frankie took me back to the scene of my attack to retrieve my vehicle, still parked along the side of the road. I was thankful I'd found it in one piece as I'd yet to find time to put any insurance on it. We'd come back to grab me a change of clothes and then to go find Al and see what new information he had for us.

As soon as she got out of her vehicle, Frankie rushed to my side and threw my arm over her shoulder so I could lean on her.

I chuckled. "I can walk just fine, Frankie."

"You look wobbly," she said, looking up at me.

"Oh, fine." I leaned my weight on her, not because I needed the help, but because she was cute and I just wanted to feel her close.

When we hit the top of the porch, I heard a screeching

voice come from the road behind us. Frankie and I both stopped walking and turned to look over our shoulders.

It was Mariposa Marrero, wailing at the top of her lungs as she ran down the path. "Where is she?!"

I tipped my head to the side curiously. "Hey, Mari. What's going on? Why are you yelling?"

She stopped at the bottom of my porch stairs and wagged a finger at me. "Where is she, Drunk? I know you have her here."

I frowned. "Have who here?"

"Giselle! I know she's here."

I tipped my head to the side. "Giselle? What are you talking about, Mari? Giselle's not here."

"Liar!" she hissed. She looked past me at my cottage. "Giselle! I know you're in there! Come out!"

"Mari. Giselle's not in there. I literally just got home."

Mari's face was set in a firm, angry line. Her face was crimson as she stuck her finger out towards me again. "I know you've been seeing my daughter behind my back!"

My heart thundered in my chest. I glanced over at Frankie uncomfortably. "Mari. I swear to you, I haven't been seeing Giselle."

But she ignored me and continued to rail. "You said I could trust you! But you haven't changed. Not one little bit!"

"Ms. Marrero," began Frankie, holding her hands out calmly. "I think you're mistaken. Danny was with me last night. He doesn't have your daughter. Honestly."

Mariposa sucked in her breath. "Bed hopping from one woman to the next. *Ay, Dios mío!* I knew that you hadn't changed! I told you!"

I let go of Frankie and slowly crept towards Mari, holding my hands up defensively. "Mari. I swear to you, I haven't been seeing Giselle. You have to believe me."

"I didn't want to believe it at first," she admitted, nodding. "But when she didn't come home last night, some of the rumors I'd been hearing around the resort came back to haunt me."

I looked at her in surprise. "Wait a minute, Giselle didn't come home last night?" Fear filled my limbs with lead and made me feel suddenly weak. We'd told Gibson that Giselle had been the one to open the giant can of worms up for investigation. What if they'd gone after her to shut her up?

"Several people saw you talking to her down at the swim-up bar this week," she continued. "And one of the cleaning girls said she saw Giselle sneaking into your cottage. I told her it couldn't be true, but she insisted. So I asked Giselle about it. She denied it, but now I know—you convinced her to lie to me, so I wouldn't know the truth!"

My head shook. "Mari, that's not what—"

"And then when she didn't come home last night and wouldn't return any of my calls or texts, I went online and looked at her cell phone usage. I saw that she'd been texting and receiving texts from a US number. So I looked up your number and sure enough, it was you!"

I palmed my forehead. "Mari, I swear to you. Yes, I texted Giselle, but it's not what you think. If you'll just let me ex—"

"But this, *this* was the final straw!" she hollered angrily. She pulled a red tank top from a plastic bag that hung on her arm and shook it in the air. "I went through her room last night and I found this!"

It was the tank top I'd slid over Giselle's head on the first night she'd come to my cottage to ask for my help finding Jordan.

"I've seen you wear this tank top, Drunk. I know it's yours, don't try and deny it! You're having an affair with my daughter! I'm going to have you arrested!"

Frankie stepped forward. "Ms. Marrero. Do you recognize me? I'm Officer Francesca Cruz. With the Paradise Isle Royal Police Force. Would you please allow me to say something?"

Mari's head rocked wildly from side to side. Tears streamed down her face. "I want this man arrested!"

"Please, Ms. Marrero, let me tell you what's going on."

Mariposa's chest heaved up and down from all the yelling and screaming and from running over to my cottage. "You're friends with him. You'll just lie to me too!"

"No, I won't. I promise. I'm going to tell you exactly what's going on. It's time you know the truth, because I think your daughter might be in serious danger."

Mariposa's face went white. Trembling, her hand went to her heart then. "My Giselle is in danger?"

"Yes, Mari," I said. "Please, just let Officer Cruz explain. Okay?"

But all the excitement was too much for Mari. Her knees buckled. Frankie and I rushed the bottom of the steps to scoop her up. We both got her by the elbow and caught her just before her head hit the ground.

"Let's get her inside, Danny," said Frankie. "It's too hot out here for her to be carrying on like this."

Together, we managed to get Mari inside and got her seated on my sofa. I went to the kitchen and plucked a bottle of water from it, took off the cap and rushed to Mari's side. "Drink this, Mari. You're overheated."

With shaking hands, Mari managed to hold the bottle and take a couple of long sips. Finally, she looked up at Frankie. "Tell me you know where my Giselle is. Please?"

"We'll find her," said Frankie. "But first I need you to believe me. Danny hasn't been taking advantage of your daughter. I swear to you. He's been trying to help her."

"Help her? Help her with what?"

"Your daughter got herself into some trouble and she didn't want you to know about it. So she went to Danny to ask for help."

Mari's eyes widened. She looked up at me in surprise. "What? She got herself into trouble and she went to *you*?!"

I held up my hands and shrugged. "Funcle Drunk, remember? I offered. She accepted. I honestly didn't think that would happen, Mari. I swear."

"W-why didn't she come to me?"

"She was scared to tell you what had happened."

Mari's hand went to her mouth. It shook as she looked at me. "*Ay, Dios mío!*" she gasped. "Does this have something to do with Jordan's passing?"

I glanced over at Frankie.

"She told you her friend passed away?" asked Frankie.

"Yes. In an accidental drowning at the beach. She's been in her room crying since it happened. But yesterday, I worked a late shift, and when I got home, she wasn't in her room."

I sighed. I hated having to break the news to Mari, but it had to be done for her to understand the direness of the situation. "It wasn't an accidental drowning, Mari," I said quietly. "We think someone killed Jordan."

Mari's head shook. "No. No. There's no way. Jordan was a sweet girl. Why would anyone want to kill her?"

"Sometimes bad things happen to good people," said Frankie quietly.

"But who? Who would want to kill her?"

"That's what Frankie and I have been working on." I held up my shirt and showed her the bandages along my side. "I just got released from the hospital, Mari. We think that the same group of people that killed Jordan tried to kill me last night. It's possible they got their hands on Giselle."

Mari's eyes widened to the side of quarters. "No! Giselle!" she whispered. She made the sign of the cross and began to pray in Spanish as tears streamed down her face.

Frankie went to the kitchen and got Mari a napkin. When she returned, she handed it to the woman. "Ms. Marrero, there's a lot to explain and I know you want to hear the whole story. You are *owed* the whole story. But right now, we need to find Giselle before something bad happens to her."

Mari blotted her tears. Her head bobbed up and down.

"Is there someone that I can call? Someone that can sit with you until we have news to share with you?" I asked.

"I'll go to the front office," she whispered. "The girls will take care of me."

I glanced over at Frankie. When she gave me a little head tilt, I nodded back. I sucked in a deep breath and gave Mari a tight smile. "Okay, Mari. Come on. We'll drop you off."

40

AFTER DROPPING MARI OFF WITH ALICIA AND ROXIE AT THE front desk, Frankie and I headed to the resort's main dining hall, where we had a meeting set up between us, Al, Big Eddie, and the Weaz. Having wisely chosen to skip the hospital's bland breakfast of cold, tasteless eggs and rubbery bacon, I was ready for a full-blown meal.

"You want something?" I asked Frankie as I went through the buffet line, filling my plate up with enough carbs to last me a week. If I was going to after the guys who took Giselle, I was going to need sustenance. I shoved a piece of bacon in my mouth. "I'm buying."

"This might be the first time I've seen you eating anything besides chocolate and soda for breakfast," she chuckled, grabbing the plate I offered her.

I chuckled. "Come on now, Frankie. It's Sunday. Sundays are for brunch. I save the chocolate and soda for dessert."

When we'd filled our plates, we made our way to the seating area. Al and the guys were seated out on the balcony. It was a warm morning, but the outdoor seating area had a roof and ceiling fans to provide a little air movement. The sea crashed against the rocks just below the balcony and gulls squawked over the water. Al waved Frankie and me over when we emerged with our food.

"There you are," said Al.

"Sorry, we're a little late. We were starving," I said, pulling a chair out for Frankie with my free hand.

Al eyed Frankie and me up and down. "Uh-huh. I bet you were."

I rolled my eyes at him. "Get your mind out of the gutter, old man."

"You two look like you didn't sleep a wink," said the Weaz, his smile wide.

"Thanks, Weaz. You know, those bags under your eyes are great, too. Are they Gucci?"

Frankie elbowed me in my good rib.

I sighed. "Frankie, let me introduce you to a couple of Al's buddies. This is Big Eddie, and this is Ralph, aka the Weaz."

"The Weaz, huh?"

The Weaz waved a hand in the air dismissively. "It's a nickname." He took her hand and kissed the top of it. "It's a pleasure to meet you, madame."

She shook his hand and grinned. "It's nice to meet you both, I'm Francesca Cruz."

"She's better looking than you said she was, Drunk," said Big Eddie, a devilish smile on his face.

I let my head fall forward, catching it with the palm of my hand. I felt like I was in high school again and my friends were doing their best to embarrass me in front of my crush.

Frankie elbowed me a little. I tipped my head slightly so I could see her out of the corner of my eye. She grinned at me. "You told them I was good looking?"

"Actually, I think the words he used were 'fucking hot,' his language, not mine," said the Weaz.

I sighed and then looked up at the table. "Can we get to the point here, fellas? Things got ratcheted up a notch since I set up this meeting."

Al looked at me curiously. "Ratcheted up a notch? What do you mean?"

"Mariposa just paid Frankie and me a visit at my cottage. She thought I was having a thing with Giselle."

Al's head bobbed. "I'm not surprised. Evie said she heard that from one of the girls that you and Giselle were"—he twiddled his fingers in the air—"you know. She asked me if it was true."

"Evie believed the rumor too?!" *Fuck!* Did *no one* on this island have faith in me that I wasn't a scumbag?

"Relax, kid. I said she *asked* me if it was true. I didn't say she *believed* the rumors."

"Well, I hope you set her straight."

"Of course I did."

"Ms. Marrero said that Giselle didn't come home last night," interjected Frankie, trying to keep us on topic.

Al's eyes widened. "What do you mean, she didn't come?"

Tension over Giselle being missing had my body wound tighter than fishing line on a new reel. "Just what she said, Al," I snapped. "Giselle didn't come home last night. Geez. Are the batteries in your hearing aids working?"

"Calm down, Danny." Frankie put a hand over mine. "We're gonna find her and bring her home."

"You think Markovitz's people got her?" asked Al.

"Pretty much. If I had to guess, I'd say that it was Gibson's guys, specifically. We told him last night that she was the one that tipped us off that Jordan was missing."

"Damn," breathed Al, clubbing his fist onto the table. "That's terrible."

"I know it is. We have to find her, Al. Tell me you figured out who's in charge of the whole operation. Tell me we have new leads."

Al looked over at Eddie and the Weaz. "Go ahead. Tell 'em what we know, fellas."

Eddie nodded at the Weaz.

"There's a whole lotta money coming in," explained the Weaz, nodding. "Far more than just for this whole sex trafficking operation. This is way bigger than that."

"Wayyy bigger," added Eddie, adjusting his glasses. "This is a multimillion-dollar operation. The sex trafficking thing was peanuts in comparison."

I shook my head. "Multimillion-dollar operation?" I glanced over at Frankie. She looked just as confused as I felt.

"Where are they getting millions from?" she asked.

"We traced the money back to the source, and you're not gonna believe what we found out," said the Weaz.

"Try us."

Ralph and Eddie exchanged a look and then both shot glances over at Al.

Al cleared his throat. "It's coming from the Paradise Isle government."

As if she'd just taken a blow to the stomach, Frankie sat back in her chair. "The government?! The government's in on this? I don't understand."

"I don't get it either," I added.

"Yeah, well, we're not quite sure what's going on either," said Al. "But that's where they traced the money back to. It's coming from a government account."

"So you think the government is intentionally funding this organization?" I asked.

Frankie furrowed her brows. "I can't imagine that they would. I mean, that doesn't make any sense. The government as a whole would *not* fund an organization such as PGC. I'm gonna go out on a limb and guess that someone within the government found a way to embezzle the money from general funds. Whoever it is is likely the one who's in charge of all of this."

"But who in the government would have access to *that* kind of money?" I asked.

"They'd have to be pretty high up on the food chain," said the Weaz, shrugging.

"And obviously if they're funding PGC, they'd be included in their own club," said Frankie. "So whoever this guy is has to be pals with Markovitz, Gibson, and all the rest of them."

That was when it hit me. I sucked in my breath. Leaning back in my chair, I covered my mouth with my hand. "Ohhh, fuckity-fuck-fuck-fuuuuck."

"What is it, Danny?"

"I think I know who it is."

Everyone stared at me.

"Well, come on, kid. Don't leave us hanging."

"Frankie, you remember that day that Al and I came to see you to ask about Jordan?"

"Before we knew she was dead?"

I nodded.

"Yeah. I remember."

"There was that guy who was in Gibson's office. The customs guy. What was his name?"

"Rupert Villanueva. He's the commissioner of customs."

I nodded. "Yeah, old Rupert. As commissioner of customs, you'd have to assume he's got access to the tariffs on all vehicles coming to the island."

Frankie nodded like she got it. "He sure would."

"You know, there was a spiffy vehicle out front that day. It was a tricked-out black Escalade. How much would you like to bet he got it at Steve Dillon's Automart?"

"You think he's skimming the vehicle tariffs off the top?" asked Al.

"I don't know. But we know he's friends with Gibson, and if he's got Steve Dillon in his pocket, then that idea is not totally off the table."

"Oh, man," said Frankie. "But how in the world do you go after a guy like Villanueva without the head of the police on your side?"

Al stabbed one gnarled finger into the table. "I think I know a way."

"But first we need to find out if that's really who's behind all this. I mean, I could be totally off base here."

Frankie shook her head. "No, I think you might be on to something."

"So what do you say? Should you and I pay the commish a visit."

"Absolutely. And if we find out that he's innocent, then at the very least, we'll let him know that Dillon's neglecting to charge his buddies the vehicle tariff. That alone is worth paying him a visit."

"Oh, absolutely," I agree. "I just wish we had an army backing us."

Al nodded. "Look, you two just work on figuring out if the commissioner is our guy. I'll work on getting you some help. Deal?"

I shoved a waffle in my mouth and held a hand out to Al. "Deal."

41

I took a quick guzzle of my Dr Pepper, then leaned back in my seat and patted my stomach. "I feel like a new man."

Frankie took her eyes off the road for a moment to look over at me and smile. "And that would be the pain meds talking. Which is exactly why I'm on this side of the vehicle and you're on that side."

Feeling the aftereffects of a large breakfast combined with relief from the pain meds, I'd allowed Frankie to drive us over to Rupert Villanueva's private residence in my Jeep. "Eh, I think it's a toss-up between the medicine, the big breakfast, and a hot shower."

Frankie nodded. She'd also changed out of her fake caterer's uniform and into her police uniform. "Yeah, I feel better too. But I'm really glad to hear that you're feeling better."

"Thanks to you," I said, reaching out to squeeze her hand. "Now, let's talk plans. We're heading over to Villanueva's place. Then what?"

She shrugged. "We'll see if he'll talk with us. I'm a pretty good judge of character. I think I'll be able to tell if he's involved just by asking him a few questions. And then we'll go from there. The number one goal is to find Giselle before something happens to her and bring her back safely."

Within minutes we'd pulled up to Commissioner Villanueva's private residence. Stopping at the gate, Frankie pressed the button.

The speaker crackled as it came to life. Latin music played in the background. *"Hola,"* said a woman's voice cheerfully.

Frankie leaned out the window and flashed her badge at the camera. *"Buenas tardes, señora. Estoy aquí para ver al Comisionado Villanueva."*

"Lo siento, el comisionado no está aquí. Él acaba de irse."

I frowned. My Spanish was rusty. I understood *lo siento* to mean *I'm sorry*, but that was all I got. "What's she saying?" I hissed.

Frankie held up a finger to shush me. *"Habla usted inglés?"*

"Oh, *sí,* yes."

Frankie nodded and whispered over at me. "He just left." Then she turned back to the speaker. "Ma'am, my name is Officer Cruz with the Paradise Isle Royal Police Force and I need to speak with the commissioner right away. Can you tell me where he went?"

"I'm sorry, but he didn't say where he was going."

"Is this Mrs. Villanueva?" asked Frankie.

"Oh no. Commissioner Villanueva is not married. This is Frida. I'm Commissioner Villanueva's housekeeper."

"I see. Frida, can you tell me if the commissioner had anyone with him when he left?"

"Mmm, not that I'm aware of."

"And he didn't give you any indication of where he might be going?"

"No. He only said he'd be gone for a while."

"A while? As in a few hours or a few days?"

"I didn't ask, but I think maybe a few days."

Frankie glanced back at me and then back at the speaker. "Why do you say that?"

"He left with a couple suitcases—tore the house apart doing it, too. I think he was in a hurry."

"Commissioner Villanueva took suitcases with him?" asked Frankie sharply.

"Yes, Officer."

Frankie let out a little sigh. "Okay. *Gracias.*"

"*De nada.*"

The speaker clicked and went silent. Frankie backed us out of the commissioner's driveway and put us back on the road.

I looked at her curiously. "Well, where to now?"

"He's got luggage. My guess is he's heading for the airport," said Frankie.

"You really think he'd fly out commercially, where his movements could be tracked? He's trying to get away before we can put the pieces together and nail his ass."

"You think maybe he chartered a boat?"

And then it hit me. I shook my head and pointed to the next turn. "Nah. Why would the commish charter a boat when he's got a private helicopter at his disposal? I know *exactly* where he's headed."

42

We pulled up to the Hidden Beaches Aerial Tours hangar, situated in a flattened basin at the bottom of a hill jutting out along the edge of the island's coastline. There we discovered a black Escalade parked out front beside a pair of police cruisers. About thirty or forty yards away from the building on the concrete pad sat a motionless helicopter. The lower half and underbelly of the helicopter were painted bright blue, with three green stripes splashed across the middle section and a white top. The doors had been removed from both sides, and from what I could see, the helicopter sat empty.

I let out a little puff of air. "Aaaand I was right." I pointed at the Steve Dillon Automart sticker on the back of the Escalade.

"Yup, you were." Frankie nodded towards the squad car in the middle. "And that one's Sergeant Gibson's."

"Of course it is. And I bet that's Jones's and Ames's next to it. Can't wait to get my hands on those two asshats and let 'em know how much I appreciate the little souvenir they left me to remember our time spent together."

Frankie shut off the engine and gave a cursory glance around the property. "Everyone must be in the hangar."

"You have to assume they aren't going to be in there for long. We've gotta get to them before they get to that helicopter."

"Are you kidding, Danny? There's only two of us." She shook her head. "No. We wait for the backup Al said he's sending over. Did he say when they'd get here?"

I'd called Al on the way to the hangar to give him an update about where we thought Villanueva was headed. He'd hardly been forthcoming with the details of our support team. "Not exactly. After I told him where we were headed, I asked him if help was on the way. He just said they were working on it and hung up."

Frankie sighed.

"I know, I know. I need to work on his phone etiquette, I got it."

She shook her head. "It's not that. All we need to worry about is getting Giselle back safely. She's our priority. I just hope she's still alive." She glanced up at the building. "But until help arrives, we don't engage with them."

"Fine. So we don't engage. That doesn't mean we can't sneak in there and see if they've even got Giselle with them. Maybe they dropped her off with Markovitz's other girls."

Frankie nodded. "That's a definite possibility. But fine, we'll sneak in there and see if we can't get eyes on her."

"Alright, let's do this."

The two of us slid out of my vehicle. With my back pressed up against my Rubicon and gripping the handle of my G43 tightly, I slid around to the driver's side, joining Frankie and ducking low behind the Escalade. She gripped her own pistol, and together we crept behind the Escalade and over to the two squad cars, making our way towards the building.

I was just about to slide from the back of Gibson's car to the other squad car when the hangar's front door flew open and Sergeant Gibson, Commissioner Villanueva, and Ziggy Thomas all came striding out, trailed by Officer Jones, who tugged Giselle Marrero by the elbow with one hand and held a gun in the other.

"Shit," I hissed under my breath, drawing back around to the side of the last police cruiser and pulling Frankie with me. I was thankful to see that Giselle was indeed alive but deeply concerned that, without our backup, we'd be unable to stop Gibson and Villanueva from leaving the island with her in tow.

Giselle had gone no more than a few paces towards the waiting helicopter when she yanked her arm out of his hold, stopped walking, and crossed her arms over her chest. "I'm not going with you."

Jones pointed his gun at her. "You'll go where I say you'll go. Now come on." He tugged her along, but she fought him every step of the way.

"Lemme go!" Giselle screamed. Angry tears rolled down her flushed cheeks. Finally, her legs went limp and she fell to the ground intentionally.

"Stand up!" Jones bent over and tried to force her back onto her feet using only his free arm.

She swatted at him. "I don't wanna gooooo!"

Jones let out an annoyed sigh and then looked up ahead at Gibson. "Can't we just shoot her here, boss?"

Gibson kept walking but tossed back over his shoulder, "No, she is our insurance policy to getting off of this island safely. Once we have gotten to Isla La Fleur, then you may do what you like with her."

Giselle sat cross-legged with her arms folded over her chest. She stared down at the ground like a petulant child.

Jones pointed the gun at her. "Get your ass up, or you're gonna end up like your friend. I sure hope you know how to swim better than she did." He snickered, glancing back at his boss.

Giselle's eyes narrowed as she looked up at him. Anger at what he'd done to Jordan seethed beneath the surface. Without a word to him, she lifted a foot and lashed it out, using the back of her heel to strike him sharply in the knee cap.

Caught off guard by the attack, Jones crumpled to the ground. The scene was reminiscent of David bringing down Goliath and made me want to cheer. Jones let out a grunt as he fell, holding his leg.

Giselle scampered to her feet and began to run back towards the hangar.

I spotted that as being our opportunity to grab her. "Giselle!" I hollered.

"Danny!" hissed Frankie, reaching for me. "No!"

But I'd already scrambled to my feet and was beckoning her to come to us. "Over here!"

Giselle's eyes widened, and an overjoyed smile covered her face. She ran towards us. "Drunk!"

Behind her, Gibson, Villanueva, and Ziggy had all stopped and turned around. I tracked Gibson's eyes as they first darted over to see my Jeep parked beside the Escalade and then slid over to me, beckoning Giselle towards us. He pulled his weapon out while, off to the side, Jones struggled to get back to his feet.

"Giselle, get down!" I screamed, training my weapon past her and on him.

When she saw my gun pointed in her direction, Giselle's eyes widened fearfully, but she did as instructed and immediately fell to the ground.

"Don't move!" shouted Frankie, now forced to her feet.

Limping slightly, Jones fought through the pain in his knee to stand upright.

"I said, don't move, Jones!"

"Bite me, Cruz!" he hollered, getting his own gun up and aiming it at us.

Villanueva and Ziggy both stared at the showdown, neither of them moving. I hoped that meant that neither had a weapon to pull out, making it a little bit more of a fair fight. I felt slightly better about our odds, but I would've felt better if Al's backup showed up.

And then I heard a click behind me. "Drop your weapons."

My heart froze.

"Drunk! No!" screamed Giselle from the ground before beginning to sob.

I let out a sigh as I caught Frankie looking at me out of the corner of my eye. "Ames?"

"Damn straight. Now drop your weapons," he ordered, shoving the barrel of his gun into my spine.

I hung my head, then reached down and put my Glock on the pavement.

Frankie did the same. "Don't do this, Ames. You're better than this."

"Oh, zip it, Cruz. I'm tired of you being a goody-two-shoes all the time. Now march. The boss wants to have a word with you."

Across from us, Sergeant Gibson holstered his gun and turned to say something to the rest of his men, then began to walk towards us.

"He's not my boss," growled Frankie through gritted teeth as we walked towards the helicopter.

"Ohhh, you hear that, boss? Cruz says you're not her boss anymore," sneered Ames as he leaned over and forced Giselle to her feet.

"He was *never* my boss."

"Awww, Officer Cruz, that saddens me to hear," said Sergeant Gibson with a bit of a chuckle.

"All that time I thought you were a good man. And I thought that I wasn't good enough," she said bitterly. "But now I know. I was wrong."

Sergeant Gibson let out a little tsk, tsk, tsk. "Oh, but, Officer Cruz, the truth is, you were right! I *am* a good man, and you *aren't* good enough."

Jones and Ames both laughed.

I wanted to lunge across the short distance between us and wipe the smug smiles off the crooked officers' faces, but Ames shoved his gun harder between my shoulder blades, forcing me to stay put, feeling helpless. "Don't listen to him, Frankie."

"Oooh, *Frankie*," said Ames behind us. "I *like* that. Makes you almost sound tough, Cruz."

"Fuck you, you piece of shit. The woman's tougher than hell. Why don't you put down the gun and come over here? She'll kick the shit out of you."

I glanced over at Frankie. I'd never seen her look so angry before. I could tell she wanted to unload on her former coworkers. Then I noticed Commissioner Villanueva making a move towards the helicopter. "You know you can't hide, Villanueva. No matter where you go, we'll find you."

Villanueva stopped walking and sighed. He looked over at Gibson. "Who is this guy, Gibson?"

"This is *Officer* Drunk. The American pest we have been hearing about," he explained.

"You're the one that snuck into my friend's party?"

"Damn straight. And we've got the evidence we need to bring you down."

Gibson chuckled and pulled the USB stick we'd given him out of his pocket. "No, *we* have got the evidence you need. You have nothing, I'm afraid."

I glanced over at Frankie and chuckled. "They really think that's the only copy?"

She shrugged, shaking her head slightly. "I guess so."

Gibson strode over to me and stared up at me, his eyes shining with contempt. "You made a copy?"

"You think we're stupid? Of course we made a copy."

"Who has the copy?"

"Oh, you'd like to know, wouldn't you?"

"Gibson, you said you had this handled," snapped Villanueva from behind him.

"Do not worry, Commissioner. I shall handle it," he said, pulling his weapon again.

But I wasn't done taunting Villanueva. "Pretty soon, the entire island will know about your precious PGC, the sex trafficking, the embezzlement, all of it. You're about to be the most wanted man in all of the Caribbean. There's nowhere you can hide, Commissioner."

"Shut him up!" roared Villanueva.

"Gladly." Jones walked over to me and punched me in the stomach, hard.

"Danny!"

My breath left my body, and it took me a moment to regain my composure. In the meantime, the men all laughed. When I was finally able to breathe, I glanced over at Ziggy Thomas. "And don't think you're not gonna be the talk of the town." Hunched over, holding my stomach, I gave Ziggy a little wink. "They're gonna write blog posts for *months* about your trial. But don't worry, looking like that, I bet you'll still find a date. Of course, it might be your cellmate, but whatevs, right?"

Ziggy's eyes shifted around nervously.

Villanueva's nostrils flared. "Get this thing started," he said to Ziggy.

"I'm on it." Ziggy got in the helicopter.

Villanueva turned his attention to Ames and Jones next. "Put the girl in the chopper and kill these two."

Giselle screamed when the two men surrounded her. Each of them grabbing her by an elbow, they began to drag her towards the helicopter. "Nooo!"

"Let her go!" I hollered, making a move towards Ames as they walked past me.

But Gibson grabbed a fistful of my hair and yanked me backwards.

"Drunk!" screamed Giselle, crying as Ames shoved her into the helicopter.

The helicopter's motor let out a high-pitched whine. It was

now or never. If Frankie and I didn't get Giselle off that helicopter now, we never would. I shot Frankie a sideways glance. We had to do something.

She gave me the slightest of nods as the motor revved up louder and the propellers began their slow rotation.

Gibson stood behind me and slightly to the side. With my adrenaline racing, I slammed my head backwards, head-butting him directly in the face. Blood spurted out of his nose, catching him off guard long enough for Frankie to grab the gun out of his hand.

She swiveled around on him and fired one round into his shoulder—making sure he would survive the shot and be able to pay for his sins. Holding his arm, Gibson fell to the ground.

Then she turned the gun on Jones, who was just climbing into the chopper. She aimed at his shoulder, but when he saw that he was in her sights, he charged at her. She pulled the trigger just as he turned towards her, sending the bullet hitting him squarely in the chest. His torso kicked back and his uniform exploded in red. His knees buckled and he went to the ground.

The propeller blades were spinning full speed now, whipping up the air around us, making dust and dirt fly. Villanueva ran for the helicopter and jumped inside.

"You stay with them, Frankie. I'll get Giselle," I hollered. I ran to the side of the helicopter and launched my torso inside the cabin just as the landing skids left the ground. There were two rows of leather seats facing each other just behind the pilot and passenger's seats. Ziggy was in front in the captain's seat. Villanueva was in the back, seated next to Giselle. Ames stood in the center aisle. Giselle and I made eye contact for a split second. "Jump!"

But I'd no sooner gotten my feet secured on the landing skids than I took a kick to the ribs from Ames. Holding on to the helicopter with one arm, I reeled back, trying to catch the air that had left my lungs. But I came back with everything I had. I lunged back into the cabin and grabbed hold of Ames's ankles with both hands, pulling his legs out from under him and sending him straight down onto his back. The force knocked the gun out of his hands. It flew backwards, out the helicopter's other open door.

Villanueva, who had until that point seemingly wanted to let Gibson and his men do the manhandling, stood up. "Get off my helicopter, you annoying insect!"

In one smooth move, he delivered a polished black shoe to the underside of my jaw. Pain shot through my face. Before I could recover, he gave me a hard shove with his other foot, and my body kicked back from the helicopter. My feet slipped off the landing skids, but I managed to grab hold of a metal bar attaching the seat to the cabin floor.

I dangled there for a moment, my feet not attached to anything and my one hand holding the weight of my body. I stared down at the ground. We still hovered only feet off the ground, but with me out of the cabin now, Ziggy began to move the helicopter to a higher altitude. I'd jump, but I'd yet to retrieve Giselle.

The earth grew further away, and I quickly realized that I couldn't hang on like this. I panicked. This wasn't supposed to happen. I saw guys hanging from helicopters all the time in the movies, and yet they managed to hang on forever, all while shooting the bad guy. But now I found my hands to be slippery, and I could barely keep my grip on the helicopter.

Fuck.

As I dangled there, trying to figure out my next move, out of my periphery, I saw my bright yellow banana boat barreling full speed ahead towards me. Frankie was behind the wheel. Was she going to try and catch me if I fell?

I struggled to hold on long enough to find out. But when I looked down once again, I saw that she'd stopped the vehicle and gotten out. Giselle was in a heap on the ground! She must've jumped out when Villanueva had kicked me off the helicopter!

It was now or never. This helicopter was never getting any closer to the earth than it was right now. I held my breath and let go. I landed on my feet, but the force of the fall sent me rolling across the pavement several times. Sitting up, I held my ribs. I was pretty sure my stitches had popped. Wincing, I glanced around me. Ames's gun, which he'd lost during our struggle, lay on the pavement just a few short yards away.

I crawled over to it, flipped over onto my backside on the pavement and emptied the entire clip into the tail rotor. I managed to shoot off one of the propeller blades, and the helicopter began to rock woozily back and forth in the air like a drunk barely able to stay on his feet. The next thing I knew, the chopper went into a spin. It rocked around and then started to make like a boomerang and head back towards me!

My eyes widened. I struggled to get to my feet, but as soon as I did, I began to run.

"Frankie! Giselle! Run!"

The helicopter was coming at us, spinning out of control.

I ran as fast as I could, helping Frankie get Giselle to her feet. The three of us veered left as the helicopter veered right and crashed into my Jeep, sitting where Frankie had parked it.

I rolled over the top of Giselle and Frankie as the Jeep and helicopter exploded behind us, sending shrapnel flying around us. My body shuddered as the violent burst of flames warmed my backside and thundered in my ears.

43

"You alright, Giselle?" asked Frankie. We'd just gotten her to her feet and had started to dust her off and check her over for blood and/or broken body parts.

Tears and dirt stained her cheeks. Her hair was wild around her face. But she nodded anyway. "I think I twisted my ankle when I jumped, but otherwise I'm okay," she said with a sniffle.

Though my own body had its own aches and pains, I helped her wrap her arm over my shoulder as Frankie did the same. "Your mom's gonna be so thankful that you're okay."

Giselle looked up at me with surprise. "My mom knows they had me?"

I nodded as we began to help her towards the hangar. "Yup. No more secrets. When we get you back to her, we're telling her *everything*."

Giselle's head shook wildly as she made a sudden stop. "Noooo. She doesn't need to know *everything*."

I winced. My own side was on fire, and I was pretty sure I'd ripped off a significant amount of skin from my back when I'd rolled on the pavement after falling off the helicopter. But I fought through the pain. "She *does* need to know everything, and she *will* know everything."

"Oh, come on. What happened to Funcle Drunk?" asked Giselle, shooting big puppy dog eyes up at me.

"Funcle Drunk died when he fell off that helicopter," I assured her. "Look, Giselle, I was wrong in keeping secrets from your mom. She was pretty upset with me. She thought we were having an affair."

Giselle giggled as the three of us hobbled together towards the hangar. "Eww. As if. You're like a million years old."

I glanced over at Frankie, who had quirked a smile at that stinging insult. I sighed. "Well, maybe not quite a million. Not until my next birthday anyway."

"You know what I mean," she said. She narrowed her eyes and stared at the pavement up ahead. Gibson's body lay on the ground next to Jones's. Giselle's body shuddered against my side.

"You alright?"

She nodded towards them. "Are they dead?"

Frankie sighed. "The big one is. Sergeant Gibson's alive, but he took a bullet to the shoulder. I've got Sergeant Gibson handcuffed, so don't worry. He's not getting back up without a little help."

Giselle put her head on my shoulder. "That big one scared me so much," she whispered as tears began to fall again. "He's the one that came in my house and took me."

I gave Giselle's side a little squeeze. "Don't worry. No one's gonna scare you like that again. Okay? Gibson's going away for a very long time."

"But what about Harvey?" she asked, looking up at me.

"Don't worry about Harvey. We're gonna get him next. I promise," said Frankie assuredly.

Just then, a line of military vehicles appeared on the main road and, turning down the driveway, started towards the hangar. "Holy shit," I breathed.

Leading the lineup was a sky-blue Toyota Land Cruiser, and an ambulance wailed in the distance.

"What in the world?" whispered Frankie.

Wide-eyed, I pointed at the Land Cruiser. "That's Gary the Gunslinger's vehicle!"

"Gary the Gunslinger?"

"Gary Wheelan," I clarified with a grin. "He's a friend of Al's."

Frankie's smile widened. "So this is the backup Al arranged?!"

I shrugged and quirked a smile. Al was full of surprises. "I guess so."

The parade of vehicles drove across the landing pad and stopped just short of us. I could see Gary behind the wheel of his vehicle and Artie seated shotgun. The back door opened, and Al slid out. I shook my head. I couldn't believe it. We all walked over to them.

"We're too late?" asked Al, looking behind me at the fiery flames that engulfed both the helicopter and my Jeep.

"No. You're just in time," I said. I nodded towards the military fleet that had surrounded Gibson and Jones, who still lay on the pavement between us and the hangar. Another pair of vehicles headed straight past us towards the fire in the background. "How in the world did you manage all this, Al?"

Al held up both hands and lowered his head slightly as if admitting a secret. "It wasn't me."

I frowned. "Not you? Then who was it?"

Al hooked a thumb over his shoulder as Artie walked towards us. "It was this guy right here."

"Artie?!"

"We got them here as fast as we could," said Artie. "I'm sorry if we're too late."

"I mean, yeah, it would've been nice if they'd come *before* their helicopter smashed into my Jeep, but now *is* better than never, right, Frankie?"

"Oh, absolutely. We could use a little help with the cleanup."

Al frowned at me. "You ever put insurance on that thing, kid?"

I groaned and let my head fall backwards. My body had been so filled with adrenaline and fear that I hadn't even had time to *think* about the implications of my Jeep being destroyed. "Ugh. Fuck! No. I didn't. When was I supposed to find time to do it? We've been busy!"

Al shook his head. "How long does it take to make a phone call?"

"Too long, apparently," I muttered.

"Shit. Now I'm out that money!" I shook my head. I was pretty sure someone in the heavens didn't want me having nice things.

Frankie squeezed my arm. "But Giselle's alive. And *you're* alive. That's what matters, right?"

I let out a little grunt. "Ugh. I suppose."

Al pointed a finger in Frankie's direction. "And Francesca's alive. *That's* what matters too, right, kid?"

I looked over Giselle's head at Frankie and gave her a smile. "Absolutely."

"So where's the commissioner?" asked Al, looking around.

Frankie gave a backwards nod. "Let's just say he went down with his ship," she said, shaking her head.

"Ziggy Thomas and Officer Ames were in there too," I added.

Al stared at the fiery inferno, shaking his head. "No one's making it outta that mess alive, that's for sure."

"Yup. I think you're right," I agreed. "The island's female population isn't going to be too excited about Ziggy Thomas getting drilled into the ground." I rubbed the scruff on my chin and grinned at Al. "Guess Paradise Isle will need a new handsome eligible bachelor to write blog posts about. Hmm... whoever will fill his shoes?"

Al grunted. "Your feet ain't big enough to fill his shoes, kid."

"Thanks for the vote of confidence, Al."

"I think you've got an overabundance of confidence. I don't think you need any more of that."

I chuckled and looked over at Frankie. "But with Villanueva, Gibson, and Ziggy outta the picture, now it's just a matter of getting the rest of the people in PGC."

"Starting with Markovitz," said Frankie.

Artie smiled. "Way ahead of you. We've already got people headed to Markovitz's to find him and the other two girls. Plus we've got people headed to Club Cobalt, and to Steve Dillon's."

Al nodded. "Big Eddie, Ralph and I made a list of all the players in the operation. We're gonna get them all. Each and every one of the scumbags." He patted me on the shoulder. "We did it, kid. We brought down the PGC. You should be proud."

I smiled. Relief washed over me. "I can't believe it."

Just then, from the back of the line, one of the vehicles' doors opened and a portly black man in a tailored suit with salt-and-pepper hair and a matching beard got out and strode towards us.

"Oh, Drunk. I almost forgot. There's someone here I'd like you to meet," said Artie with a smile on his face.

"Oh, yeah? Who's that?"

When the man got close enough, he extended his hand towards me. "You must be Mr. Drunk."

"I am," I said, looking at the man curiously. "And you are?"

"I'm Governor Bustamante. I've heard a lot about you. Artie's kept me abreast of your escapades since you've been to the island. It's a pleasure to finally meet you."

My jaw dropped. So *this* was the contact they had! Artie's

connection to the governor. I shook his hand. "It's nice to meet you too, Governor."

"Artie and I spoke extensively this morning about the PGC organization, and I must say, I can't thank you enough for bringing the situation to light."

Stunned, I cleared my throat and looked over at Al. "Well, thank you very much. But I have to be honest, I didn't do any of this alone. I had a ton of help. You probably already know Al Becker?"

"Yes. Mr. Becker was in on the conversation this morning," said Governor Bustamante, extending a hand to Al. "It's nice to meet you in person, Mr. Becker."

"And, Governor, this is Officer Francesca Cruz with the Paradise Isle Royal Police Force. She helped Al and me bring down Sergeant Gibson and Commissioner Villanueva. Without her, *none* of this would've been possible."

Governor Bustamante reached a hand out to shake Frankie's hand. "Is that right? Well, then, the citizens of Paradise Isle and I thank you for your service."

"Thank you, Governor. I appreciate the opportunity to serve my government," said Frankie proudly.

I looked at Artie then, shaking my head.

Artie smiled. "What?"

"I just can't believe you called the *governor*."

"I had no other choice," said Artie with a shrug.

"Yeah, kid, who else could take down the police department *and* the customs commissioner?" said Al.

I frowned at the governor. "So, Governor, I assume Artie and Al explained to you that we think Commissioner Villanueva was skimming the vehicle tariffs off the top. Do you have any idea how he was able to do it? I mean, that's a hefty amount of money he was syphoning into his own accounts. How did he do it without anyone noticing?"

Governor Bustamante sucked in a deep breath. "I'm gonna be honest with you here. I came onto the job a little over a year ago. As you might know, Governor Schilling, the previous governor of the island, was killed in a mugging, leading to the vacancy. I was appointed not long after, and because I'm still learning the ins and outs of the organization, I trusted Commissioner Villanueva to handle the tariff collections properly." He shook his head. "I assumed I had good people working for me, and I took the reports he submitted to my office at face value. Of course, I would've gotten around to auditing each agency sooner or later, but I've been so busy just learning the ropes that I wasn't aware of what he was doing."

I frowned. "As you are aware, I'm fairly new to the island. I hadn't heard about Governor Schilling's death."

Frankie nodded. "It was a big deal when it happened. He was getting ice cream with his family on the boardwalk when he was the victim of a mugging. He chased after the thief and was stabbed along the boardwalk. Unfortunately, he didn't make it."

Governor Bustamante winced. "It was a very difficult time for islanders. Governor Schilling was very well liked."

"A mugging, huh?" I said, curling my lip. "Knowing what we know now about Commissioner Villanueva's embezzlement scheme and PGC, does anyone else wonder if maybe Governor Schilling's death was not just a mugging gone bad?"

The governor's eyes widened. "I sure hope not."

I shrugged. "Might be worth investigating."

Frankie's head bobbed. "Absolutely worth investigating. Maybe the governor discovered what Commissioner Villanueva was up to."

"Yeah."

The governor sighed. "I definitely think it's worth investigating. I'll put together a team to look into it." He looked at me a little more closely then. "Now. I think it's time we get the three of you some medical help." He pointed at the blood that stained my shirt. "We'll meet to discuss all the details of

Villanueva's operation once you're feeling better. For now, I'll get our medics over here to check you out."

I gave him a tight smile and looked down at Giselle. "If it's all the same to you, I think we'll just head over to the hospital. I need to give a friend of mine a call to let her know that this one is okay. And then Frankie and I need to follow up on some promises we made."

The governor looked at me curiously. "Promises?"

Frankie nodded. "We promised two of the girls that were working for Markovitz that we'd go back for the remaining girls. We can't quit until we've found them and brought them home safely."

"Oh!" said Governor Bustamante with a grin. "I guess I didn't get around to that yet. Just before I walked over here, I got word that both girls have been recovered and Markovitz and Dalton are both in custody. I know we've got a ways to go before we sort out everyone that was involved in PGC, but Mr. Becker and Artie both stressed to me that finding those girls was our top priority."

"You got the girls already?" I asked, stunned.

The governor smiled at me. "We sure did."

"Oh, thank God." I exhaled. For the first time since we'd discovered that Jordan truly was missing, I felt true relief loosen my shoulders. I walked over to Frankie and practically fell around her shoulders.

She hugged me. "See, Danny? We saved them. *You* saved them." Then she got on her tippy-toes so she could nuzzle her mouth up to my ear. "You're a good man, Danny Drunk."

44

THE NEXT DAY, AFTER GETTING MY STITCHES REDONE AT THE hospital, I lay on a lounge chair down at the beach. Artie had ordered me to take a few days off work so I could recuperate, and I didn't argue with him. The last couple of days had been hell on me, and I definitely needed time to heal.

Al lay beside me in a white ribbed tank top and khaki shorts. I was shirtless and soaking in the sun. The air smelled of coconut oil and iodine, and music played at the swim-up bar about forty yards behind me.

The heat felt good on my body. As if the sun's rays were taking away my aches and pains and healing my wounds. I had an ice-cold beachcomber in one hand, lying beside me, and my other hand rested on top of my fedora. The water crashed on the beach only a couple yards away from my feet— it was so close that I could feel a fine mist of tepid water settle over my body with every big crash.

I felt good.

Relaxed.

At peace.

I'd just exhaled a deep breath when I heard my name.

"Excuse me. Drunk?"

Behind my knock-off Ray-Bans, I closed my eyes. I recognized the voice. I lowered my arm, allowing more of the sun to distort my vision, and looked up at the face above me.

"Hey, Mari."

She seemed hesitant as she stared at me. Not quite like the self-assured woman I was used to dealing with. "Umm, Drunk, may I have a word with you for a moment?"

I covered my face again with the crook of my elbow. "Pull up a lounge chair."

With my eyes closed, I could hear the sound of her dragging a chair through the sand. When she hadn't said anything after a minute, I turned my head and peered at her. She was sitting on the edge of the chair, like a bird on its perch. She sat there quietly for a couple of long seconds.

Finally, I broke the ice. "So what's up?"

"Drunk, I—" she began, her voice faltering.

I didn't say anything. I had no intention of making things easy for her. I'd spent the last several months bending over backwards trying to make friends with the woman, only to be rebuffed at every turn.

She sighed and tried to begin again. "Drunk, I don't even know—" Her words trailed off again, this time I was sure I heard the distinct sound of sniffling.

Behind my sunglasses, I pinched one eye open and looked over at Al. His face was turned up towards the sky, but he had both eyes shut, like he was sleeping. I closed that eye and opened the other eye, so I was looking at Mari behind the darkness of my glasses.

She had her mouth open, trying to get words to come out, but only tears rolled down her face.

I sighed. "I accept your apology."

"No, Drunk," she whispered. "I don't get off that easy. Let me say what I came here to say."

I nodded and pressed my lips together.

She swallowed hard, blotted her tears with a tissue she'd

brought along, and then took a deep breath. "Drunk, I thought you were a horrible man," she said, her voice low. "I thought you had no moral compass and no integrity as a man."

"Thanks?" I said, curling my lip and wondering when the apology part would start.

"But I was wrong about you," she continued, her words quivering in the air as she spoke. "I was wrong about everything. You are a good man. You might be a bit of a playboy, and you might like to act like you're cocky, but underneath all that, you have a tremendous heart. I know this now."

I turned my head slightly to look at her. Tears streamed down her face. I reached a hand out to her. She took it and covered my hand with hers. "Thanks, Mari, that means a lot to me."

She shook her head. "Giselle told me everything. *Everything*," she whispered. "I understand why she was scared to come to me. But I'm so thankful that she went to *you*. *You* protected my baby from those monsters."

Hearing Mari cry tugged at my heartstrings. I sat up on my beach chair then and swung my long legs around so that they were in the sand beside hers as I faced her. I squeezed her hands in mine.

"If you hadn't offered your support to her, I don't know what kind of dumb decisions she might have made. She might have ended up like Jordan did." She was having a difficult time keeping it together.

"But she didn't," I said quietly. "She's safe and sound."

"Because of you, Drunk." She shook her head. "I'll never doubt you again. You have my word. I was so wrong, and I'm very sorry for that."

I scooted around so I could sit next to her. I put my arm over her shoulder, and she wept into her tissue.

"Can you ever forgive me, Drunk?"

"It's water under the bridge."

Mari's head bobbed as she dried her tears and blew her

nose. Finally, when she was more composed, she sat up a little straighter. "I brought you something. Just a little thank-you for everything you did for my family. I know I can never repay you, but I thought I'd start with this."

I clapped my hands and rubbed them together anxiously. "I do love presents," I said with a grin.

She let out a little nervous laugh and then turned around and grabbed a long box she'd put on the other side of the beach lounger. She handed it to me.

"Oooh, I think I know what this is," I sang, unwrapping the box.

"I thought it was my turn."

I pulled off the lid to unveil a box of chocolates. I chuckled. "You found my kryptonite."

"I know. I bought these at that little tourist boutique downtown. They're imported from Germany."

"Niiice! Thanks, Mari." I put my arm around her shoulder and gave her a little squeeze. "You want one?" I offered her the box.

She giggled. "No, no. Those are just for you."

My head bobbed. I looked down at her. "So, how's Giselle doing? Aside from the sprained ankle."

"She's okay. She had kind of a rough night, some nightmares and stuff, but she'll be alright."

"Good. I'm glad. I really like that girl. She's strong, just like her mother. You did a great job raising her."

"Thanks, Drunk. Your mother did a good job raising you too."

We sat quietly, watching Al sleep on the chair next to mine. Finally, I looked down at her. "So. Does this mean we're friends now?"

Mari shook her head. "No, Drunk. It doesn't."

I frowned. "Oh."

She wrapped her short arms around my waist then. "It means we're *family*. *Funcle* Drunk."

45

"WHAT TOOK YOU SO LONG?" I ASKED AL AS HE RETURNED TO the bar. "And please don't tell me the shitter was broken."

Al shrugged. "It wasn't broken *before* I went in there. I can't be so sure about it now."

I chuckled and then looked out at the group of people that had assembled at the Blue Iguana. Al and Evie were both there. Mari was there with a couple of the other front desk girls. Artie had come, surprisingly with Val on his arm. All the Cruz brothers were there, some of them with girlfriends and wives. And Frankie was there. She stood next to Solo, with his arm draped around her shoulder.

I held up my drink then. "I'd like to make a toast!" I said over the music playing in the background.

The chatter quieted down as all eyes turned towards me.

"First of all, I'd like to thank Al Becker for being the best partner a guy could ever want. He seems to know how to get me out of sticky situations before I've even gotten into them."

The room let out a collective chuckle.

"So cheers to Al and his beautiful wife, Evelyn."

"Cheers to Al and Evelyn!" the toast went up as glasses rose all around the room.

Then I turned my eyes on Frankie. "And now I'd like to congratulate our very own *Inspector* Francesca Cruz on her promotion. She's spent *years* working the Paradise Isle Royal Police Force, with little recognition for the effort and hard work she's put into her job. But now, finally, she's being recognized for everything she brings to the table. And I couldn't be prouder! So, cheers to Inspector Cruz!"

"Cheers to Inspector Cruz!"

"Congratulations, Panchita," said Solo, embracing his sister.

"Thanks, Solo."

When he let her go, I snuck in next for a hug. "I'm so happy for you, Frankie," I whispered in her ear.

"Thanks, Danny. I couldn't have done any of it without you. You should be playing detective right alongside me."

"Oh, the way my luck has been going since getting to Paradise Isle, I have a feeling I will," I said smiling.

She shook her head, grinning from ear to ear. "It was really great of Governor Bustamante to recommend me for this promotion. I think I'm still in shock."

"If it hadn't been for Sergeant Gibson and his crooked police crew, you probably would've made inspector much sooner. I promise you."

"Maybe."

Solo squared up to me then. "You know, my brothers and I noticed you returned our van."

I groaned. I had a feeling that topic was going to come up sooner or later. "You mean *our* van, right?" I drew a line in the air between us.

Solo pursed his lips. "Yes. It's got bullet holes all over it."

"Looks pretty badass, huh?" I said, grinning.

The rest of the brothers all chuckled behind him. Only Solo kept his perpetual frown steady. "I don't think badass is quite the word I was looking for."

"Kickass? Awesome? Hard-core? Am I getting closer?"

He glared. "I think we're going to have to talk about the *rules* when using our equipment."

I patted him on the back. "Set up a shareholders' meeting, Solo. I'll have my secretary put it on my calendar."

Then I tossed an arm over Frankie's shoulder and spun her around. Wanting to put distance between me and Solo's hound-dogging, I pulled her along with me towards the bar. I bent down and whispered in her ear, "Well, that was awkward."

She laughed. "Listen, Danny. Speaking of vehicles, have you gotten anywhere with the insurance company yet on your Jeep?"

I groaned. "Ugh. No. Supposedly, they want you to put insurance on the vehicle *before* a helicopter crashes on it." I shook my head. "I don't get it, but what're you gonna do? I guess I'll have to find me a junker to drive around from now on."

She patted my stomach. "Well, to ease the pain, I've actually got a surprise for you."

My face brightened as the memory of Mari handing me a box of chocolates sprang to mind. "A surprise? For me?"

She nodded.

"Great! I love surprises." I looked around. "What is it?"

She tugged on my arm. "Follow me." I noticed her giving a little wink to Diego, who made a quick dash towards the exit. Then she glanced over at Al and gave him a little nod too.

Furrowing my brow, I tipped my head sideways curiously. "What's going on, Frankie?"

"You'll see," she said, a sly smile on her face. "Come on. Your surprise is outside."

I let her lead me out of the building. Al and the rest of our guests all followed us. Parked right outside the front door was the Cruz brothers' white van, dotted with bullet holes. I laughed nervously. "I think it looks good, don't you, Rico?"

I looked over at Rico, who was standing next to me. "It looks legit, man. Not like those fake bullet hole stickers."

I glanced over at Solo. "See? Rico likes 'em."

Solo rolled his eyes as Diego pulled the van away from the curb.

"Hey. Where's D going?" I asked Frankie.

"Oh, he's just moving the van," she said lightly.

"Why is he—" My words trailed off when I saw what was parked in the parking lot across the street from the Blue Iguana. An entire parking lot of shiny new vehicles. I lowered my brows as I stared at them. "What in the world is that about?"

Frankie took me by the hand and led me across the street. "These were all seized by the government," she said. "They're all the vehicles that were acquired with PGC money."

"No kidding?"

She nodded. "Yup. And Governor Bustamante was so pleased with you for figuring out Commissioner Villanueva's embezzlement scheme that when he realized that you didn't have insurance on the Jeep, he wanted to do something to help you out."

"No way!" I said, shaking my head.

Smiling broadly, Frankie nodded. "He said you can pick one."

My eyes widened as I stared at the assortment of vehicles in the parking lot. "*Any* of these?!"

Her head bobbed excitedly while the crowd that had formed behind us all cheered.

"Any of them, Danny."

"Wow."

Al came hobbling out of the crowd and sidled up next to me. "Don't forget what you said, kid."

"What did I say?"

"That if you were ever to get a new vehicle, you'd go with something a little less flashy."

I swallowed hard and nearly choked on my own saliva. "Surely I didn't say that."

Al frowned at me. "You did."

"You sure that wasn't you?"

With his hands behind his back, Al tipped forward so he faced the ground. "I'm positive."

"Huh. That doesn't sound like me."

"Drunk."

"Al."

"Kid."

"Dad."

"Make a wise decision."

I grinned. "You mean pick the flashiest one?"

Al palmed his forehead.

"Hey, Al. You like that green one over there?" I pointed.

"Kid. Don't you dare."

I tapped a finger on my chin. "You know, I've always liked green."

HEY THERE, IT'S ZANE...

I'm the author of this book. I've got a huge favor to ask of you. If you even remotely enjoyed Drunk, Al, and their predicament, I'd be honored if you left a review on Amazon. I'd love to see this book reach more readers, and one way to do that is to have a whole bunch of feedback from readers like you that liked it.

Leaving reviews also tells me that you want more books in the series or want to read more about certain characters. Or, I guess, conversely, if you didn't like it, it tells me to either try harder or not to give up my day job.

So, thanks in advance. I appreciate the time you took to read my book, and I wish you nothing but the best!

Zane

MANNY'S BEACHCOMBER RECIPE

2 oz light rum
3/4 oz orange liqueur
3/4 oz lime juice
1/4 oz maraschino liqueur

Combine rum, liqueurs, and lime juice in a cocktail shaker, add
a half cup of crushed ice, and shake vigorously for ten seconds.
Pour into a chilled martini glass. Enjoy!

ALSO BY ZANE MITCHELL

Other Books in the Misadventures of a Drunk in Paradise Series:

Drunk on a Plane, Book 1

Drunk on a Boat, Book 2

Drunk Driving, Book 3

Drunk on the Job, Book 4 (Coming Soon)

If you'd like to notified when new books in the series are released, then consider joining my newsletter.

I swear I won't spam you, I'm really not that ambitious.

I'll only send out an email when I write a new book or have something to give away that I think you might like.

So what is that?

A couple emails a year?

You can handle that, can't you?

Go to www.zanemitchell.com/news to signup!

ABOUT ZANE

I grew up on a sheep farm in the Midwest. I was an only child, raised on Indiana Jones, Star Wars, and the Dukes of Hazzard. My dad was a fresh-water fish biologist and worked on the Missouri River. My mom was a teacher when I was young, and then became the principal of my school around the time I started taking an interest in beer. My grandpa, much like Al in my Drunk in Paradise series, actually owned a Case IH dealership, and I thought the world of him and my grandma.

I've been married twice. I'd say the first was a mistake, but that marriage gave me my four kids. Marriage numero dos came with two pre-made kids. So yeah, we're paying for Christmas presents for six and college for three. So buy my next book, *please*. I'd say that was a joke, but jeez. College is expensive.

In a former life, I was a newspaper columnist, and I actually went to journalism school but eventually dropped out. I did go back to school and eventually got a teaching degree, but let's face facts. I sucked at being a teacher. I was just as much of a kid as the kids were.

The love of my life and I live in the Midwest. We go about our boring lives just like you do. We parent lots of teenagers and twenty-something-year-olds. We watch superhero movies and Dateline on TV. We're a little obsessive in our love for the Kansas City Chiefs. We take yearly visits to the Caribbean because hey, tax deductible. And now, I write books - sort of a life long dream, to be honest.

So thanks for reading. You have no idea how cool I think it is, that you picked *my* book out of all of the choices you had to read and you made it to the end. You rock. Don't ever let anyone tell you otherwise.

Zane

Oh. P.S. I don't do Tweets. Or Insta. I do have Facebook and a website. www.zanemitchell.com. You're welcome to come over and hangout. BYOB.